Bandit
queen

Bandit queen boogie

A MADCAP CAPER OF TWO ACCIDENTAL CRIMINALS

SPARKLE HAYTER

THREE RIVERS PRESS · NEW YORK

Published by Three Rivers Press, New York, New York.
Member of the Crown Publishing Group, a division of Random House, Inc.
www.crownpublishing.com

THREE RIVERS PRESS and the Tugboat design are registered trademarks of Random House, Inc.

Printed in the United States of America

Design by Karen Minster

Library of Congress Cataloging-in-Publication Data
Hayter, Sparkle, 1958–
    Bandit queen boogie : a novel / Sparkle Hayter.—1st ed.
    1. Americans—Europe—Fiction.   2. Fugitives from justice—Fiction.
3. Female friendship—Fiction.   4. Female offenders—Fiction.   5. Women
travelers—Fiction.   6. Young women—Fiction.   7. Backpacking—Fiction.
I. Title.
PR9199.3.H39B36 2004
813'.54—dc22

2003025853

ISBN 1-4000-4744-7

10 9 8 7 6 5 4 3 2

First Edition

FOR
ALL MY
ROAD
FRIENDS

CONTENTS

"There was lately a lad in the University of Oxford who was, by his poverty, forced to leave his studies there, and at last to join himself to a company of vagabond *Gypsies* . . . after he had been a pretty while exercised in the trade," this scholar-gypsy chanced to meet two of his former fellow-students, to whom he stated:—"that the people he went with were not such impostors as they were taken for, but they had a traditional kind of learning among them, and could do wonders by the powers of imagination, their fancy binding that of others; that himself had learned much of their art, and when he had compassed the whole secret, he intended," he said, "to leave their company, and give the world an account of what he had learned."

JOSEPH GLANVIL,
Vanity of Dogmatising, 1661

WATCH OUT FOR THOSE RATS AND MASHERS

For nine years, Michelle "Blackie" Maher and Chloe Bower had been best friends, and in that time, neither knew the other was born a thief. If they hadn't gone to Europe the summer after college graduation and become accidental criminals they might never have known, though if Chloe had thought about it, she would have seen it in Blackie all along. Blackie always underpaid on dinner tabs, borrowed money without paying it back, had an amusing and largely harmless amoral side to her, and a great ease in rationalizing it all. She liked to quote something her father said when she was twelve and they were wrestling a side of beef into the back of her Dad's chevy after he swiped it from a meat wholesaler who had shortchanged him on some construction work:

"It's a sin to be too generous with the greedy, Blackie."

Many people would have been surprised that these two very different girls had that of all things—crime—in common. Outside observers could never quite figure out how these two had ever bonded, matter and antimatter as one of Chloe's boyfriends would later refer to them.

In fact, lawbreaking had been at the root of their friendship, nine years B.E., Before Europe. In eighth grade, they'd both been caught smoking in the john and sent to the same Stop Smoking program after school. They were the youngest reprobates in the class. After everyone else in the circle had talked about why they started smoking and how long they smoked, it was Blackie's turn and she said, "All I can think of right now is that there are 30 smokers in this room and we could all be smoking and having a lot of fun."

When they had to pick a "buddy" to help them through the course, Chloe picked Blackie. After class, they went off to smoke behind the 7-11—Marlboro reds for Blackie, Benson & Hedges menthols for Chloe. Neither wanted to quit smoking and they conspired to fake their smoke sheets for class and lie about their progress until they were sprung from the program. With this small, and unhealthy, act of rebellion, they became co-conspirators, the first step toward friendship.

Their pact required celebratory cokes, and the smoking of more cigarettes. Blackie showed Chloe how to "French inhale," blowing the smoke out her nostrils like a dragon, and Chloe showed her how to blow smoke rings, perfect, silky gray O's. As they sipped and smoked, they discovered they liked the same bands and TV shows. More important, they disliked the same people, particularly one mean clique of girls who had invited Chloe to a premium slumber party recently then withdraw the invitation publicly the next day.

"I didn't want to go anyway," Chloe said. "I was afraid I'd fall asleep during the night and they'd call me dead and eat my heart and liver."

"And suck the marrow from your bones," Blackie agreed.

Nobody could have been more shocked that they had anything in common than they themselves were. They'd seen each other in school and just always assumed they were in parallel universes. Chloe was cool, blonde, quiet, bookish, ambitious, and came from an upper-middle-class family with a well-known photography business that handled class photo and yearbook contracts in three counties. They belonged to a (not overly exclusive) country club, lived in a big two-story house in an established part of town and had fine china that not only matched but had been passed down two generations almost intact, with just the loss of a gravy boat.

Blackie looked tougher, a bit feral, with dark hair, dark eyes, a tattoo. She was friendly, got good grades without trying and never did more than she had to in school. Her father was a carpenter who had started his own business, her mother a homemaker and part-time Avon saleswoman, and they lived in a more modest house in a newer subdivision. Long after her father's construction business became successful the family still drank out of mismatched glasses, two of which were survivors from a set Blackie's grandmother won at bingo, which Blackie jokingly referred to as the "heirlooms."

— — —

Their differences, as much as their similarities, helped them stay friends through high school and college. They had different ambitions, so there wasn't any negative competitive energy between them. They went for different kinds of guys, eliminating a common friction point between friends. They never much liked each other's boyfriends, but this was less of a problem than if they had liked them too much, and at breakup time it was easy to say, "You're better off without him," and "He'll never find another girl like you," and sound convincing.

Or, as Blackie said after Chloe was dumped by John Carey in senior year of college, "This is the best thing that ever happened to you. You're free of that weighty albatross at last. Get dressed. I'm taking you out to celebrate."

Blackie was not surprised by these events. John Carey had been a yo-yo since Christmas, when his best friend got engaged to his pregant girlfriend. Chloe was infected with the matrimonial virus around the same time John, watching his buddy go down, was inoculated with the antibodies. One day he'd be withdrawn and aloof to Chloe with no seeming reason, then he'd feel guilty or turn needy and be loving, warm, and solicitous. Her confidence in herself was steadily eroded by the increasing drip-drip of his ambivalence. It had been a sad thing to watch.

A couple of months later, when Chloe caught the bouquet at a same-sex wedding reception for her favorite professor and his boyfriend, John's ambivalence turned to cold hostility. It was obvious to everyone but Chloe. As Blackie noted, you could almost see that gotta go light turn on inside his head.

"What reason did he give for the breakup?" Blackie asked now.

"He pitched it as an artistic imperative—a great writer needs to have a lot of different experiences, he needs to know a lot of women, he can't be hemmed in by conventional relationships. Look at Kerouac, Lord Byron, Hemingway, Henry Miller, Ted Hughes," Chloe said, mimicking John's voice. "It's dangerous to keep a wild thing like him in a cage. . . . He'd only hurt me worse down the road—this was for my own good."

"FUCKER! But he's right about the last part, it's for your own good."

"So I listed all the great artists who were greater for being married, like Gustave Mahler."

"Chloe, you don't for one moment think this guy is going to be Jack Kerouac or Ted Hughes."

"He's got talent."

"He's clever and superficial. I bet you a buck he ends up in his dad's investment business. He's a tourist."

"Do you think John will come back to me?"

"If he has any taste and intelligence at all, honey, he would. So in other words, no. Oh God, I hope not."

"Don't say that, Blackie. I love him."

Over tequila poppers and tapas at a campus bar, Chloe cried and drank and wondered aloud what to do with the rest of her miserable life if John didn't come back to her. They were both enrolled at Columbia grad school in the fall, but how could she go to New York if they were no longer together? Risk seeing him with some other woman, or women? And that summer they had planned to go to Europe together, but how could she go now—

"You're not going to cancel Europe because of him, or Columbia in the fall, Chloe. That's insane. Just abdicate your dreams to him?"

"Fu-uck it," Chloe said, hiccupping. "You're right. I should go to Europe anyway."

"You should," Blackie said, and an even better idea suddenly occurred to her. "I should go too."

"Yes," Chloe said. "Please."

"God, yes. A little Italy, a little France, a lee-tle romance."

The first sign that there might be some trouble on this trip was the choice of guidebooks. Chloe bought the upscale *Mousseline Travel Guide*, with its subtle, blue matte cover bearing no picture whatsoever, just the words, "Mousseline Guide to France" in plain white letters, an understated style reflecting the discerning, just-the-facts approach inside.

Blackie bought the backpacker's Bible, the *Lonesome Roads Guide*, which was chatty, frank, and included offbeat advice on which hostels had chiggers and where to find the black market in Marseilles.

Neither one thought anything about it. They prepped for the trip with maps, web sites, and by watching old movies set on the Riviera, most starring either Audrey Hepburn or Grace Kelly, and of course Cary Grant who, they agreed, played a great heterosexual. Though still depressed about John, planning for Europe took the edge off for Chloe.

The only person who felt any foreboding about this trip was Blackie's father. He didn't want her to go, claimed it was because he couldn't replace her in the office. He was afraid to say the real reason out loud because of superstition that saying it might bring it about—that as an American she was a walking bull's eye when she stepped outside her nation's borders.

So she wouldn't be identified as an American he bought her a backpack with a big glaring Canadian flag on it, two maple leaf lapel pins (in case she lost one), and several T-shirts. One said

"Canada" in big red letters above a red maple leaf. Below that it said, "We're not America." It was supposed to be a joke motto, poking fun at America and at Canada's own mythical lack of identity at the same time. To her father, who came from Canada, it was a kind of shield.

When he and his girlfriend and Blackie's mom and her boyfriend came to see her off at the airport, he said, "You watch out for those rats and mashers over there."

Mashers was his old-fashioned term for a wide variety of pickup artists, continental seducers, and white slavers. It was the same thing he said before she went to her first mixed party, to New York sophomore year, and before every first date.

Blackie said what she always said, "And they'd better watch out for me."

CHAPTER 2

The madcap Audrey-and-Grace enthusiasm Chloe had shown back in America vanished when she actually set foot in Europe. The first video made with Blackie's camera, *La Dolce Vita: Chloe and Michelle Do Italy*, opens with Chloe Bower, reading with the Roman Coliseum behind her. Next we see her in front of the ruins of one of ancient Pompeii's many brothels, sad, her hand by her side with a book in it, the place carefully kept with her thumb so she can return to it as soon as Blackie turns off the camera.

There's a rough cut, snow, then we see Chloe, looking sad, holding a book as she listens to the unseen Blackie. The Leaning Tower of Pisa is behind Chloe, far enough away that she appears almost as tall as it.

"Come on, stand sideways so it looks like the tower is straight and you're crooked," Blackie says.

Chloe refuses and suggests Blackie do it, and Blackie obliges, handing the camera off to Chloe. Blackie then puts her hand up as though gripping the shaft of the tower and jerking it off, but at that point, Chloe picks up a couple in the background, and zooms in on them. She curses.

"It's HIM, with some woman. Oh my God, how could HE come to Italy when he knew I was coming anyway. He's probably using the hotel reservations in Florence, too. We can't go to Florence, Blackie, not if HE's there!"

Blackie sighs deeply and says, "Well, then we won't go to Florence. We'll go to the beach."

— — —

Chloe turned off the camera and started crying.

"He's here in Italy, Blackie, he's with someone, and he's going to go to Florence, I know it."

"Is it the same girl you saw him with at graduation?"

"A different woman."

"He's not worth worrying about. Whoever this guy marries is going to catch him in the broom closet with the nanny before their first kid is weaned," Blackie said. "Let go."

"You think he's going to marry someone else?"

"I don't know. What do you care? If he wants to tom-cat around, then the only thing for you to do is to she-cat around. What do you say we find ourselves a couple of nice Eye-talian fellows—"

"That's the last thing I need right now."

"No, the first thing. Vitamin XXX."

"I'm not ready."

"Soon?"

"Soon enough."

"Let's go back to the hostel, have some dinner. Tomorrow we can go to Livorno."

But Chloe didn't want to eat, she couldn't eat, she was too angry and nauseous after seeing John Carey. This level of grief was puzzling to Blackie. She'd had her heart broken, and remembered being miserable briefly, but not this miserable for this long, and not over someone like John Carey. Chloe found him charming and sensitive and believed he was going to be a brilliant novelist one day. Blackie thought he was pretentious, controlling and repressed, wound so tight his eyeballs bulged a little. He could talk for five minutes without blinking. When he did blink, it was in a very deliberate way, as if to say, "I am not a space alien trying to pass as one of you." Blackie knew he'd drift into investment banking, get dinged for white collar crime and go to a minimum security prison where he'd discover he actually preferred having sex with men, and would finally write his novel behind bars. There was just something about him that reminded her of the Enron execs and others of their ilk she'd seen on the TV news.

Before Pisa, it was enough that Chloe was hyperaware that she was in Europe WITHOUT John. The trip she would have been having with him hovered over this trip like a ghost, and the littlest things could start her lips to tremble and the tears to flow. Now that she'd seen him here, it was going to be so much harder to have any fun, especially if that fun involved any other men. If Colin Farrell himself had tried to chat her up, she would have either burst into tears or stared him down with a cool, accusatory look for the crime of not being John.

It had now been three months since the breakup and Chloe was only getting worse. Nursemaiding Chloe for another two months in Europe was not what Blackie had planned. She wanted to have fun, meet guys, have a romance or two.

But Chloe showed no sign of wanting to find another man, or men. On this trip so far, Chloe had scared away every reasonably nice man and the only men who had persevered past her dark glare were married, middle-aged men looking for a threesome, a persistent hazard when these two friends were together.

In better times, they met more guys together than they did when alone. On their own, they were attractive to men, but in combination they were irresistible. Alone Chloe seemed inaccessible, and Blackie seemed a little tough. When together, the ethereal-looking Chloe could be approached through Blackie who seemed very friendly next to Chloe.

The combination of styles and tones was magnetic. On the downside, their differences made some men assume they were opposites-attract lesbians, in cases of serious wishful thinking. They did feel each other's breasts once in eighth grade, to see how they felt, and Blackie had once French-kissed a girl at a frat party to see what it felt like, but beyond that curiosity neither had felt any same-sex urges, thus puncturing the porno-lesbian fantasies of scores of men with a fetish for having sex while feeling obsolete. The Playboy Mansion Curse, Chloe and Blackie called it, the idea a lot of men had that they were entitled not to just one woman or a selection of equally free women, but more than one at a time, preferably young and beautiful—the same kind of guy who would complain about how superficial women were after he'd been blown off by a gorgeous model "because my wallet wasn't fat enough." These types were annoying Chloe and Blackie to no end this summer in Europe.

Blackie took a table alone on the terrace of the hostel ristorante, overlooking the river and a low-rent marina where rusty but still serviceable fishing boats bobbed and creaked in the water. The hostel ristorante had that same rusted appearance but buoyant spirit. The tablecloths were old, faded and bearing the shadows of ancient tomato and coffee stains. Almost all the tables had some sort of wedge propping up a too-short fourth leg to keep the table balanced. The china was chipped. But nightfall was starting to smooth all the rough edges and blur the blemishes with dimming light. The entire terrace was lit by nothing but strings of cheap multicolored carnival lights, which gave it a romantic cast. *It would be nice to be here with a guy,* Blackie thought.

Then destiny moved. A young man sat down at the table next to her. He was nice looking, appeared to be in his mid-to-late twenties, with blue eyes and brown hair cropped very short, as if he had shaved his head and the hair was just starting to grow back. He was carrying a sketchbook and a knapsack. After he sat down and ordered a glass of wine, he took out a charcoal pencil and began to sketch the marina.

"Do you find that inspirational?" she asked.

He looked up, surprised that she had spoken to him. "Yeah," he said. "It's real. Sincere."

"I'm Michelle. My friends call me Blackie," she said.

"Eddie."

"Where are you from?"

"Canada."

"No shit. Are you really from Canada?"

"Yeah."

"Where?"

"Sudbury."

"Really. Who sang 'Sudbury Saturday Night'?" she asked.

"Stompin' Tom Connors," he answered, sketching as they talked. He drew very quickly, with fast, freakish strokes. "Where are you from?"

"I'm American."

"How do you know Stompin' Tom?"

"My father is Canadian, he has some Stompin' Tom vinyls. Dad wants me to try to pass as a Canadian while I'm traveling."

"Are you passing?"

"I'm not trying. I mean, I don't tell people I'm Canadian, but they assume I am because of the maple leaf on my backpack and some T-shirts and pins my father bought for me. I mean no disrespect to your native land—"

"I know. I've been on the road two years," he said. "I've met a lot of 'Canadians' who turn out to be from Buffalo and Virginia Beach."

He showed her his drawing. She couldn't tell if he had serious talent.

"Can I draw what you think God looks like?" he asked.

"You asked the wrong girl," she said. "I'm an agnostic."

"Even atheists have some image of God in their minds, something they absorbed in childhood from the church or the culture."

"Let me think about it."

"Don't think about it, just tell, like you'd describe a suspect to a police sketch artist. Male or female?"

"Male," she said. "I want to say female, or androgynous, like Warhol or 1970s Bowie, but I'm seeing a man in my mind. I'm a victim of socialized patriarchy."

"Shape and size of head?"

"Round and small."

"Hair?"

"Bald."

"Facial hair?"

"None."

"Eye shape, size, color?"

"Oval, average, black."

"Smiling, frowning, weeping, somber, raging—"

"Smiling. Wickedly," Blackie said.

He showed her what he'd drawn.

"No no no. That looks like Billy Bob Thornton. The eyes are too psycho and he needs a slightly bigger nose and bigger ears," she said.

"What is he wearing?"

"Flowing blue robes, and a hat, kind of like the pope wears, but blue and more conical. You've been on the road two years?"

"Almost. I started in Tokyo, taught English there for six months, worked like a dog, made a ton of money and then headed slowly west with no map and lots of detours. How long have you been on the road?"

"Almost two weeks," she said. "Where have you been in two years?"

"All over Asia," he said. "The 'Stans, Russia, Eastern Europe . . . "

In Prague, Eddie ran out of money and slept in the train station for two nights before he met some people who put him up in the storage room of their bookstore. Since then he had been supporting himself by drawing portraits of tourists and busking with people he'd hooked up with on the road. To economize, he had stayed in the cheapest hostels or slept on the beach or in train stations. Occasionally, he got a tip about a nice "squat" and was able to slap down his sleeping bag there for a while.

"Have you been drawing God the whole way?"

"I've been drawing God since I was 14."

"Hey," Chloe said. She had come up from behind, and now looked at Eddie coolly, before sitting down across from Blackie in a way that shut Eddie out.

"I decided to eat after all," she said.

"Good. Chloe, this is Eddie. He's from Canada. Really."

"Hi," Chloe said, giving him half a glance over her shoulder.

Blackie leaned to one side to look past Chloe at Eddie. "Care to join us, Eddie?"

"I'd love to, but I have to go meet a friend at a bar on the other side of town. You want to come?"

Chloe shook her head at Blackie and half smiled, beseechingly.

"Can't tonight," Blackie said. "Chloe is in relationship rehab and I have to get her drunk."

"Sorry to hear that, Chloe. Well, maybe tomorrow Blackie?"

"We're going to Livorno tomorrow."

"I'll be there in a couple of days. Where are you staying?"

"The Paradise."

"I'll look for you," he said, and turned the sketchpad toward her. "This is your God. He looks a lot like Merlin the Magician."

"I always get the two mixed up."

They smiled at each other.

As soon as he was out of earshot, Chloe said, "Drawing God since he was 14. Oh brother. What a line."

"I spoke to him first," Blackie said. "He didn't try to pick me up. I liked him."

"You think he's one of those post-millennial, post-ironic Jesus freaks?"

"No. I don't think so. He seems sincere."

"They always do at first, don't they? God, Blackie, John's here, in Pisa, right now, with some other woman."

"He's a dick. We'll go to Livorno, and we'll leave him far behind, okay?"

"Is there any more wine?"

CHAPTER 3

The hotel in Livorno, La Paradiso, was typical of the cheap hotels they were staying at. There was a small lobby with a small registration desk, a coin-op internet machine, a pay phone, a rack of brochures for nearby tourist sites and four small tables for breakfast. There was no elevator, just an (invariably) winding staircase covered in red carpet worn down by the feet of two generations of backpackers. The rooms were small, clean, with two double beds, toilets, and showers. On the wall was a framed print, usually of a seascape or an impressionistic field of flowers.

In the room at La Paradiso, the painting was of furniture, an empty chair beside a small table bearing a telephone in an empty room.

Outside the window of the real room were the red, rolled-tiled roofs of Tuscany, stepping down irregularly toward the masts of fishing boats in the blue sea. It was sunny, the beach was a mile away. But Chloe wanted to stay in the room with the curtains closed, reading or writing postcards or staring at the painting of furniture in an empty room.

"It's a waiting room." Chloe said.

"What?"

"In the painting. The room looks like it is waiting. What is it waiting for?"

"Two red-blooded American girls to return from having fun at the beach?"

"You go without me."

"No. Come on, it's a beautiful day."

"You go without me," she said.

"Okay. Have fun with the painting," Blackie said.

She was about halfway to the beach when Chloe caught up with her. Without speaking, they walked down an old stone lane surrounded by old houses and flowering vines, then Blackie said, "This is perfect weather, hot but not too hot with a nice cool wind coming off the sea. And look at the scenery. Isn't this just fucking beautiful?"

It was the wrong thing to say. Anything pleasurable or beautiful just reminded Chloe that she no longer had John to share it with.

"Yeah," Chloe said, her voice quivering.

Except for a few pained and shivered sighs from Chloe, they walked in silence the rest of the way to the beach, where they claimed two beach chairs and set up their suntan lotion, paperback novels, magazines, and MP3 players.

"Do you want to read *Hello* or *OK*?" Blackie asked.

"Neither." Chloe lit a cigarette and picked up a pen and some postcards. "Why do you read that trash, Blackie?"

"It's fascinating to me."

"You don't even know who most of those people are."

"That's why they're fascinating. Celebrities you've heard of are boring. Celebrities you've never heard of from other countries are fascinating. Like this girl. Who is she? What is she famous for? It doesn't really say. As near as I can tell she's famous for having enormous fake boobs and a baby out of wedlock with a British football player. Or this one, famous for being the badly behaved daughter of a wealthy man," she said. "Oh oh. Don't look, but to your left, there's a masher walking toward us."

Without turning her head, Chloe watched as an older man in sunglasses picked his way across the sand like someone walking on fresh tar, stopping every ten steps to shake the sand out of his sandals.

"We are irresistible. Why is that?" Chloe said.

"Is it because we're attractive, but not too pretty, so we're accessible?"

"We're pretty. Don't you think I'm pretty?"

"Yeah, but we're not scarily beautiful. Anyway, we don't care excessively about our looks, right?"

"Do you think the girls we've seen John with are prettier?"

"No."

"Is this seat taken?" the man asked in English, nodding toward an empty beach chair next to Chloe.

Blackie was almost relieved to have him interrupt her and Chloe. But Chloe wanted the man to leave. Pointedly, she glared at him, and when this didn't penetrate, she tried to ignore him.

Without waiting for an answer, he sat down.

"Do you speak English?" he asked.

"Yes," Blackie said, before she caught Chloe's forbidding look.

"Oh, thank God. Bob Parker."

"I'm Audrey, and this is Grace," Blackie said.

"Where you girls from?"

"The United States."

"Me too. California. Fresno. I'm here on business."

"What is your business?"

"Advertising," he said.

"What kind?" she asked, picking up her digital video camera and pointing it at him.

"Oh, don't tape me please."

"Why not? I'm documenting the people I meet on my travels."

"I'm just . . . I don't like being on camera."

"Okay," Blackie said. She put the camera down. "So what kind of advertising do you do?"

"Internet advertising," he said, quickly and too defensively. "I'm a pioneer in it. Keeps the net free for people like you."

"How exciting," she said. "Do you have a card?"

"Sure," he said, and handed her one from his wallet.

She noted the tan line where his wedding ring should be. It was worse than an obvious tan line. It wasn't a white bar of skin, but a slightly less tan strip, as if he had taken the ring off recently in order to conceal his marital status and tried to tan the ring line away, or, worse yet, filled the blank space with fake bronzer.

This was a deliberate con.

"Business good, Bob?"

"Great. Because I specialize in low-cost avenues of marketing, business is booming for me in America," he said. "Now I'm expanding into Europe, with French and German versions of my programs. Next, Japan and China. So I'm over here a lot doing sales meetings and conventions. What about you two?"

Chloe tried to tune him out. Every now and then she looked at him over her sunglasses as if he had just snapped a fly out of mid-air with his tongue. But Blackie was the friendly one, usually, so she listened politely, and asked an innocuous question now and then.

"You girls go to school or what?"

"We're going to flight attendant school in the fall," Blackie said.

"You're both single?"

"Yes. Are you married?" Blackie asked.

At this point, he made a mistake. He could have said he was divorced, and they would have perhaps believed him. That would have explained the tan line . . . he had taken off his ring because his divorce had just come through and was now trying to erase the evidence of an unhappy marriage.

But instead he said, "I'm a widower. My wife died."

"Sorry to hear that."

"Yeah," he said, looking somber for a moment, then quickly recovering. "You girls staying . . . together . . . here?"

Chloe shot Blackie a look.

"I'm going swimming," Blackie said, jumping up quickly to

run into the sea, leaving Chloe alone with Bob Parker. Served her right. Maybe after a spell alone with an asshole, Chloe would come to appreciate her.

"I like your friend's tattoo," Bob said. "What is it, a pink rose?"

"No," Chloe said.

"What is it?"

"I don't know, but it's not a rose!"

"Oh. Okay. Didn't mean to upset you. It's cute the way she has it, with her navel as the center of the flower. Whatcha writing?"

"A postcard."

"Do people still send those? I send e-postcards, using my own digital photos."

Chloe said nothing. She put down her pen and postcard to light a cigarette, and Bob grabbed the postcard.

"Don't read that," Chloe said.

"I'm just looking at the picture," he said.

When he went to put it back down, the wind picked it up, and blew it about ten feet away, toward an empty beach chair. Chloe got up to retrieve it, but just as she got close, a bigger wind blew in and carried it another ten feet. This happened a third time before she angrily slapped the card down with her foot to secure it.

She took her time walking back, glancing now and then at Blackie, splashing in the sea. She wanted to cry, but not in front of Bob Parker.

Blackie waved and began to walk in from the water. Chloe paced herself so she'd return around the same time as Blackie, and she wouldn't have to be alone with the Playboy.

Bob Parker, meanwhile, was thinking that he already had the nice dark-haired one on his side, he just had to win over her chilly blonde girlfriend.

When they returned, Blackie smiled politely, and Chloe rummaged in her purse for another smoke. Bob asked if they were with boyfriends or if it was "just you girls," and Blackie was about to invent two young men who would soon be joining them when Chloe said, "The money is missing."

"What money, Chloe?"

"Our money."

"All of it?"

"All of it. Cash and travelers' checks."

"Why did you bring all our money to the beach?"

"Well, I didn't want to leave it at that cheap hotel."

"You're sure you brought it?"

"Yes. I know I put it in my purse. I can see myself doing it in my mind, very clearly."

"What are we going to do, Chloe? Wow. All our money? Our cards are already maxed . . ."

Remembering Bob was watching, Chloe shot him a cold look.

"The only time I was away from that money was while you were swimming and I was chasing my postcard," Chloe said, keeping her eyes on Bob.

They both realized that Bob was the only one left alone with Chloe's purse. He shifted uncomfortably, guiltily.

"How much was it?" Bob said.

Chloe said, "$2500," and she said it as if he already knew how much was there.

"$2500?"

"All our damned money," Chloe, said, vaguely accusing.

"That's a bad break. Look, let me buy you dinner at my hotel," Bob said. "Maybe I can figure something out over dinner. A loan or something."

At his five-star hotel, it turned out that Chloe and Blackie weren't dressed properly for the restaurant, as they were not wearing stockings. But no problem, according to Bob. They'd just have dinner in his room. This proposition sounded pretty shady to Blackie. But Chloe wasn't willing to let him out of her sight. She wanted her money back, and she knew he had it.

When they got to his room, Bob apologized for the foofy French decor, poured them some wine, then said he had to "freshen up."

Chloe and Blackie sat in the matching pink satin chairs while he used the washroom.

The room was pastel pink and green with too much gilt and what appeared to be real antiques. There were magazines and business papers on the coffee table, along with an opened bag of pistachio nuts from the minibar and an empty beer bottle.

"This is nice," Blackie said. "He obviously has money."

"That he took from tourist girls."

"That's a tough way to make a living."

"Maybe he doesn't need the money. Maybe he does it to render young women vulnerable," Chloe said.

"That's sick. You know, I don't care what married people do, and I can't even fault a married guy for hitting on another woman. I mean, who knows what he's got at home. Maybe she's bored with him. Maybe she's doing the UPS guy. But—"

"But, play fair," Chloe said.

"Check this out: 'Captivate Your Audience, by Bob Parker,'" Blackie said, handing the brochure to Chloe.

"There's a bio. Hmm. He really is a pioneer in internet advertising, mass e-mail, pop-ups, and spyware to determine consumer tastes. Recently, he's added an element to break spamblocks to his mass mailing package," Chloe read. "He won an AIM award, whatever that is."

"Assholes in Internet Media."

"And he resides with his wife Patricia and his two daughters in Tucker Estates, a small town near Fresno, California."

"I guess the brochure was printed before the wife died."

"The man has daughters, Blackie. Maybe our age. What a jerk."

"Don't be too quick to judge the poor man," Blackie said. "Maybe the daughters died in the car crash too. And he took our money as a way of getting us to spend time with him because we remind him of them. He means no ill will, he just wants a little platonic companionship in his time of loneliness and grief."

"You're right, Blackie. How insensitive of me to assume otherwise."

Bob returned and poured some more wine, urging them to drink more, and more quickly, in order to "loosen up."

"I'm too preoccupied, worrying about the money we 'lost' today," Chloe said.

"You need another drink," he said.

Before he could give her one, a call came in and he took it, mouthing, "Business," to the girls before turning his back to them and walking across the room to talk very quietly.

"Did you hear that?" Chloe whispered.

"What?"

"He said, 'Sure, I miss you too, honey.' You don't whisper, 'Sure, I miss you too,' in a business call unless you're a total freak. It's the dead wife."

"We're going to get our money back," Blackie said.

"How?"

"First we get him naked, which shouldn't be too hard to do," Blackie said, and then outlined the rest of the plan.

"Business, can't escape it," Bob said when he returned. "You need more to drink."

"We need some music," Blackie said. She fooled with the radio till she found something she could dance to, provocatively.

"I like that," Bob said.

"Dance with me," she said to Chloe.

"Oh that's nice," Bob said.

Blackie slipped her sundress off over her head, revealing her bikini.

"Very nice, very nice," he said. "Nice tattoo. The way it surrounds your bellybutton. It's provocative."

"How would you like us to bathe you, Bob?" she said.

"Bathe me?"

"Yeah. Is there room in your bathtub for you and me?"

"It's a Jacuzzi," he said. "There's room for all three of us."

"Perfect."

Bob followed her into the bathroom, unbuttoning his shirt as he went. Chloe hung behind, picking up his clothes. She removed his wallet and pocketed his Rolex.

"Get in," Bob said to Blackie.

"I must clean you first," Blackie said, kneeling over the tub with a washcloth and a bar of soap. "You're a dirty, dirty boy, Bob."

While Blackie methodically scrubbed his back, Chloe rummaged through Bob's suitcase and garment bag in the other room. In the Jacuzzi, Bob cooed and said, "Oh yeah, that's nice, a little lower, no, to the right."

"I'm going to run downstairs to get cigarettes," Chloe called to them, and hauled both Bob's bags outside, putting all his clothes on a service elevator bound for the basement.

When she returned she took Blackie's digital video camera and held it, hidden, under a folded beach towel. She turned it on and walked to the bathroom, recording Bob, naked, as Blackie soaped him up, her body turned so only her back was visible.

"What do you like, Bob," Blackie asked.

"Two beautiful girls naked in a Jacuzzi with me."

"Of course you do. More wine?"

"Thanks."

"Have you been in a lot of Jacuzzis with a lot of loose women, Bob?"

"I've been around."

"Tell us about your dead wife. You must miss her."

"You don't want to hear about her."

"I feel a little guilty, having so much fun with a widower. You must miss her."

"My wife and I, we were getting a divorce when she died. I'm sorry about what happened to her, you know, but the marriage was already over."

"I see. How did she die?"

"Car accident."

"That's terrible. Did she die instantly, or did she suffer?"

"Can we talk about something else?"

"We don't have to talk at all," Blackie said. "Chloe, will you turn up the music?"

"Sure. Be right back."

Then Blackie said, "I'll just get some more wine for us, and maybe I should call room service and order up something to nibble on."

"I'll do that," Bob said. "Hand me the phone."

Smiling, Blackie handed him the bathroom phone before she went out into the living room and put her sundress on. Chloe wrote a note, which she left on the table with his passport and credit cards. Quietly, they crept out, leaving Bob in the bathtub, shouting down the phone at room service to be heard over the blaring music.

When Chloe and Blackie didn't return right away, he called for them, and called for them again. Then, he got out of the Jacuzzi and found a note.

We know your wife's name, address and phone number, and we have a videotape of you naked in the bathtub with a young woman soaping you up. So please don't make any trouble for us. If you're good, we'll send the wallet back to your wife, and we won't mention this incident at all. She looks very nice for a dead woman, btw. But who is Maria in Rome?

As they walked back to their hotel, Chloe showed Blackie the wallet.

"Which one is his wife, the naked drunken woman or this nice smiling one in the Peter Pan collar?"

"I bet it's the hot naked one," Blackie said. "You got our money back?"

"There's just a little over 500 euros in the wallet. He must have hidden the rest when he went to the bathroom. But I got his Rolex too, and that's gotta be worth something if it's not fake."

"Gold Rolex?'

"Looks like silver. But it's better than nothing."

The whole episode put Chloe in a good mood, relatively speaking, all evening. At dinner, in a classic lamplit ristorante with tablecloths and mustachioed waiters in white aprons, shirtsleeves, and black bowties, she smiled a Mona Lisa smile and ate a full meal, which she hadn't done since her breakup.

But she didn't get wildly excited about it until later that night, when she opened one of the books on her bedside table and found their money. She had pulled it out of her purse and stuck it there while looking through her bag for a Tylenol, then forgotten to put it back in before she left for the beach.

"Oh my god. Bob didn't take it," Chloe said. "We made an enormous mistake!"

Blackie laughed. "We've made an enormous profit!"

"Right. And he can call the police and have us arrested."

"He knows we have a video, and that if he rats us out, we rat him out to his wife."

"You're right," Chloe exclaimed. "Who's going to take his side anyway? My God, he's responsible for spam! But we can't stay in Livorno. I don't want to risk running into him again. Let's go to Portofino tomorrow."

"Yeah, but we told that guy Eddie we'd meet him here tomorrow."

"Leave him a note."

"Okay."

"Whew," Chloe said, and took several deep breaths. "I am feeling a real buzz from it now."

"What do you mean?"

"From ripping off Bob Parker. Wow. That was fun. It's the perfect crime, Blackie."

CHAPTER 4

DIANE BENHAM

Chloe Bower and Michelle "Blackie" Maher were among thousands of young women all over the world who decided to spend their summer "on the Continent" that year. From cramped Tokyo kitchens to Moscow bedrooms to campus bars in Ohio, they read through the guidebooks and plotted their Byronic tours, highlighting the must-see sights and events while dreaming between the lines of adventures beyond those a 20-buck guidebook could promise.

Take for example, Wendy Kapp, of Nickelsburg, Arkansas, sophomore at East Arkansas Christian College, founding member of the Godsmacked youth organization, and witty roving correspondent for the XGRRRL show on Christian Rock radio. For a full year, Wendy had planned for her trip, reading the history of France, studying French intensely and researching the current state of religious affairs in the country. She pitched a series of feature stories to XGRRRL, including insider coverage of the Godsmacked convention in Cannes, and got enough assignments to pay for the trip and then some.

Her guidebook of choice for the trip: *The Christian Traveler in France* by Pastor and Mrs. George Phillips. Wendy was thinking of doing her own guidebook to France, something more up-to-date for young people like her. And perhaps, she thought, it could be the first in a series of Godsmacked guides . . .

Crime was not on her itinerary.

An English heiress who would make the papers that summer,

Diane Benham, was not going enthusiastically, or voluntarily, to the Continent, but as part of a plea bargain that would send her to rehab in Switzerland. Her guidebooks of choice: her laptop computer, her phone book, and a Frommer's road map of Switzerland, Italy, and France. Certain victimless, consensual crimes were most definitely on her itinerary. Bank robbery hadn't even occurred to her.

The night before she flew to Switzerland to check into Le Petit Château, Diane Benham threw herself a Caligulan party in her apartment in Knightsbridge. A few dozen of her favorite people—this week—drank champagne, snorted coke, swallowed E, danced and tranced to DJ Vapourtrails and coupled recklessly until 8 A.M., three hours after the hostess Diane was taken by car to the airport to catch a flight to Geneva.

A nurse from Le Petit Château and a functionary of Diane's father met her at the airport and drove her to the clinic. On the ride in, the functionary said nothing as he took faxes and answered business e-mail. The nurse smiled and assured her she was going to grow to love Le Petit Château and her life would be better because of it.

Her incarceration was not voluntary, though the deal worked out with Crown prosecutors in the UK stated that she would "voluntarily" admit herself for eight weeks of rehab followed by a year of probation. Then all she would have to worry about was the lawsuit resulting from the big flap-up at the Indulgence club, which led to her arrest, the discovery by police of five grams of coke in her purse, and tabloid photos of her screaming abuse at cops.

Because she was just 17, she might have gotten off lighter if this were a first offense. But, this was the third time she'd gotten into trouble, and this time she had massive quantities of drugs on her person.

Le Petit Château looked like a Swiss Miss picture postcard chalet crossed with Guantánamo Bay, but it was better than juvenile jail. Located in the country outside Geneva, the beds were comfortable, with 300-count French linens and antiques in the rooms. She had internet, a selection of old and new movies on DVD, cable TV, and every day at three there was a chocolate tea, at which 15 kinds of tea and two dozen different chocolate desserts were served. Chocolate and cigarettes were all she was allowed, but it wasn't enough for Diane. She didn't like being cooped up, she didn't like the other residents, and she wanted something harder than Earl Grey and mousse. Every day she had to listen to the others in her group talk about their rotten childhoods and bad marriages and it bored her ass off. She didn't want to talk about her childhood or her family to strangers. In her short, intense life, she had already trusted too many people and given away too much personal information to them, thinking it would help them understand her, when in fact all she'd done was point out her vulnerable points and given others the daggers to stab her there.

As far as Diane Benham was concerned, everyone she'd slagged off, slugged, or "assaulted with a deadly weapon" (a stiletto shoe) had it coming. The drugs had nothing to do with it and anyway, she could afford to snort up half of Colombia if she wanted. She was rich and irresponsible. It wasn't like she was a surgeon or a motorman on the tube.

After a week in rehab, she decided it was time to leave. But Le Petit Château had top-notch security. Crack armed guards with German shepherds patrolled regularly. The fence around the grounds was electrified, and there was no tree close enough to use to jump over the fence, the way she had escaped over the high stone walls of the convent boarding school she was sent to for a year. The only time the gates opened was when the guards admitted a vehicle or let one out—except on visiting day, Sunday.

Nobody had come to visit Diane the first Sunday, but she had watched the procedures carefully. The gates were kept open for most of the day, but always manned by four guards. Nobody had ever escaped Le Petit Château. But then nobody had ever escaped Stalag 17, the Nazi prisoner-of-war camp in one of Diane's favorite

Billy Wilder films, until J.J. Sefton did with the help of a distraction . . .

For the next visiting day, she arranged for her parents to come, separately. Knowing her father was always precisely punctual, she asked him to come at 11 A.M.

"Has your mother come to visit?" he asked.

"God no. She's doing a sleep cure I think, before her next operation. She's supposed to come by next week before she goes in to the clinic."

Her mother was always recovering from some form of plastic surgery, and was always a half-hour late, so Diane told her to come at 10:30 A.M.

"Is your father coming?" she asked, when Diane called to invite her.

"No, he and Lily Sue are entertaining this weekend."

"He owes me money."

"I'll give you money if you come visit. 10:30 A.M. Don't be late or I won't be able to see you," Diane said.

At 11, her father Lord Lawrence Benham and his second wife greeted Diane at the gate. His face was a mask of complete control. Lily Sue Benham, attempted to squeeze a beneficent smile through her utter antipathy for Diane, which made her look like a stroke victim.

Before either could open their mouths to disapprove of Diane her mother Prue showed up, stumbling out of her car, drugged up on something legal but highly effective. She looked stunned to see her ex-husband there with Lily, though ever since that botched forehead lift she looked permanently shocked.

"Prue!" Lord Lawrence said.

"Larry, DON'T TOUCH ME!"

"I wasn't going to touch you. What are you doing here?"

"I came to see Diane. Where's my check?"

A crowd had begun to gather around them.

"No doubt you spent it already and don't remember. But this isn't the time—"

"Liar! Showing up here with your . . . Is she still shagging that Jamaican jockey—"

"You're disgusting," Lily said.

"DON'T TOUCH ME!" Prue shouted.

Nobody was touching her. She sputtered and swung wildly. Her motor control, if not her temper, was dulled by her medication but she managed to land a slap on Lily's face. Lily instinctively slapped her back, her hand shooting out as if propelled by a spring.

While silently cursing whatever hormonal madness had led him to impregnate and marry Prudence 18 years previously, Lord Larry tried to get between the two wives and took a rapier-sharp fingernail up his nose, causing a blood vessel to burst. Blood streamed down the front of his suit as Lily and Prue tore at each other. The security guards finally managed to restrain the warring parties physically, though Prue continued to scream.

"Don't touch me! DON'T TOUCH ME!" Prudence shrieked at the two men holding her back. Nobody was allowed to touch Diane's mother except licensed physicians who had put her under general anesthetic. Twice a year, she had some sort of invasive surgery. Lily Sue liked to say it was the only way Prudence could get a man inside her, and even then she had to be unconscious and it had to be followed by a week of IV medication.

"Diane told me you weren't coming," Lord Larry said.

"Diane told me you weren't coming," Prue spat.

They both, at the same moment, looked around for Diane. But Diane was gone. She'd slipped out during the melee, taking her laptop and a small valise, and jumping into a taxi she'd booked in advance to meet her in front of a farmhouse down the road. She made one stop about ten miles from Le Petit Château, at an ATM so she could withdraw money from five different accounts to supplement the cash she had sewn into her clothes. The rest of her money had been transferred to her boyfriend Woy's name, for her to collect when they met up later.

After a second stop to purchase hair dye, it was on to Geneva, where she had the keys to a mate's apartment. She wasn't sure if she and the schoolmate, Kate, were friends at the moment, but it hardly mattered, as Kate was in New York for a wedding so Diane had the place to herself. She took a shower, found the keys to Kate's car and her emergency stash of coke—ten glorious grams—then did a few lines and packaged up the rest to take with her. After she cut her hair pixie-short and dyed it, she put in her blue contact lenses, changed into one of Kate's outfits, packed some clothes, and left.

The car had a full tank of gas. *So do I,* Diane noted with satisfaction, after cutting herself another line and snorting it up. She pulled out and drove east. The cocaine hit her heart and her brain at the same time, and she pushed her foot down harder on the gas.

Yeah, that felt good. She was in charge again. To hell with her family, she was going to start fresh. It was the new Europe and she could move fairly effortlessly all over the continent, as long as she laid low, kept to the back roads, and didn't run out of money. Or cocaine.

In a few weeks, she had to be in Paris to meet her boyfriend. They'd faked a breakup to mislead the newspapers before she went into rehab. He'd already gone underground. Nobody knew where he was either. It was so romantic.

For now, she just drove. The road was golden in the sunshine and she drove into the night, when the road turned silver in the moonlight. During the darkest stretches, the landscape on each side seemed to fall away and the road looked like a ribbon of light, floating in space.

CHAPTER 5

MUMBAI (formerly Bombay), INDIA

The heat had been building all day in Mumbai. The dirt powdered in the heat and rose, the sea water steamed, and the two mixed so at its most oppressive the air felt like an invisible muddy mist. Everyone in the city was hot, dirty, and angry. Those who could, bathed often. Those who had no access to showers waited for the monsoon with a piece of soap in the pocket, ready at a moment's notice for a spontaneous street shower.

In the newspapers and on TV, the commentators talked worriedly about the late rains and the implications for agriculture and the tourist industry. Thousands of free-spending Gulf Arabs had come to Mumbai after a year in the dusty desert to enjoy the rain, the way people from cold places like Canada and the Northern U.S. flocked to tropical beaches in the winter. While others ducked inside to dodge the wall of water, the Arabs flung open their balcony doors and went out to revel in it.

"Papa" Ganesh Dajgit sat hidden on his verandah behind a lacy wooden screen that let the air in and kept prying eyes out, watching the afternoon sky, not for the monsoon, but in a plea to the gods, bring this baby forth ALREADY. To ease his tension, one of his beautiful mistresses massaged his genitals.

His first grandson, Baby Ganesh, like the monsoon, was late. Until recently, there hadn't been much suspense in the pregnancy. Thanks to technology, the family had known for months that the fetus was healthy and a boy. An astrologer had determined that the estimated due date was an auspicious day. All seemed assured.

The champagne was on ice and the eunuchs were rounded up, in order that they might dance and sing near the family house, thus bringing good luck to the child, a tradition his daughters found freakishly old fashioned.

The due date came and passed. A week passed. The champagne remained on ice and the eunuchs drifted away. Two weeks passed. There were two false labors and doctors recommended inducing. But the astrologer cautioned against it. The baby had to come naturally, or they would never know its real birth date, its true destiny.

As he awaited the birth of the first son the Dajgit family had produced since him, Papa Dajgit tried to go about his business. There were pressing concerns to distract him, but somehow the urgent state of his affairs made him focus more and more on the birth. It became everything.

The only surviving son among three sisters who were all now the mothers of girls, Papa was the father of seven daughters himself, five with his wife and two with mistresses. He was the grandfather of six more little girls.

He couldn't get a son to save his life. The best he could do was to find sons-in-law. On the plus side, he was rich, and could offer a young man a comfortable life and opportunities for career advancement. But since his business was crime, many good husbands were kept away. Then there were the problems of caste.

For his generation and background, Papa was a relatively ecumenical and westernized Indian. All the same he would have liked for his daughters to marry up and to observe more of their Indian and Hindu traditions, if only for the sake of appearances.

The daughters were a big problem. Willful, spoiled, overly romantic, over sexed, raised on movies, MTV India, shopping trips to London and pop music, they refused to marry the men their father found for them. They united against him and their mother, tearing to pieces any potential husband they brought home. Eventually, he had to give in and let them choose their own husbands—because he desperately needed men in the family just to keep him from drowning in an estrogen fog.

Though the husbands they found for themselves were useful in different ways, none was the spiritual heir he wanted, let alone the blood-heir. And they seemed incapable of delivering a Y chromosome. They fathered girls too, though not so many of them. His daughters were modern and didn't want to be eternally pregnant, spilling forth a sea of daughters in hopes of getting a son, or having abortion after abortion until a male fetus arrived.

Finally, Amit and Farha came through for him. Of course, it was Amit who did the job. Amit was smart, obedient without being subservient, and full of ideas about modernizing the business by moving black money into real estate speculation, corporate extortion rackets, and internet porn. Papa wasn't convinced and had held back approval on everything except the internet porn idea, which he gave his blessing once he learned Farha's unborn child was a boy.

About three that afternoon, the heat and humidity had built to an inhuman level and the smell of brazier smoke and rot drifted up from the streets, rotting fruit, rotting meat, rotting wood. The mistress would have preferred to be inside the house, where there was air-conditioning, but Papa loved the smell of the street and the feel of the air. He kept watching the sky.

The mistress was getting impatient. She sighed a little too deeply and changed hands because the right hand was starting to cramp. Vigorously, she began to pump, like she was scrubbing barnacles off a pole.

"Not so hard!" he said, and she slowed down and relaxed her grip slightly, so she now seemed to be pulling up a very tough weed by its roots.

When he complained again, she finally deigned to use her mouth and brought him to a barely satisfactory conclusion.

This woman, Rakha, was his wife's day nurse and was not his favorite mistress. That would be Veena, but she was not available today, and hadn't been available much since she won that Filmfare award. He made a note in his Palm Pilot to send one of the men to remind her who got her into movies and who could get her out of them just as quickly.

"V. In-Out," he typed. Then he added, underneath: "GENTLY." He wanted someone to shake her up, but just enough to restore her respect, so he would again be wanted in her bed. This would be a job for Sanjay, the nicest of his sons-in-law.

The mistress excused herself to freshen up—to gargle, wash her hands, and see what she could pilfer from his wife's closet and jewelry chest. Mama Dajgit, immobilized by two strokes, could do nothing as she watched this thievery but blink curses in a Morse code nobody understood since Papa fired her previous day nurse for asking too many questions.

Papa stared at the sky until he saw the telltale monsoon clouds spread on the horizon like a dark stain, sweeping swiftly over the Arabian Sea toward Mumbai.

According to Papa, the first drops were just falling when Amit called with the news: Ganesh was born, was healthy, had all his toes and fingers, and let out a fierce, warlike yelp when he came into the world. Farha and the baby were in the post-natal unit now.

In fact, the rain fell for three-quarters of an hour before the call came, but close enough for a family legend, that Ganesh Kapoor was born at the exact moment the monsoon began. At other times and in other places, rain on the day of birth might seem a bad omen, but not in Mumbai.

Before he left for the hospital, Papa stopped in his private shrine to the god Ganesh from whom he and his new grandson took their names, to give thanks and burn some incense and flower petals in front of a new statue of the elephant-headed God of success, education, knowledge, wisdom and wealth, destroyer of evils and obstacles.

After he locked the safelike steel door that kept his shrine private, he went downstairs, surrounded by a cordon of well-paid bodyguards. All had been recruited in the slums at Bandra when they were young boys, 12 and 13, with muddied feet, red teeth, and parasites. Not one of them could then read or write. Their life expectancy was 30, perhaps 35 for the wily ones. For them, the opportunity to come work for the Dajgit Rowdydom was irresistible. They were fed, housed, debugged, and schooled. Everyone had to learn English, which was not only the official language of the world at large, but India itself, even with its 18 official languages and thousand dialects. They were put in clean suits and received salaries that, though modest, were more than they had ever dreamed of. Then, of course, there was the glamour.

In return, they were required to take a bullet for Papa if shot at and, ever since the Goonda war began with the Mumbai police, taste his food.

For now, all they had to do was surround him as he moved from the house to the limo with its bulletproof, smoked-glass windows.

From his car, Papa called his sons-in-law Sanjay and Doo and instructed them to pick up his widowed daughter Tara and bring her to the hospital.

Doo took the call. When he hung up, he said, "Farha had the baby."

"Little Ganesh is born," Sanjay said. "We are uncles of a nephew!"

It was touching how Sanjay was genuinely happy about having a little boy in the family. Doo was genuinely happy too, but not about the grandson. It would have been different if he had sired the long-awaited male heir to Papa's empire, but Doo could no longer ejaculate except under very specific conditions and in any event, his wife wouldn't sleep with him anymore and, after her daughters, didn't want any more children by anybody.

So now Amit was the golden boy. There was no chance of career advancement for Doo, the father of no sons and a foreigner to boot. It was either live his days as a glorified errand boy for the Dajgit family, or get gunned down on the street by the cops or rival gangsters, as hundreds of "goondas" had in the past two years, including Mohan, one of Papa's sons-in-law.

Or he could make off like a bandit, which is what Doo had chosen to do. A month earlier, he had set his plan in place when Papa worried aloud about protecting what he called "a family treasure." Papa worried a lot, but he was more worried than usual because of the heightened police threat and because some valuable things had been stolen from the house recently. This was the one thing he could not lose, which had to be preserved for Baby Ganesh and future Dajgit-Kapoors.

So, Doo suggested that since Papa wanted to have a new statue of Ganesh struck to honor the birth, he might hide the thing inside the statue. They never spoke about the "thing" in specifics. Papa was very mysterious and protective of it and didn't want any of his greedy children to know what valuable thing he possessed. Doo, however, had known about it for a long time.

The day of the casting, Papa had personally inserted a small, well-padded package into the statue's hollow center, and then supervised as the statue was sealed, soldered, and dipped in molten gold. After he left, Sanjay and Doo watched as the gold hardened, and was dipped twice more. They didn't leave until the statue was ready to take home and the mold broken in front of their eyes.

No matter about the mold though. The smith had already made a duplicate statue and given it to Doo the day before in exchange for 50,000 U.S. dollars. The duplicate had just one layer of the gold. Unlike the real statue, this one had nothing in its hollow core but some crumpled-up pages from the matrimonial section of the *Hindustan Times*.

It was the duplicate he and Sanjay delivered to Papa that day.

Then Doo bided his time, playing the slap-happy Aussie son-in-law Papa enjoyed so much, the cooperative, devil-may-care brother-in-law that Amit, Sanjay, and Chunky relied on, and the husband who was never around except when expressly called for that his wife Madhuri had trained him to be. The truth was, he was none of those things. He wasn't even a slap-happy Aussie named Doo McGarrigle. But he played all those parts well, for as long as he had to.

Behind the scenes, he got in touch with a former employer he knew in Europe from his days in Franco's Spain, where he had gone to sell mutual funds before getting sucked up into lucrative smuggling between Europe and Central Asia. While the Dajgit family was anticipating the birth, Doo bought dollars and euros on the black market to finance his trip, along with a counterfeit Australian passport in the name Harold Carpenter, a private joke.

Now that the baby had, finally, been born, launching weeks of celebratory mayhem, Doo could put his plan into action. He called to see when he could get a flight to Dubai. The only seat available was for a flight in three hours. He'd have to leave the hospital early, take the real statue from the trunk of his car, and get on the plane, leaving the Dajgit family and Doo McGarrigle behind.

But first they had to pick up Papa's daughter Tara, who for six months had been playing Ophelia for her late husband Mohan, gunned down by cops on Mumbai's Chowpatty Beach.

Traffic was terrible in the rain. Doo and Sanjay got stuck behind a man on foot hauling a cart stacked high with bags of cheap candy, a popular kind made of boiled sugar and water and sold in bazaars for a few paise a sack. The rain was melting the candy, and the man was moving as fast as he could, hoping to get to his destination before his cargo turned to syrup and disappeared into the gutters. But fast for him was painfully slow for Doo.

When they arrived, Tara was still in her pajamas, despite two phone calls from Sanjay to remind her that he and Doo were coming to take her to the family home for dinner tonight.

"Do you have a cigarette?" she asked.

"No. Your father wants you to quit, remember? Now get dressed."

"I don't think I'll go," Tara said, sliding into an armchair suddenly, as if all her bones had instantly melted like the candyman's cargo and left her unable to hold herself up.

"Come on, put on a pretty dress and come celebrate with the rest of the family," Sanjay said. "After the hospital we are all going to the Oberoi for supper. There'll be champagne and those little crepes you like."

"No, I can't. I don't want to. I didn't ask to be part of this family, you know."

"Papa said you have to be there."

"I am a widow because Papa said. Who do *I* have to kill to get *out* of this family?"

"Don't make jokes. Get dressed."

"It's not safe."

"All security has been arranged. Think of this as a way for the family to celebrate the end of Papa's complaining about not having a male heir," Sanjay said. "If you don't come, you'll miss the karaoke at the house after dinner."

"Tell him I'm sick. I think I have SARS, and cholera . . . and chlamydia."

Doo was losing patience. His flight was in less than three hours, and it was a fair hike from the hospital to the airport in the rain. Traffic would be bad, and he couldn't afford any more delays.

"Tara, you don't want to make your father angry today. Shall I call Madhuri to come help you?" Doo asked, referring to his wife and Tara's oldest sister, the family bully.

"No, don't call Madhuri. Please."

"Then get dressed and come to the hospital."

Tara surrendered, but slowly, moving to her bedroom as if she were walking through deep water. She took a long time in there.

"You can put your makeup on in the car," Doo said, surprising Sanjay with the sharp tone in his voice.

"Relax," Sanjay said. "Papa won't even notice that we are late to hospital. He is too happy."

Finally, Tara emerged in pink capri pants and a black blouse, wearing a toe ring, dark sunglasses, and a red bindi on her forehead. Doo and Sanjay took her to the hospital, where the whole clan was gathered to look at the squinting, frowning newborn.

After he and Sanjay touched the feet of Papa and Mama, a sign of respect, Doo said all the right things. Farha he commended for her beauty after her difficult ordeal. Amit he took aside to offer a jovial, guylike, "Good shootin', buddy." And Papa he hugged, looking genuinely delighted that there was finally a blood-heir, and predicting a new golden age for the Dajgit Rowdydom and for the great Papa Dajgit.

The old fool. If he knew what Doo really thought of him ... if any of them knew what he really thought. Of his brothers-in-law, Chunky was a gorilla, Sanjay an ass-kissing idiot, Amit a priggish operator and a snob. His own wife Madhuri was a stupid, spoiled bore who confused money with being intelligent and having sex appeal, and thought those B-list film stars she slept with kept her around because they actually found her attractive and interesting.

If only she knew how they mocked her behind her back. He had secretly overheard two of them at a Juhu Beach cafe, talking about Madhuri Dajgit and her legendary lovemaking skills.

One of the men was a character actor named Chota Pandit who often played a gangster and liked to hang around with the Dajgit boys for "character research." Doo thought he was a condescending ass, but Chota redeemed himself with his cruel impression of Doo's wife Madhuri during sex, looking like a donkey, belly up, limbs twitching like she was about to die. The details were perfect, right down to the freakish overbite and shrill orgasmic bray.

And Papa . . . a bully who imagined himself to be some sort of wise, paternalistic warrior like Don Corleone who had righted a wrong by taking from the rich and giving to the poor, himself and his own. That he was now rich and his business included shaking down poor people, like rickshaw drivers and prostitutes, didn't seem to occur to him. That wasn't shakedown. That was "protection" from other goondas.

Before the family dinner, Doo slipped away and drove to Bombay's Sahar Airport to get his plane for Bahrain. From there, he'd fly to Monte Carlo, meet his contact, get his suitcases of cash, and begin his new life.

On the plane, as he watched the lights of Mumbai recede into the dark of the Arabian Sea, he thought of the dinner they'd now be starting at the Oberoi. If they noticed he was not there, they would wait, but only for as long as Papa's patience lasted, perhaps five or ten minutes. Then dinner would begin without him. Papa would start with a long speech that would include the story of his father the dhobi, the washerman, who had a lifelong plan to rob the richest family in his town but died before he could fulfill it, and how Papa had taken up the cause and robbed the family, thus obtaining the seeds of his empire.

"I was born in the mud and raised into the sky," Papa would declare.

After that, Sanjay would lead an ass-kissing toast to Papa-ji, and then to Amit, who would thank Papa and the rest of the family. Tara would sneak off to smoke every half-hour. Amit and Madhuri and Chunky would argue about the cinema. At that point, he imagined, they would begin to wonder about his absence. In another hour they would begin to worry and try him on his cellphone.

By the next day, they would have called the family brothels to see if he'd embarked on a drunken walkabout and passed out there. Failing to find him, they would suspect he'd been shot by police in a setup and await notification by the police or the newspapers.

After two or three days, when it didn't come, they would realize the truth.

PART TWO

SAVE THE TOBLERONE FOR ME

After they ripped off Bob, Blackie and Chloe were going to quit. It was a one-time thing, the perfect crime, which had dropped into their lap. And that was it.

But there was no shortage of married men who wanted to seduce young women in Europe that year, or any year, anywhere, especially two women who were as magnetic as they were. After just two hours in Portofino, they landed in the middle of another perfect crime, this one in the form of a Mr. Slowenz, whose first name sounded like the word "Brackish" with a Slavic accent. It reminded Blackie of a joke she'd heard once about "the eighth dwarf, Brackish," and so did he, as he was on the short side and had tried to make up for it with a lot of hair and a hat.

They had first spotted him in a restaurant on a hill overlooking the beach, where he was dining with his wife, son, and daughter, eating like they hadn't eaten in days, but looking like they'd been eating quite well for some time, all plumped out in a shiny, skin-smoothing way. Blackie's quick assessment was that they were from some former Communist country where they had grown up eating poorly and were now making up for it, storing fat in case bad times came again.

The next time they saw Brackish was on the beach, alone. Blackie caught his eye and recognized him from lunch, which he misinterpreted as flirtation and an invitation to approach.

"Uh oh, it's that man from lunch," Blackie said. "He's coming our way."

"Bonjorno," he said.

"Hello," Blackie said.

"You speak English."

"Happily, so do you evidently."

Without waiting for any invitation, he sat down on the beach chair next to Blackie.

"Brackish Slowenz," he said.

"I'm Audrey, from Canada, and this is my friend Grace from the United States," Blackie said. "Are you here alone?"

"Yes."

"Didn't we see you with your family at lunch?" Chloe asked.

"My family?" he said, repeating the phrase to buy himself time to think of an answer. "No, no, my sister and her children. I'm divorced."

"Your sister's children call you Papa?" Chloe interrogated.

"Yes, they . . . I suppose they think of me as their father, since their father died."

"How did he die?" Chloe shot back, giving him just a little more rope.

"In a . . . he fell from a roof."

"When did that happen?"

Blackie felt it was now time to step in and play good cop.

"That's sweet. Aw. You've been looking after them since their father died?"

"Yes."

"That's really admirable, Brackish. Isn't that admirable, Grace?"

"Let's go swimming," Chloe said. "We'll be right back, Brackish. You relax."

They left their belongings under the watch of Brackish, and when they returned, Chloe claimed all their money was missing. It worked like a charm. Brackish immediately wanted to turn suspicion from himself and, at the same time, find a way to turn their loss to his advantage.

"I am very rich, I will loan you some money," he said.

But first, he had to "find a hotel room." Yes, because he could not take them back to the suite he had now where his wife and children were in residence, probably eating a room service turkey right now as an afternoon snack to hold them until dinner.

When they arrived, he went into the bathroom to make their drinks, a special cocktail he said. Chloe went in right after him to wash her hands and found the only thing he'd brought with him to this hotel was a shaving kit. Inside was an unmarked bottle of white pills. More tellingly, by the side of the sink was a trace of white powder, as if a pill, or pills, had been crushed there.

"Don't drink anything," she whispered to Blackie when she returned. "Where's Brackish?"

"Ordering room service in the bedroom."

Chloe emptied her glass into a potted plant. She switched Blackie's glass with that of Brackish.

"What's going on?" Blackie asked.

Chloe opened her hand and showed her a white pill.

"What is it?"

"I don't know. Viagra? Date rape drug? It's not a roofie, they have something in them that turns the liquid blue."

"But there are new date rape drugs that don't, like GHB."

"We'll find out, I expect, when he takes a sip."

When Brackish returned, he lifted his glass in a toast to them and drank. He spoke of his great business successes back in Slovakia, how he now owned a lot of real estate in Bratislava, and then he cited case after case of women madly in love with him, as if he knew they would not believe he was attractive without a lot of anecdotal evidence. When their glasses were empty, he went to make "new cocktails," weaving his way to the bathroom. On his way back, the pill—or pills—kicked in, and he crumpled to the floor, the glasses sliding off his tray and spilling onto the bed.

"What a loser," Chloe said. "We should call the cops. He's probably done this before, like that Max Factor heir who drugged and raped all those women and then went on the lam."

"Can we do it anonymously?"

"Duh. And we'll put it on tape. You narrate while you video him with the bottle of pills. I'll wipe for fingerprints."

"This man, who is on vacation with his wife and children, attempted to drug me with these pills," Blackie said off-camera, affecting the same southern accent she used when she played Blanche DuBois in a high school production of *Streetcar*. "I switched his drink with mine, and he subsequently passed out. I believe he has done this before. His wife and children are staying at another hotel."

They left the tape and left the wallet too this time, so as not to muddy the case with accusations of theft. Chloe took all but two of the pills and slipped them into her purse. After they cleared the hotel, they called the Italian police on a public pay phone, and went back to their hotel to pack.

— — —

In an elevator in a hotel in La Spezia, Italy, Chloe discovered a talent for picking pockets. A German man who had been hitting on them bent over slightly to get a closer look at Blackie's cleavage, which exposed the wallet in his back pocket to Chloe, standing behind him. Chloe feigned a small trip, pushing the man into Blackie while she nipped the wallet out and into her purse. When they disembarked on the ground floor, they slipped away from him and caught a train for Genoa.

In Genoa, while shopping in an old-fashioned paper store located in a medieval cobblestone lane that twisted back from the Old Port, they both became inspired, in different ways, by the delicate blown-glass pens and jewel-like jars of colored and perfumed ink.

"I see this stuff and I just want to write florid, heart-spending love letters, with a quill," Chloe said, sadly, having nobody to write love letters to now. "While sitting in my fairy-like nightdress at a desk by an open window overlooking the sea. I wonder where John is now—"

"Indelible ink!" Blackie said.

"What?"

"Indelible ink. Next time a guy tries to drug us, we write a note on the man with indelible ink. What do we write? I have it— I prey on young women. Simple, to the point."

"This one is peppermint scented," Chloe said, picking up a jar of green indelible ink. "We could use it even on the pervs who don't try to drug us. We just have to put it in a different container and say it's sex lotion. Paint a guy's dick with it."

"Explain that to your wife when you get home."

"How could he? He'd have to hide it and make up a story . . ."

"I have this terrible rash I picked up in Genoa."

Once they'd purchased ink and paint brushes, they couldn't wait to use them. But they had rules. They couldn't seek out their "victim." He had to find them.

There were more misses than hits, promising marks who went bust. They let a guy go in Savona because he was just a lonely guy whose wife hadn't wanted to sleep with him for a long time, and told them this outright. The girls believed him. They felt bad for him and his wife—but not enough to sleep with him.

Another married man looked like a rich prospect but he didn't con them, and he wasn't cheating on his wife. He wanted the girls to join him and his wife. They were swingers, working their way west towards Cap d'Agde, which, he told them, was a veritable nudist paradise in summer. The town was divided between the "nude side and the prude side." This time of year, the nude side numbered about 40,000 people, with its own nude apartment buildings, banks, shops, and restaurants.

"Are there a lot of ugly revolving-door accidents?" Blackie asked.

The man didn't get the joke, or he wasn't really listening. He went on, telling them that the nude side was subdivided into the "family" side and the "swinger" side. He and his wife were heading to the swinger side. Blackie and Chloe declined his invitation, and laughed afterwards that one of the most honest people they'd met so far was a wife-swapper.

In San Remo, they finally had a chance to use the ink. His name was Ali, and he was an Oxford-educated businessman from the Gulf, and though he had no wedding-ring line, he was likely married. At least forty and wealthy, tall and nice-looking, chances were good he had at least one wife back in Saudi Arabia. Like the other marks, he found Blackie and Chloe on the beach and shortly afterwards he fell for the missing money scam. It seemed like a routine job for the girls, until they got to his suite for dinner and his friend Abu was there waiting with him.

Blackie looked at Chloe. They'd never done two guys at once before. It was risky. But the men looked rich, Chloe wanted to git 'em, and Blackie was just dying to use the indelible ink.

As usual, Blackie played the Good Cop, but she was just a little extra friendly to the two gentlemen. Chloe was a little extra chilly. Silently, her face a mask, she endured the men's business boasts, Ali's condescending manner, and Abu's roaming eyes and sinister grin until she couldn't take it anymore. Everything these men did was, in their own view, superior to most mortals. Everything they owned was "limited edition," "one of a kind," or "top-drawer."

"This hotel is historic, the best hotel in San Remo, and this is the best suite in the hotel," Abu said. "And the food is top-drawer."

"It's all just wonderful," Blackie said.

"Are you enjoying your first trip to Europe?" Ali asked. "Do you find Europe more civilized than America and Canada?"

"Do you think America is uncivilized?" Chloe spoke up, an edge to her voice. "Less civilized than, for example, Saudi Arabia?"

"We come from a great, ancient tribe of people," Ali said defensively.

"So do we," Chloe said. "We all come from an ancient tribe of people somewhere. Americans didn't just evolve out of the bogs three hundred years ago."

Abu didn't like the way this was shaping up. He and Ali had expected an easy seduction of the naive young North American women. An argument would ruin any chance of that. They'd have to use drugs, and that would take some of the thrill out of the conquest.

"Ali didn't mean to offend," Abu said.

"No. I simply meant to say that Europe has a much older culture than America, more steeped in history—"

"So?"

"That there's art everywhere here, beautiful architecture."

"We've got art in America! We've got architecture!"

"Europe is very civilized," Blackie chimed in cheerfully. "Lots of art, lots of architecture. I really like that about Europe."

"Of course," Chloe said. "But it isn't as if America is a complete cultural wasteland inhabited by savages."

Room service rang at the door and saved poor Ali. Before the waiter left, he opened one bottle of wine and poured it in front of them. It was safe; the girls drank it with confidence. They were beginning to wonder if this was just a plain old, boring dinner with a couple of traveling businessman on the make, and not an opportunity for a juicy crime. In other words, a wasted evening.

But when it came time to open the second bottle of wine, Abu took it into the outer room to pour it, away from their view. He claimed he wanted to rinse out the glasses so the new wine wouldn't be contaminated by the previous stuff, which was a different vintage.

Ali stayed with Blackie and Chloe. When he began to speak, Blackie said, "Sshh. Listen to that, the sound of the sea." Then she listened to the sound coming from the next room: the tinkle of metal hitting glass, of something being stirred into liquid.

Now they needed a way to get rid of both men while they switched glasses, and they were going to have to do it without consulting each other.

Chloe looked at Blackie and nodded slightly. She had the plan.

When Abu returned with four glasses of wine on a tray, Chloe said, "I'm out of cigarettes. Damn! I'm so cranky without cigarettes. I have to go downstairs to get more."

"I'll go with you!" Blackie said.

"Don't be silly," Abu said. "I will call room service for cigarettes. Dunhill Green? Fine. Excuse me."

After he left, Blackie pointed and said, "Ali, what is that painting on the far wall? Is it a Renoir?"

Ali laughed. "Oh no, no. This is a reproduction of a Raphael. He and Renoir are from completely different schools and eras!"

Blackie walked toward it. Ali followed.

"It's very vivid, isn't it," Blackie said.

While their backs were turned, Chloe switched her glass with Ali's. Before she could switch Blackie's glass, Abu came back with cigarettes. Chloe picked up his glass and hers, and handed hers to him casually.

"We have a head start on you," she said, as if she had already drunk from her glass. "This is an interesting wine. It's going straight to my head."

When Blackie and Ali returned to the table, they all toasted to Italy and beautiful young women and the moon over San Remo. Then they ate. Soon, the men's speech was slurring, and before long their legs slipping under them. Ali collapsed first. Abu held on for another five minutes before passing out.

"What would you have done if we couldn't have switched glasses?" Blackie asked as they stripped the men naked.

"Spilled my wine. What about you?"

"I'd almost puke on one of them, call it the flu, or food poisoning, and you'd take me back to our hotel."

"Can you throw up on command?"

"I can fake almost throwing up," Blackie said. A spasm jerked her upper body and her cheeks puffed out at the same time. She put her hand over her mouth as her body heaved.

"That's great. How come I didn't know this about you?"

"I only learned it last March, at a frat party. I haven't had a lot of cause to use it yet. Whoa. I have an idea."

"What?"

"Let's put them in an oral sex scenario with each other," she said.

"Oh my god. Yes."

"But first, we paint their dicks with indelible ink, peppermint green for Ali I think, and red for Abu. That way, their mouths will be stained too, and they won't be able to look at each other for days without being reminded of their night of tender manlove."

They left a note for the cops with the bottle of pills they found in Ali's jacket pocket, less a few they kept for future mashers. Then they helped themselves to 2,300 euros.

After that triumph, they hit a dry patch. Not a mark in sight for three days.

In Ventimiglia, just shy of the border with France, Chloe almost ripped off a rich Arab woman because she so harshly berated her Filipino maid, or lady-in-waiting, or whatever she was. Her purse, something Gucci, was just sitting there, on the table at a cafe while she lacerated the poor young woman in accented English, her hands clenched into fists at her side as if she were forcing them down, trying to keep them from rising up and hitting the maid in public. The maid cowered and bit her quivering lip.

Chloe reached for the bag, but Blackie grabbed her arm to stop her.

"The rules," Blackie reminded her. This was not a married man trying to con them, and so it was outside their victim pool.

Blackie exacted a better justice. While the woman stood and shrilled cuttingly at her employee, Blackie discreetly poured some water on the woman's chair, so when she sat down and stood again, it would look like she'd peed her pants.

"She deserved to be ripped off," Chloe said afterwards.

"Yes, but how would that have helped the maid? She might have accused her of it," Blackie said. "And remember . . . the rules."

By now, Blackie was tiring a little of crime. It had been fun and had helped them move up from no-star backpacker lodgings to comfortable three-star hotels with dazzling views.

But here they were, in a landscape of sea and terraced grape vines, olive groves, and whitewashed buildings covered in brilliant bougainvillea and roses, whose aroma filled the warm lamplit evenings. It seemed a place for romance, or at least sex, but that wasn't likely as long as they were spending their time with rich perverts.

Chloe, though, wasn't ready to give it up. It had been strangely empowering for her. Since their crime spree had begun, she hadn't mentioned John Carey once, though sometimes at night she went out on the balcony of whatever hotel they were in and cried.

And then, on the train to Menton, France, she thought she saw John getting into the adjacent car. It turned out to be a Swedish guy on his way to meet his boyfriend. Whatever. It was enough to snap Chloe back into her old self, listless, ungrateful, wondering aloud far too often where John Carey was, who he was with now, what he was doing and seeing, and if Blackie thought he might marry someone else.

"I think he'll burn through a dozen more women before he finally finds the one he'll put through the wood chipper ten years later in order to get the insurance money to cover his stock market losses," Blackie said.

"Please don't do that."

"What?"

"Say mean things about him. It doesn't make me feel better."

Nothing did, except for crime. In Menton, a sleepy, rich little seaside city just over the French border, Chloe practiced picking pockets at the Cocteau Museum, just for fun, returning the wallet to the victim with a polite, "Did you drop this, sir?" Sometimes, she'd offer one man another man's wallet to see if he was honest.

If he took it, she'd pick his pocket again, twice, taking the other wallet and his own as well. It relieved her agita, but only temporarily. Blackie did not approve.

Menton was a tedious parade of gracious elderly gentlemen, with not a mark among them. Then came Doug Mason, an elderly retiree from Ohio, looking like he'd stepped out of a Duane Hanson painting, wearing Bermuda shorts, white sport socks with sandals, and a gray T-shirt that boasted, "World's Greatest Grandfather." He was carrying a shopping sack as he trudged toward them on the beach.

Chloe saw him first. "Oh here he comes," she said, snapping out of her moody lethargy. "Our next victim, and just the way I like them too, fat and pink-cheeked."

"Hello, you speak English?" he asked.

"Yes," Blackie said.

"Thank God. Can I sit down?"

"We wouldn't want to turn away the World's Greatest Grandfather," Blackie said. Chloe was silent.

He plopped down on a beach chair. "Thanks. Doug Mason, from Ohio."

"Audrey and Grace."

"Audrey and Grace, do you enjoy poetry?" he asked.

"We sure do."

"How would you like to buy a poem?"

"Well—"

"Before you answer, listen to me. You can read the poem before you pay for it. You only pay if you like the poem."

"How much is it?"

"Two euros."

"You're selling poetry? For real?"

"I believe if something has value, you can sell it! And I'm provin' it."

Chloe turned from his view, lowered her glasses, and looked at Blackie. She was all charged up.

Blackie bought his poem without reading it and asked him the usual polite questions. Why was he in Europe? Where was he from in Ohio? Was he married?

"I'm from Chagrin Falls, Ohio. I'm a widower," he said. "Two sons and two daughters-in-law, five grandkids. They bought me this trip, a summer in France."

"Oh really," Chloe said. "It's astonishing how many widowers there are on the Riviera this year."

"Are there? Maybe I'll meet up with some more."

"When did your wife die?' Blackie asked.

"A little over a year ago."

The way he said it made Blackie wonder if he was sincere, but Chloe was suspicious of him. She initiated the missing money scam, dragging Blackie into the water and proclaiming her money lost when she returned to the beach and Doug Mason. As usual, the scam and their Good Cop–Bad Cop routine worked. Mason immediately offered to loan them a little money.

"The poetry's been sellin' well, and I don't need the money. I'm retired and I have enough in the bank. What do you need, a hundred bucks?"

Blackie stopped the game. "Chloe, I have our money in my purse."

"I don't think so."

"Oh yes, I do. See."

"Let me buy you girls lunch anyway," Doug Mason offered, and Blackie accepted for both of them.

They ate at a restaurant on the beach, and Chloe had a salad with preserved duck in it, which inspired Doug Mason to announce that he used to be a champion duck carver. Chloe scorned his boasting.

"Decoys. You make wood . . . duck decoys," she said.

"My ducks were art," he said. "And I didn't use just any wood. Tupelo Gum. That's the best wood for carving, but the hardest to carve."

"Why?" Blackie asked.

"It's a tricky wood, you really have to get to know it, develop a feel, because it's as soft in spots as balsa and as hard in others as walnut."

"You said you 'used to be a champion duck carver,'" Chloe said. "Lost the crown to an up-and-comer, did you?"

"I gave up duck carving."

"Why?"

"Not enough money in it," he said.

Chloe looked at Blackie as if this confirmed she was right about the guy.

"You gave up duck carving because there wasn't enough money in it, and you took up . . . poetry?" Blackie said.

"Yes."

"And is there money in poetry?"

"Like I said, it's selling well. I've sold over a thousand poems since I started at two bucks a crack. Or two euros. Nice even number. Then I've sold a few hundred copies of my book of poems through my website. Ten bucks. The address is at the bottom of the poem I sold ya. You haven't read that poem yet by the way."

"I wanted to talk to you instead, Doug. I'll read it now."

This poem wasn't really a poem. It was more of a prose piece. It was about his narcoleptic brother who would have drowned in his soup in front of the television in 1964 if his wife in the kitchen hadn't heard Ed Sullivan announce Topo Gigio and gone to watch. She loved Topo Gigio. Topo Gigio saved his brother's life. Blackie handed it to Chloe.

"So tell us about your family," Blackie said.

His wife Mona had died of uterine cancer—a dog shouldn't have to die the way she did, he said. He had two grown sons, Jeff who built loghouse vacation homes and John who sold pharmaceutical products, both married, with five kids between them. They all helped him get through the last year. Just as he was starting to tell them how he met his wife, three other elderly people from his bus tour came by to remind him they had to go inland to a castle.

"I told you he wasn't trying to make us," Blackie said after he'd left.

"Okay. He wasn't trying to make us," Chloe said. She sounded completely deflated by this. "Menton's a bust. Let's blow this town, Audrey."

"Monte Carlo, Grace?"

— — —

Sons-in-law Sanjay and Chunky were in Elephanta, waiting for papa's favorite mistress Veena Nata to finishing shooting her scene with Partap Krishnan.

"Papa suggests if you are overworked he will arrange to lighten your shooting schedule," Sanjay was to say to Veena, in the nicest possible way. But he didn't get the chance. Before he and Chunky could see her, they received a text message from Papa: "URGENT. HOME. NOW!"

"They found Doo's body," Sanjay guessed sadly and was wrong.

It was two days after Doo's disappearance and everyone suspected he had been gunned down. Only Papa was starting to suspect something else. Nobody's fool, he sent his sons-in-law Sanjay and Chunky around to retrace Doo's steps. It took only five minutes to learn of the duplicate statue from the goldsmith— five minutes with Chunky's gleaming dagger poised beneath the poor man's testicles. Sanjay had to look away—he hated the rough stuff and breathed with great relief when the goldsmith spoke and Chunky pulled his knife back and sheathed it.

When Papa learned about the statue, he had Chunky break it, knocking off a piece of the bottom with a sledgehammer and inserting a wedge that, when struck, broke the bottom off, exposing the hollow center.

"This is not my statue," Papa thundered, pulling out the crumpled pages from the *Hindustan Times*. He turned to his two sons-in-law. "Go to Bahrain, find out where Doo went from there. Kill him and bring back Ganesh."

Oh how Papa hated to send these two. For a job this tricky, he would have rather sent Amit, but Amit was needed here with Papa's daughter and grandson, and to get the family's new internet porn business up and running. Tara's husband Mohan was dead. Doo would have been the next option and he was obviously not available. Papa was left with no choice but to send Sanjay and Chunky. Sanjay was a jolly son-in-law, but not too bright, though next to Chunky he was a rocket scientist.

But they got off to a promising start, learning in Bahrain that Doo, now passing as a guy named Harry Carpenter, had gone to Monte Carlo, and so Sanjay and Chunky did too.

— — —

Menton is a rich town, but it looks like a poor relation in off-the-rack next to the wealth of its nearby tax-haven neighbor of Monte Carlo, Monaco. Suddenly, the pristine blue sea fills with yachts, tall luxury apartment buildings and imposing mansions rise out of the landscape of modest tiled roofs, and you pick up the heady tang of hard currency and the bleachy smell of money laundering in the salt air.

Monaco, a few acres on the shore, proudly calls itself a country (awwww), and is ruled by a "serene" prince in a pink palace. Its motto, displayed on buildings around Monte Carlo, is *Deo Juvante*.

—from *The Lonesome Roads Guide to France*

"*Deo Juvante*. What does that mean?" Blackie wondered after reading this passage to Chloe.

"Deo Juvante: 'Nice country, doesn't take up much space'?" Chloe suggested.

" 'You can eat off our streets, but please don't, it would make us sick to see that.' "

" 'Bring us your jaded, your wealthy, your swaddled masses yearning to be tax-free—' "

"Let's go shopping."

At the Monte Carlo Casino, it is important to look classy. It is a pale peach-colored castle with turrets, waving banners, ornate gilt, painted ceilings, and staff dressed like ladies and gentlemen, just as one might imagine a fancy French gambling den where both Mata Hari and Elizabeth Taylor had gambled. You couldn't play the slots in your bathrobe and curlers here, like in Vegas. The Monte Carlo Casino had a dress code. Men had to wear jackets. At the door, they charged ten euros admission to help weed out the voyeurs and riff-raff and reserved the right to refuse service to anyone.

Backpacker dress-up clothes—a simple sundress and ballet slippers or Mary Janes—just wouldn't make the grade. With some of the cash they'd taken from perverts, Chloe and Blackie bought new dresses and shoes. Chloe bought an ice blue sheath, classic and understated. It provided the subtlest contrast to her pale skin and white-blonde hair, but the overall effect was stunning.

Blackie bought a fitted red dress with half-sleeves. Not so subtle, but it made her look a little less Lara Croft and a little more Liz Taylor.

They stuffed their old clothes into their fancy shopping bags and wore the new clothes to lunch in a little cafe overlooking the bay. Blackie flirted with the waiter. His name was François Albert, and he told them he was saving money to move to Paris to be an actor. Blackie would have lingered to talk to him more, and maybe picked him up, if Chloe hadn't dragged her away to the casino.

If you're in Monte Carlo for a day, the only game to play is roulette, just like James Bond or the late King Farouk of Egypt. Blackie sat between an intense, nervous man with red hair and a middle-aged woman wearing pearls and enough perfume to fog an Iraqi battalion. Chloe sat between two men who looked at her at the same time when she sat down. The whole table seemed to do a double-take when she appeared, before the roulette man resumed business, closing all bets and spinning the wheel.

The woman within the Chanel forcefield was evidently winning and the nervous man losing. Then the situation reversed, the woman began to lose and the nervous man began to win.

Both Blackie and Chloe were losing. Blackie stopped and got up. The nervous man put some of his chips in front of her.

"Stay, please," he said in English with an accent she couldn't identify right away.

Chloe had that glittering cold-water-shark look in her eyes. Blackie sat back down.

After a couple of martinis and a healthy winning streak, the nervous man was no longer so nervous. He continued to ply Blackie with gambling chips, until she got bored and stood up, in defiance of Chloe's look. Chloe had him picked out: He was their mark.

"Stay," he said.

"I'm starving," Blackie said.

"Let me buy you dinner."

"I'm with my friend," she said, motioning toward Chloe.

"I'll buy you both dinner. Harry Carpenter."

"Audrey and Grace."

This guy invited them to go have dinner in his hotel, the Blanca, but when they got there, they didn't have a reservation so he offered to feed them in his suite—big surprise—which had a great view he wanted them to see anyway.

"A view of him naked with his dick in his hand, I bet," Blackie whispered.

Something made Blackie not want to go. He was too intense, too dark. They hadn't had a chance to pull the missing money scam in order to test his reactions and size him up. He had no ring line, said he wasn't married, and didn't seem married. With most married men, it's pretty easy to guess. They just smell like husbands somehow.

The whole thing felt bad to her.

"Why don't we just go eat somewhere near the harbor," she suggested.

"We'll never get a table anywhere decent," Chloe said, and went with the man to the elevator. Blackie wasn't about to let Chloe go alone so she followed. They ate a cold seafood dinner in his smallish suite, they poured their own wine from a bottle they'd watched him open, and he told of his adventures traveling the world, some of which would turn out to be his, and some of which he stole from people he met along the way.

"I was raised in Mollywat," he said, with an off-Aussie accent. "It's near Adelaide. My father owned a garage and wanted me to work in it, but he died when I was 17 and we had to sell it. My auntie Alice said without that yoke around my neck I was just an untethered balloon, waiting for the first big wind to take me somewhere."

"What kind of accent do you have?" Blackie asked with barely contained suspicion. "It sounds weird."

"Well, I haven't been in Oz in many years. My accent has been worn down and warped by traveling."

Chloe encouraged him. "So you were saying earlier that you sold mutual funds in Franco's Spain?"

Without meaning to, Chloe and Blackie had switched roles.

"Yeah. But it wasn't the right job for me. I made a lot of money, then I headed to South Africa to mine diamonds. Made a fortune there, and headed to Pakistan to spy for the CIA and learn to play Buzkashi in the refugee camps during the war against the Soviets. You heard of the game?"

"No," Chloe said. "Tell us!"

"It's like polo, for real men. You play on horseback with the headless corpse of a goat. Brutal game. If you're not covered in blood by game's end, you haven't really played. The Afghan players said I was almost as good as Sher Ali, the Joe Namath of Buzkashi."

Then he said he had a special wine for after dinner, and he went into the bedroom to get it. "What a charmer," Blackie said.

"A rich charmer."

"Let's get out of here."

"No."

"I'll tell you the rest of his stories later. After Pakistan, he went to Thailand to learn a game played with the headless corpse of a child prostitute, then he made a fortune in SARS masks in Taiwan. . . ."

"Good, then he deserves to get ripped off. Let's stay."

"It doesn't feel right, Chloe. Let's go."

"You go. I'm staying." She was all lit up.

"I won't leave you here alone with him."

"Is there a full moon or something? You're so jumpy."

The next thing they heard was the sound of metal hitting glass.

"He's stirring something," Blackie said. "Drugs."

He returned with a small tray bearing three glasses of something golden and a bottle of the same.

Chloe was ready to fake-trip in order to spill her wine and cause a distraction so Blackie could switch glasses, when the phone rang. He stepped into the bathroom to take the call on the phone by the toilet.

Blackie switched her glass with his, while Chloe emptied hers. Then, to "be on the safe side," Chloe added a crushed pill from her private supply of pills to Harry's drink, mixing it until it was fully dissolved.

In the bathroom, he raised his voice. "I can sell it anywhere."

Pause.

"No. All of it. No more excuses. I've waited long enough. Tomorrow or it's all over."

"Let's go," Blackie said.

"No, I want to see if he falls asleep after he drinks."

"Okay, then let's go."

When he returned, he was wearing his hotel bathrobe. He toasted the girls and drank.

"I want to dance," Chloe said, taking off her shawl and letting it slide to the floor. She kicked off her shoes. "I want to dance in my underwear. Harry, will you unzip me?"

He had been drinking steadily all day and had at least one pill in his system now. But he showed no effects. He was like Rasputin. Encouraged by Chloe's striptease, he began telling stories about his sexual exploits, as Chloe cooed and subtly encouraged him to wilder and wilder stories—Yes, he had had two girls at once, three even, never had sex with a man, watched a woman with a goat—culminating with the time in Macao when he'd first had sex and played Russian roulette at the same time.

"They say auto-erotic asphyxiation is the greatest sexual high ever, that's why people risk killing themselves for it. But pulling that trigger while you come . . . that's it, I'm telling you."

He was starting to sweat. His bathrobe barely hid his hard-on when he stood to go to the john.

"Let's make a run for it," Blackie said.

"He'll be out soon. Relax."

"Please, let's go. He had sex while playing Russian roulette! He's a fucking psycho."

Reeling, Harry came out of the bathroom, his bathrobe wide open, waving his member with one hand and a gun with the other, slurring, "Come here, beauties." Chloe was about to scream, when he wobbled forward and collapsed.

He was a big man, and it took plenty of dragging to get him on to the bed. After they videotaped him in compromising positions, their faces hidden but his exposed, they wiped his gun for prints and put it back in his hand for more videotaping.

Chloe cleaned out his wallet—1400 euros—and took a gold ring she found in the drawer of a bedside table.

"A wedding ring," she noted. "He was married. I knew it."

They found no bottle of pills or any other evidence that he had tried to drug them and there wasn't much else to take. There was one other thing, in the closet, in a box behind his shoes, a small gold statue about a foot high of an Indian God, the one with the head of an elephant.

"Think it's worth anything?" Chloe asked.

"I dunno. I like it," Blackie said. "It's cute."

"Take it."

Blackie shoved it into her shopping bag and they left, passing two men on their way to the elevator, one smallish and dark, one burly and pale with dark hair, both in a big hurry to get somewhere. The men noticed them, but barely, something far more important on their minds.

Afterwards, Chloe and Blackie went to celebrate at the casino, winning some money, drinking too much, and passing out when they got back to their hotel. So, it wasn't until morning that they got around to making an anonymous call to the police to tell them there was a pervert with a gun in room 1211 at the Hotel Blanca. After breakfast in the hotel, the girls hoisted up their backpacks and hiked to the gare to catch the next train to Nice where, according to an internet search, there was a good pawn shop.

CHAPTER 7

Sanjay and Chunky found Doo in Monte Carlo in one day just by asking a few questions at the casino.

To make their job even easier, when they broke into his hotel room, he was already unconscious, and with his own gun in his hand. While Chunky stood guard over Doo, Sanjay searched the room.

"I can't find it," Sanjay said.

"The statue?"

"No, the Taj Mahal. Yes, the statue. He must have sold it already."

"What should we do? When will he wake up?"

"I don't know," Sanjay said. He sat down on the bed and thought. "Hand me Doo's cellphone."

In the last three days, Doo had called one number, twice. Sanjay pressed the autodial button and it brought up a name: "Sophisticated Ladies." The woman who answered the phone evidently saw the number calling and recognized it. She didn't even wait for Sanjay to talk.

"I told you not to call here again," she said. "If you do, I shall call the police." She swore in French and the line went to dial tone.

While they waited for Doo to regain consciousness, Chunky raided the minibar.

"Hey, save the Toblerone for me," Sanjay said, flicking for the Pay-TV movie channels.

After they'd watched Gigli and eaten their way through the

Toblerone, the cashews, a mini ballotin of Godiva truffles, and some cheesy biscuits, Doo finally stirred. It was almost dawn.

He didn't quite wake, so Chunky sped up the process with a bucket of water and half-melted ice.

"Ohhh, God," Doo groaned.

"Where is the statue?" Chunky asked.

Doo half-opened his eyes.

"Oh no," he said. His throat was dry and his feeble, raspy voice sounded like it was coming from a very old man.

"Where is the statue?" Chunky asked again, putting Doo's own gun to his head.

"In the clo . . . clo . . . closet."

"No, it is not," Chunky said.

"Oh oh no . . . Two girls . . .

"Which girls?" Sanjay asked.

"Grace. Audrey. A blonde and a brunette—"

"Where are they now?"

"I don't know. Oh God. Papa—"

"Yeah, Papa is angry," Chunky said. He pushed the gun barrel harder into Doo's skull. "Tell us more."

"I don't know anything else. Please, we are brothers," Doo pleaded.

"Just one moment," Sanjay said, turning the satellite TV to a music channel and boosting the volume to the max. The gun had a silencer, but contrary to popular belief, a silencer doesn't render a gun completely silent.

After putting the gun back into Doo's hand, Chunky shoved the gun into Doo's mouth. During a particularly clanging percussionist portion of a rock song on MTV France, he pulled the trigger.

The cleanup was the toughest part. Sanjay had brought a dust buster to help pick up any hair or fiber evidence that might help identify them. He ran it over the carpet, the bedspread, and even over Doo's dead body. He didn't bother to clean up the blood and bits of bone and brain tissue splattered on the headboard and the wall. After Sanjay had vacuumed, he sprinkled hairs and fibers they had collected from people in Mumbai, people from their plane, people in the hotel. On the table, they found a videotape. Sanjay pocketed it.

Before they left, they pressed the Do Not Disturb button on the phone and hung the Do Not Disturb / Ne Dérangez Pas sign on the outside of the door. They hoped to buy some time before the discovery of the body.

▬ ▬ ▬

Papa was in a lousy mood before he heard about Doo and the missing statue. That morning, leafing through his copy of *Movie Majick* magazine, he read this:

> Success hasn't changed Veena Nata. Now she has fame and crores of rupees, but our Veena is still the simple, down to earth orphan girl who used to sell flowers outside the SiddhiVinayak Temple at Prabhadevi, before her breakout role as the *Desi Doll* in Boney Sharma's blockbuster, *Pagal Hah Pagal.*
>
> We caught up with the beautiful phenom at the International Pub and Grill where *Movie Majick* magazine hosted a cocktail party and photo shoot for the Stars of Tomorrow, and where the talk was all about Preity Padit's seven on-screen kisses with Anil in *Chori Chori Pyaar.*
>
> " 'I don't like to kiss on-screen,' " Veena told us. " 'But I don't rule it out completely. If the role I was playing absolutely demanded it then yes, I would kiss, but only to preserve the integrity of the character. I will never gratuitously kiss just for cheap titillation. I leave such gimmicks to other young actresses who must rely on them, like Preity and Saraswati.
>
> " 'Recently, I met with an American director who wants me for his next movie and he said the part involves some nu-

dity. Well, I said I refuse to do nudity unless it is absolutely necessary to play the role fully and is filmed in an artistic manner. Otherwise, he would have to find another actress. I would rather lose a great role than compromise my morals. I do not need to be the next Mandikini. I can always sell flowers again.' "

Hah, she is sweet, our Veena. But what is this about an "American director?" Is our Veena going to become NRI, kya? Say it ain't so, Veena!

" 'No, no,' she tells us. "It is just one role in one movie, and I haven't decided if I will do it. I could never move from India. Mumbai is my home.' "

That's right she would never move from Mumbai. And why did she even discuss this role outside India without consulting him? Papa had been so wrapped up in the beautiful new grandson and Doo's betrayal, he hadn't had a chance to send someone out to speak with her since he'd sent Sanjay and Chunky to Europe. After the birth of Baby Ganesh, she had sent a warm letter and a lovely gift and expressed the wish they could see each other soon. But whenever he called, her assistant told him she was in the middle of a scene, or away or so exhausted from shooting three movies at once she could not be roused from a deep sleep.

And how he needed her now, as the pressures were building. He needed to hold her, to be held by her, to come inside her. It was funny, after he made love to Veena, he always felt like he had not released anything into her, but had withdrawn something from her. He always felt stronger afterwards. With other women, he fell right to sleep once he had finished. After her, he wanted to build something and then smash it to pieces.

Before he could decide which of his goondas to entrust with this, he got a text message from Sanjay: "Done. But it's gone."

Done meant Doo. When Doo was dead, he was "done." And "gone" referred to the statue. The statue was gone?

"GONE WHERE?" Papa messaged back. "GET IT!"

It was early evening now, time to visit his silent, stroke-ridden wife who could see and hear, but could no longer communicate except by blinking her eyes in Morse code.

Mama couldn't scold the servants anymore, let alone snap the tops of their ears between her thumb and forefinger to punish them. She couldn't tell her daughters how badly dressed they were, how they should live their lives, how spoiled, unhealthy, badly mannered their children and husbands were, nor complain to them about each other, the weather, politicians, or the programming on Doordarshan TV, which was all she could watch because she couldn't ask anyone to change the channel.

She couldn't tell them . . . That's not true. She could *tell* them. But they couldn't understand her.

For some reason, neither the daughters nor the servants got around to learning Morse code. Papa said he had, and pretended to know, but he'd always get it wrong. If she blinked, "Your hair awful," he would say, "She says she is very happy to see you."

So Mama Dajgit blinked her thoughts out and nobody understood. She couldn't make them understand that one of Papa's young mistresses, her day nurse, was stealing from her, right before her own eyes, or that the night nurse called her nasty names when nobody else was around.

"Doo is finished," he said to her now. "But the statue is missing."

Though she now tried to tell Papa that Doo's little plot against the family was nothing compared to the plots cooking around her at the moment, he didn't get it.

"Yes yes, I love you, too," he said, impatiently.

— — —

Doo's intended buyer had a very close call. Maurice Salt was in the lobby of the hotel, carrying two briefcases full of cash toward the elevators, when the police arrived. The hotel manager directed them to the same room he was going to: 1211.

A woman in the lobby gave him some of the story.

"A man, shot, on our floor, and he's dead."

"Did you see him alive?"

"Yes, in the elevator yesterday morning."

"What did he look like?"

"Pale, red hair—"

"Who shot him?"

"I don't know."

That was all Salt needed to hear before he beat it out of there.

As soon as he had heard the voice on the phone, he'd had a bad feeling. After all these years, his old errand boy had returned, claiming to have in his possession the very thing Salt had sent him to find those many years ago. It was suspicious enough that Salt had tucked a gun into the second briefcase along with the banded stacks of money, in case his prodigal friend was planning to burn him again.

Apparently, he'd tried to burn someone else, and that someone else had shot him. Was there a Ganesh statue that contained the treasure, or was that made up? Had he come with nothing and planned to rob his old employer Maurice?

No matter. There was a corpse now. Salt didn't want to get involved.

THE SUN IS SETTING ON THE GOONDA RAJ

The first day in Nice was a disappointment. They arrived late, and Blackie had to skip her daily swim and sun to hit the pawn-shop. They had decided to divide up the booty. Blackie took the Ganesh statue, which the pawn broker told her was merely gold-plated, not solid gold, and worth very little. A "sapphire and diamond" bracelet turned out to be glass, though she got 100 euros for a gold bracelet she had taken off one of the Saudis.

The next day, Chloe took the Rolex and a gold ring. The Rolex, she thought, was silver, until the man at the pawn shop said, "Ah yes, platinum, Limited Edition, state-of-the-art chronometer, Black mother-of-pearl face. I can give you 20,000 Euros."

The way he said it made it clear to her the watch was worth much more.

"It was my father's," Chloe said. "And it's in excellent condition. Can you give me 50,000?"

"I'll give you 25,000."

"40."

"No, I cannot."

"It's worth so much more than that," she said.

"30."

"35."

"D'accord. Okay."

The man wanted to write her a check, but she insisted on cash, and waited nervously while he sent someone "for that much money." What if he has sent for the cops, she wondered, and what would she tell them if they came? Perhaps that a shady man who'd taken her for dinner had given her the watch as a present, and that he must have been the one who stole it . . .

But the money came, no problems, and Chloe walked out of there with 35,500 euros (500 for the gold ring). She had no idea what the watch was really worth, and whether she'd settled too soon. The pawnbroker seemed very eager to buy it and didn't balk at paying her cash, so her guess was that it was worth a lot more than she got.

It didn't matter. It was stolen property after all. She thought she'd get a few thousand for it, provided it wasn't a total fake, and instead she'd hit the jackpot.

But as she walked back to the hotel, she began to feel bad, though she couldn't put her finger on why. In front of an old church, she suddenly stopped and wheeled into it. There she dropped a bunch of money into the poor box, folding up the 500 euro bills and poking them down through the wooden money slot.

She wasn't even Catholic, but she figured the money would help the poor and that's what counted, though she then worried about promoting a religion she didn't believe in and that, like any religion, had the potential of causing as much harm as good.

She was moody by the time she got back to the hotel.

"How much did you get for the watch?" Blackie asked.

"I got 25 grand for that Rolex," Chloe muttered.

"No shit."

"Seriously."

"That's great! What's the matter?"

"I dunno."

"That's amazing, Chloe. You should be happy. We earned that money."

"Yeah."

"What's wrong?"

"I dunno."

"Let's splurge. Let's call the Negresco, see if we can check in there. You'll like that, a fancy old hotel for our last night in Nice.

We'll hit the private beach, have a wicked dinner in that restaurant with the carousel horses, and then go dancing."

"I'm tired."

"Fuck you. We should celebrate. The whole world could blow tomorrow so let's have fun tonight. We got 25 grand for that watch. Wow."

"It was a Limited Edition," Chloe said, but didn't mention that it was platinum or that she'd been paid even more for it, but had stuffed five grand in euro notes into a church poor box and kept aside five grand extra for herself. She hadn't done that last thing consciously. When she returned to the hotel, she intended to tell Blackie she'd received 30,000 for the watch, but somehow 25,000 came out of her mouth and she didn't bother to correct herself.

The Negresco only had a couple of vacancies, both of them high-priced two-bedroom suites with sea views for a little over 1200 euros a night. Chloe booked one immediately. She'd pay for Blackie's share, and that would make everything all right.

"Good news," she told Blackie. "I got a deal on a two-bedroom suite at the Negresco. And it's my treat."

"We're rich. I can pay."

"I know. I want to treat you," Chloe said.

The Negresco was a huge, whitewashed old hotel with a distinctive red dome, sitting on the palm-fringed Promenade Anglais overlooking the Bay of Angels. Under a glass and wrought iron canopy, they were greeted by a man in a uniform trimmed with gold braid, and ushered into a lobby full of Belle Epoque tapestries, art, and crystal chandeliers.

"Built in 1912 by Henri Negresco, a Roumanian immigrant, the Hotel Negresco immediately attracted guests like the Rockefellers and the commoner daughters of American Sewing Machine Mogul Isaac Singer, daughters who, thanks to Pop's riches, were soon known as Duchess Decazes and Princess Scey-Montbeliard," according to Blackie's *Lonesome Roads*.

Their suite was a full two bedrooms with a balcony overlooking the promenade. Just past that was the private beach full of blue-and-white-striped umbrellas. Beyond that, the sea. Each bedroom had a view of the sea and big windows that opened up so the sea breeze could billow the sheer, opalescent undercurtains.

"This is so Grace and Audrey," Blackie said. "Cary Grant is going to burst through that door at any moment in a red scarf and ask us to hide him from the police."

"Beach?"

"Mais oui."

On the beach, an attendant checked their key cards to make sure they were registered guests, and then he pointed them to two free lawn chairs. Men in crisp whites carrying trays brought them tall cold drinks as they lay with the hoi polloi and read, Chloe quietly, Blackie describing the contents of her European celeb magazine.

"Who is Mr. Rock and Roll?" Blackie asked.

"Elvis," Chloe said.

"No. Johnny Hallyday."

"Who?"

"He's France's biggest rock star." She showed Chloe the picture.

"Seriously?"

"Hard to believe, looking at him, but it says so right here."

"What magazine is that?"

"Oh la!"

"You're reading French magazines now? What happened to *Hello*?"

"I know who those celebs are now. I'm bored with them. So I'm moving on to the "Spaniards and the French." She nodded at a copy of *Paris Hola!*

"You don't speak French."

"You don't need to really. It has a lot of pictures, and you can pretty much get the gist from them. Have you ever heard of Momo Dridi and Massimo Gargia?"

"No."

Chloe put her book down and scanned the beach, wondering if there was a mark about, but saw only men with other women, or other men. She tried to write a postcard but was blocked. She felt strange, guilty about profiting from crime, and yet anxious to commit another. The only thing that seemed to take the guilt away was the thrill of doing it again. She didn't want to give up crime—and, she rationalized, their victims all deserved it—but she did want to give up this guilt.

Then she wondered where John Carey was. The idea of him being with anyone else still made her ill, the idea that he didn't want her made her feel dark and small.

Blackie took a while to notice the chilly aura Chloe was now projecting as she stared at the sea. When she did notice, she chose to ignore it. Frankly, Blackie felt she'd been more than understanding with Chloe so far, and Chloe refused to snap out of it completely because she got some masochistic pleasure out of it or something. Blackie was tired of enabling her.

But now that she'd noticed, she had a hard time tuning it out. She was hyperaware that Chloe was breathing a little heavily and out of the corner of her eye she could see Chloe's face droop. By now Blackie knew the signs. Chloe was about to burst into tears in a public place.

"Chloe, for God's sake, what's wrong now?!"

"John—"

"Don't say his name. I can't stand to hear that asshole's name one more time. He's Lord Voldemort for the rest of this vacation," Blackie said.

"Lord Voldemort?"

"He whose name must not be spoken."

"Easy for you—"

"No, it's not easy. Jesus, we should be having a wonderful day in a fancy place. Can't we just fucking enjoy it without having the

ghost of John Carey—who incidentally is infinitely more interesting than his bodily version—along."

"I can't explain—"

"Don't cry. Don't cry! Jesus. You need to get laid. Why don't we
find guys tonight. Have a fling. Come on, what do you say to a couple of tanned French dock workers who don't speak English—"
Blackie smiled wickedly.

"Our eyes will speak for us," Chloe sniffed.

"Exactement."

Before they went out to pick up dock workers, they dressed
up in the frocks they'd bought in Monaco and went for cocktails in the hotel Brasserie, La Rotonde, which was decorated with
old wooden carousel horses—brightly colored, grotesque animals
frozen mid-gallop—some mid-snarl.

In theory, Chloe liked the idea of picking up a French guy and
having a one-night stand, but that was before she saw a potential
victim walk into the brasserie alone, look around, and stop when
he saw her.

He whispered something to the maître d', who then led him to
a table next to theirs.

But he didn't speak to them right away. It wasn't until Blackie
got up and went to the ladies' room that he leaned over and said
to Chloe, in British English, "Hello again."

"Hi."

"It is you."

"None other," Chloe said.

"Good accent," the man said, thinking she was disguising her
true way of speaking. "You've changed since I last saw you."

"Really?"

"Put on a little weight, a little older now. Don't worry, your secret is safe with me," he said.

The way he was looking at her made her feel very uncomfortable, like he was desirous and contemptuous of her at the same
time. She had seen this in all their marks, but never so nakedly.

"How's your wife?" she asked, guessing he was married and this was a "where have I seen you before?" line to pick up chicks.

"She's fine. She's in London. So Diane, do you remember where we last met?"

"Sorry no."

"Outside Brown's. You were verbally abusing a bouncer who ejected you and then you threw up."

"On him?"

"No, in the gutter. I'm the man who held your hair."

"Were you? Thank you. Well, that bouncer shouldn't have kicked me out."

"You were underage."

"I'm much older on smaller planets," she said. "Or is it larger planets?"

Blackie returned and Chloe turned to her and mouthed the words, "My name is Diane."

Then she said, "Is it the greater the gravity, the slower the atomic deterioration and so the slower one ages? Or is it the lesser the gravity the slower—"

"What the fuck are you talking about, Ch—Diane?" Blackie blurted.

"Physics. Am I older on smaller planets or on—"

"You must forgive my friend," Blackie said to the man. "She's the victim of a proper education. My name's Audrey. I'm from Canada."

"Ian. London."

"Are you staying in the hotel?"

"No, at the Bougainvillea Inn down the road."

Blackie spotted his wedding ring.

"You're married," she said.

"Yes."

"You have anything to drink at your hotel?" Chloe asked.

"Yes, I suppose, in the minibar."

"Maybe we should go there—" Chloe began.

Blackie cut her off.

"Not tonight. Remember, we're going to the Old Town to pick up French dock workers."

"Really? Will you hold that thought? I have to make a phone call," Ian said, stepping away from his table but keeping one eye on the girls.

"I so want to roll this guy," Chloe said. "It's perfect. He thinks I'm someone else. We can do dock workers tomorrow night."

"He admits he's married, he didn't invite us to his hotel, you invited us there—it's entrapment."

"Damn. You're right."

"Let's get the bill and lose him."

After Chloe signed for their drinks, they left, waving good-bye to Ian, who trailed them out, his phone to his ear.

"Diane, Diane, wait," he said

As the car pulled away, he called after it, "Wait, Diane."

He waved for the next taxi on the line. The driver, standing outside the car, took one last puff of his cigarette, held it in his lungs, slowly exhaled, ground it out purposefully, then got in and pulled slowly forward. Ian ran to meet the car.

"Suivez-vous le taxi là," he said in his bad French.

The driver looked around.

"Which taxi, monsieur?"

It had disappeared.

CHAPTER 9

Sanjay and Chunky had turned up no good leads to the statue in Monte Carlo until they sat down for lunch at a local Indian restaurant. The previous diner had left a copy of an English-language newspaper, the *Azure Coast Chronicle*, on Sanjay's chair and when he picked it up his eye caught on a picture of Doo. He showed it to Chunky, who had picked up another newspaper left behind, this one an Indian paper, the *Maharashta Express*.

"Wow. Doo made the news here in France."

"Oh. What does it say?"

"I haven't read it yet."

"Oh no," Chunky said.

"What?"

Chunky showed him the headline in the Indian paper:

THE SUN IS SETTING ON
THE GOONDA RAJ
"ROWDYISM IS IN ITS FINAL DAYS,"
SAYS CHIEF MINISTER.

"It says Garun Awli's bodyguard Vijay Ghosh has been arrested in Mumbai. He went to the police and asked them to arrest him, and when they refused he went to court and got a court order forcing the police to arrest him."

"Let me see that," Sanjay said, and read aloud. "Two of his gangmates were gunned down in Dagdi Chawl three days ago. He asked to be arrested to prevent the police from provoking an encounter so they could kill him. He is safer in jail."

"The police are killing us in cold blood. It's unjust," Chunky said. "What are things coming to, that we are safer in jail than on the streets these days?"

"We're lucky to be here in the South of France," Sanjay said. "Hand me that local paper again."

"What's in the statue?" Chunky asked.

"I don't know."

"You keep saying that. You must know. Doo knew."

"I don't want to know," Sanjay said. "Doo always knew too much."

"I never liked that guy. I always sensed there was something wrong with him."

Sanjay nodded, but they were both lying and they both knew it. Everyone had fallen for Doo. It took a long time for anyone to turn on him and when someone did, it was his wife, hardly unusual for Dajgit women. Sanjay liked him up to the end, when he found out he'd been played like a patsy.

"It makes me so mad I'd like to kill him again," Chunky said. "Remember the time he—"

"He was seen in the company of a blonde and a brunette, it says here. He had called Sophisticated Ladies. I am thinking that two women from that organization may have gone back on their own and robbed Doo. Or they know who did . . . Tonight, we'll call the Sophisticated Ladies and ask them to send over two women and after a good dinner, we'll see what they can tell us."

CHAPTER 10

E-MAIL FROM HOME

To: MichelleMaher@apu.edu
From: Gillian@maherconstruction.com
Subject: Hi Kiddo!

Glad to hear you're enjoying France as much as Italy.
Your father wants to know if they are nice to
Americans there, and to avoid crowd scenes with other
Americans, English or Australians, like discos
because they are tempting targets for terrorists. My
sister says you can tell if they spit in your soup in
the kitchen because there will be a telltale spot of
tiny white saliva bubbles from the spit. They will
look different from soup bubbles and will be stickier.
FYI.

We are fine. The peas are up in the garden. Your father
says to tell you that "the jackass next door is having
a mid-life crisis and has taken up the clarinet." He
means the jackass on the north side, Brett Steadman,
bless him, he could have had an affair or bought a
motorcycle. Your father says Donna Steadman probably
wishes he had, the whole neighborhood does. Brett's
not very good, and plays the same song over and over,
so your father is fighting back by blasting Artie Shaw
out the window. He's trying to shame him I think.

Do you have enough money? Let us know. We miss you.
Your friend,
Gillian

— — —

To:	MichelleMaher@apu.edu
From:	Mom <evelynmaher@pinkthink.com>
Subject:	Fwd: Fwd: Fwd: Nice Poem

Hi Blackie. You're already in Antibes? I have a map up
in my office and I'm plotting your route with colored
pins. You've covered a lot of ground. Sounds like you
are having a great adventure.

I got this poem from a woman on my customer mailing
list and it seemed appropriate for your current
situation (see below). All is fine here. Business is
good. We have not felt the recession as much as other
businesses because of our low prices. If you don't find
a job I can always use an extra saleswoman, but I'd
prefer you went to law school. Think about it. Your
dad and I can help you out with the tuition. Write
soon, love, Mom

===== Forwarded Message =====
>>>"All experience is an arch
>>>Wherethrough gleams that
>>>Untravelled World
>>>Whose margin fades
>>>Forever and ever
>>>When I move"
>>> - Alfred Tennyson
===== End Forwarded Message =====

www.pinkthink.com, "Penthouse cosmetics at bargain basement prices"

— — —

To: MichelleMaher@apu.edu
From: Greenmachine@aol.com
Subject: <No Subject>

Is my Poison Lips CD in the boxes you stashed in Dad's
basement? Which box? The Jiffy Lube closed lost my job
have to fucking work for Dad this summer. How's
France? Don't kiss any frogs. Later, Kev.

— — —

To: MichelleMaher@apu.edu
From: Godslefthand@earthlink.net
Subject: This is Eddie

Hope this is the right e-mail. It looked like aou.edu
in your note but the e-mail bounced back from that
address. Where are you now? I am in Grasse for a few
more days, then head to Avignon. Would love to see you.

— — —

"My father never e-mails. It's always Gillian," Blackie complained.

"Well, at least she says something when she writes."

Chloe was finished reading and answering e-mail long before
Blackie. Chloe had an e-mail from her parents—they loved her,
they missed her, they had a list of places she should see, places
they had visited when they were a young married couple, before
Chloe was born. They attached some photos of the two of them in
Europe. The pictures that included her were those where she was
an unseen fetus, taken after the island town of Ste-Marguerite,
where she was believed to have been conceived. There was also
one forwarded from a favorite professor and a note from her aunt,
none of which required more than a brief response.

"I wish Dad would write, but I like Gillian," Blackie said. "I think she might be his last girlfriend. God, I hope so. I couldn't break in another one."

"Do you think your father cheated on your mother the way our patsies cheat on their wives?"

"He cheated on her, but he did it proper," Blackie said. "He cheated with a married woman he built a deck for."

"That's proper?"

"Married people should only cheat with other married people."

"But then he left your mom."

"Well, she cheated back first, and then they decided they didn't want to stick it out. That's different. My parents aren't like your parents. In fact, most parents aren't like your parents. Your parents are freaks. Your grandparents, too."

"They are. They are freaks," Chloe said.

"How are they?"

"The same."

"Happy, good-looking, and in love?"

"Yep."

Love was on Blackie's agenda too, but she hadn't yet figured out how to look for it without upsetting Chloe or setting back her progress in getting over John Carey. The dock workers had been fun, in a Harlequin romance stereotype meets *On the Waterfront* way, two guys named Nicolas and Bruno who bought them jasmine flowers from undocumented aliens cruising the cafes, and took them dining and dancing before screwing their brains out. Bruno spoke a little English. Nicolas could only say, "Hello," "What is your name?" and "Do you like sports?" but that seemed to be more than enough for their needs at that time.

But now Blackie was feeling an urge for some real romance, and she was thinking of Eddie. He was her type, the nice guy bad boy, bad because he was going against the grain, living outside the system, just bumming around busking and drawing portraits of tourists and God. And he smoked. But at the same time, he seemed like a good person in the ways that counted. Bottom line: He sparked her up when they met, and she wanted to get to know him better . . . and sleep with him.

"Can we go to Grasse?" she asked Chloe.

"When?"

"Now? Antibes is a bore. It's like Spring break in Florida only fewer people speak English."

"Don't you want to go to Cannes?"

"Not so much."

"There won't be any crime in Grasse," Chloe said. "It's all around the beaches."

"Can we take a break from crime?" Blackie said. "I don't want to spend my whole summer ripping off perverts. Let's go inland for a while."

"After Cannes. It's practically on the way to Grasse," Chloe said.

It would be hard to convince Chloe without specifically mentioning the e-mail from Eddie, which Blackie hadn't done, trying to be sensitive. But if they didn't go soon, he might head out to Avignon.

"Why don't you go to Cannes and I'll go to Grasse, and we can meet up there or in Avignon in a few days?" Blackie suggested, figuring Chloe wouldn't want to go to Cannes alone, and would ultimately agree to Grasse.

"You want to split up?"

"Just for a day or two. I really don't feel like going to Cannes. But you should go."

"I don't want to go alone."

"Just for a day or two. Stay in a nice place, have the masseuse come up, read in the sun."

"No, if you're going to Grasse, then I'm going to Grasse," she said.

"You don't have to. I know you want to go to Cannes."

"Do you want to split up?"

"A day or two wouldn't hurt."

"I don't want to be alone in Cannes. I'll come to Grasse, as long as we can go to Cannes later—"

"Okay. Um. That guy, Eddie, might be in Grasse."

"That's why you want to go to Grasse," Chloe said. "Why didn't you say that up front? Man."

"I don't know. I thought it might—. Oh shit, Chloe, I—I didn't want to upset you."

"Well, now I'm upset that you tried to weasel around that fact. It makes me feel crappy, foolish and . . . untrustworthy. I'm what, this fragile thing you have to treat with kid gloves?"

"Yeah."

"Sorry I've been so much work for you."

"You're not. But you're still pining for that jerk Carey, and the only thing that takes your mind off it is robbing pervs," Blackie said. "You know, there's no rush to rob, Chloe. We've gained skills we can use for a lifetime. Crime can wait. I want to meet guys and, you know, people our own age and see museums and all that crap."

"Okay then. We'll go meet guys and see museums. We'll go to fucking Grasse. Start packing."

"Do you have room for my sweaters?" Blackie asked.

"Yeah. You would too if you didn't lug that statue around. You're going to bring it to Grasse?"

"Yeah."

"Why?"

"I like it. And, I dunno, I thought Eddie would get a kick out of it, because he's drawing those pictures of God."

"You really like this guy Eddie? What about him?" Chloe asked. She wasn't really interested in Eddie, but she felt like she'd better throw Blackie a bone.

"I don't know. I just liked him when I met him, right away. When I spoke to him the first time, he looked surprised, but in this shy, little boy way, like he'd just been caught doing something..."

"Naughty."

"No, like he'd just been caught doing something sweet. I find that so irresistible."

CHAPTER 11

The Harry Carpenter case was becoming a real bear for the French police. First of all, there were no records of a Harold Carpenter in Australia. The man simply didn't exist there. Then the coroner's report came in. The dead man had a popular date rape drug, GHB, in his system along with a great deal of liquor. He'd likely been unconscious when he was killed. This, and the fact that the room looked like it had been robbed, turned the case into a probable homicide.

Prints, the victim's passport photo, and eyewitness descriptions of the two young women seen with him the night he died were sent to Police Bureaus all over Europe, and to the rest of the world through Interpol.

The first break came not from any local source, but from a cop in Mumbai who saw the passport photo on the Interpol website and sent an urgent e-mail:

> "That man is an Australian named Donald 'Doo' McGarrigle. He is married to one of the daughters of Mumbai crime boss Ganesh 'Papa' Dajgit and worked for him running the family's brothels, extorting money from Bollywood personalities, and doing other errands. Please let me know how we can cooperate in this investigation. Sincerely, R.J. Sharma, Sub-Inspector, Mumbai Police Department."

The dead man now had a name at least. Or did he?

Back in Mollywat, Australia, Doo McGarrigle's friends and relatives were stunned to hear the news. They had heard nothing

from Doo in many years, and had long believed he had died somewhere in his travels. Now they grieved with certainty. Doo was
a friendly, adventurous guy, according to the testimonials of his
friends, without a "lot of consumer urges," who wanted to be a
writer but never managed more than a handful of back book cred-
its in the *Lonesome Roads* travel guides.

They were even more stunned when they saw the picture of
the dead man and read the police description.

It wasn't Doo McGarrigle. Doo was short, plumpish, with brown
hair and brown eyes. A grown man could lose weight, dye his hair,
even change his eye color temporarily, but he couldn't shrink in
height. If this wasn't Doo, then where was Doo? What had happened to him?

Now the police were back almost to square one, a mysterious
man, murdered in a top-flight Monte Carlo hotel after being seen
in the company of two mysterious women. About all they knew
for certain was that this man had posed as Doo McGarrigle while
living in Mumbai in an Indian crime family.

If they could just find the two English-speaking girls ... but
there were so many young Anglo women on the Riviera, and the
eyewitnesses hadn't been able to agree on the details so police
sketches were very different.

The dead man's body remained on ice at the morgue, the summer sun grew hotter, the police were distracted by the daring midnight robbery of safe deposit boxes at a five-star hotel in Monte
Carlo, and the murder case was pushed to a back burner.

— — —

MIKE HANDEL

While Mike Handel was flying from New York to Nice, "Bonnie
Parkavenue" struck again. The soccer mom bandit hit a Chase
branch in suburban Rivervale, New Jersey. But Mike didn't learn
of it until he was already on the ground in France, riding in his

buddy Buzzer's limousine, watching CNN on satellite TV in the back. He was on his way to Buzzer's French villa, just outside Nice in the village of Eze.

Immediately, Mike called Sharp, his managing editor at the newspaper.

"Bring me back," he said. "That's my story."

"It's Smithy's story too, Mike, and he's handling it from here on in with Masha. There'll be other stories."

"Not like this one. I've worked this story since day one. I'm the guy who coined the term 'Bonnie Parkavenue' for Chrissake."

"You're on suspension, Mike. Let go. Take your vacation. In a month you can come back, and there'll be a whole new story for you."

"I'm flying home."

"I still won't put you on the story."

"I'll write it for someone else."

"You can't write for anyone else without our express written permission and you can't quit because you're under contract. Violate that and we'll sue your ass."

Sharp said this in a disturbingly calm and matter-of-fact way. Sharp, of course, felt threatened by Mike. Anyone could see it.

"Fire me then."

"No. I won't. I suspended you for a reason—because you need to take some time off and think about things. You're very close to a nervous breakdown. You're at the edge."

"I've made my deadlines, Sharp."

"Sure. But you were becoming bigger news than your stories. I gotta call from Washington, Mike. We'll talk later. You relax there in France. Get yourself together." Sharp hung up without saying good-bye.

The first thing Mike did was check to see how soon he could fly back to New York, but there were no available seats until the next day, and even then he would have to fly through Toronto to get to

New York. It was no use. Sharp meant what he said. If Mike tried to work this story outside the newspaper, Sharp would sue him.

It wasn't fair. He had broken the story of the well-groomed, designer-clad woman in the George W. Bush mask who robbed five suburban banks over a seven-week period, then went silent for over a month. Now she was back, and he'd lost her to Smithy and Masha. Quite the team, those two were.

The sky was blue, the sea was bluer and sparkled as the sun hit the points of its gentle waves. Buzzer's house looked down on it, and with the windows open, Mike could smell the salt in the warm air along with the perfume of the flowered vines that covered the terrace facing the Mediterranean. It was so calm, so peaceful, the perfect place to relax.

But why relax when he could be eaten up instead with envy, regret, and anxiety? Why go out and enjoy the idyllic beauty of the flowered hills and the orgasmic cuisine of France when he could stay inside watching CNN International, reading the newspapers and wire services online, eating frozen dinners he had ordered in from the nearest supermarket?

There was terrorism, war, disease, economic trouble in the news during his first few days in France, but he noticed it only peripherally as he sought obsessively for updates on Bonnie Parkavenue and how Smithy and Masha, in particular, were covering it.

If he wasn't checking the wires and watching CNN, he was watching movies and TV shows shot in New York, like *NYPD Blue* and reruns of *Sex in the City.* He was missing the city and all those hungry women, missing what he had called in an article "the high-voltage cold blue current that crackles under Manhattan like lightning and strikes you from the soles up."

While he was here *losing energy* his competitors were tapping into it, growing stronger, leaving him behind.

On top of getting the front page at least twice a week, Smithy and Masha were doing TV talk shows about the story and being

quoted by other newspapers. Then he got an e-mail from another reporter, a troublemaker in the newsroom. Rumor had it
Smithy had signed a big deal to write a movie based on a book
about his previous story, the mysterious slaying of a famous upper
east side orthodontist, known as Mr. Smile in his subway car ad-
vertisements. The working title of the book was *Dead Man's
Smile.*

Reading this, Mike felt a mule kick to the gut. He could
hardly breathe, he was shaking, and even though he had the air-
conditioning turned on he began to sweat.

He pushed himself away from the computer and the offending
e-mail that set off this attack, and caught his breath. This is what
it took to get him away from the computer. He stood up and, after
steadying himself, walked into the kitchen to get another beer.

The skittish little housekeeper who worked for Buzzer had
come in that morning and brought the local papers and a bag of
croissants before she ducked out, without him even hearing her.
He ate one of the croissants with his beer while he flipped idly
through the French papers and thought about how Smithy and
Masha could get a book and movie deal out of Bonnie Parkavenue
too, the deal he hoped to get, the deal that would have redeemed
his ass with all the people who counted. How could he get even
with Sharp, Smithy and Masha? There wasn't much he could do,
he realized. He was pretty powerless in this situation. They won,
he lost.

He was a loser.

But how could that be? He was smart, he was quick, he could
write a sow's ear into a Louis Vuitton. Well, that was the real problem, he was just too talented, and of course the others felt threatened and went out of their way to hold him back. It was one thing
to yank him off the story. It was another for Sharp to suspend
him, keep him to his contract so he couldn't work for anyone else,
then claim it was for Mike's "own good." Weasel-fucker.

He took another bite of dry croissant and washed it down with beer—a surprisingly good combination—putting the bottle down on the English-language paper, the *Azure Coast Chronicle*, which was published May through September for the summer Anglos. The bottle covered the face of a guy named Harry Carpenter, found shot in a Monte Carlo hotel. Next to it, spared the damp bottle ring, was a file photo of a young woman with the headline, "Missing Rehab Heiress in France?"

Mike started reading and soon had devoured the story about Diane Benham, the scandalous heiress who, thanks to her hard-partying life, looked much older than her 17 years, or so the story said (the picture was fuzzy). In the past few days, there had been a reported sighting of her in Nice—she was said to be traveling in the company of a dark-haired Canadian woman.

Wow. A rich little bad girl who had danced with Princes William and Harry at posh balls, who had stolen a boyfriend from super-model Trisha Collingwood, then dumped him for Woy Simpson, the frontman for the Bean Counters, with whom she had a tempestuous relationship and from whom she had most recently split just before she went to the Swiss clinic. What a story. And now she was on the lam from court-ordered rehab . . .

He stuffed the rest of the croissant in his mouth, grabbed the beer and paper, and ran back to his computer. Anxiously, impatient even with the speedy DSL connection, Mike searched to see how the U.S. media were covering it. So far, there was nothing. Benham, though a gossip-column favorite in the UK and now a budding celebrity on the continent, was unknown in America, which had its hands-full with its own heiresses. Well, that would change, once he pumped up the story a little.

His only serious competition at the moment were the UK media and some guy from the *Daily Splash* named Ian Darius who claimed to have spoken with her at La Rotonde in Nice before she and her Canadian friend went out to pick up French dock workers.

Half of Fleet Street might be tracking her, but that wasn't much of a problem for Mike. More than once he'd led the competition astray with a few fake sightings of his own . . .

He did a Dow Jones Newswires search of Benham, her family, and the various celebrities she had been in contact with, pulling 53 major stories and bookmarking the rest. Then he Googled Benham to see where she came up in the web and newsgroup gossip forums. He downloaded photographs of her. Over the next two days he read every story, making voluminous notes and lists, and studying every detail of her appearance. She didn't like to show her face, he noted. In almost all the photographs, her face was somehow disguised, altered, or shielded by her hand, hats, shadow, wild makeup, or just an extreme facial expression.

She wanted attention, he thought, without being seen.

He then Googled some of the friends named in the various articles, and, more important, her self-proclaimed "former friends" and followed that up with an internet white pages search for them. Many were unlisted, but they also had friends and former friends who might be less circumspect.

Before he made his first phone call, he had enough information to post a false lead on her in a British fashion magazine's gossip message board. First he planted a blind item about a rumored reservation for later that month made at a romantic hideaway on the Corsican coast by "the guy *counting* on stardom." Mike knew from the Bean Counters' web page they had no concert dates or public appearances until the next month—one Woodstock-style concert date at the Bois de Vincennes just outside Paris—so his subtle allusion to Woy would hold water.

In another forum under another name, he quoted the story about Benham from the *Azure Coast Chronicle*.

The next day, after talking to some friends of friends of hers, he went back to the British fashion magazine's gossip board to reported a second sighting, this one on a ferry bound for Corsica. In Mike's work of fiction, Benham claimed her name was Terry

Randall, that she was from Essex, and she was spending her gap year traveling around Europe. At the time, she was in the company of a dark-haired Canadian girl whose name was not given. Before long, others reported sightings in Corsica and added their own details.

— — —

In Rome, Diane Benham sat in her room watching satellite TV, doing coke, and prowling the internet on her laptop computer. She had checked into a mid-range hotel, part of a budget chain headquartered in America, and except for the DO NOT DISTURB sign in Italian and English, she couldn't tell if she was in Italy or Kansas.

This was the last place one would look for Diane Benham, which was part of the reason she had checked in. The other was, she was trying to save money until she got to Paris, something she didn't have a lot of experience with. By now her credit cards had been cancelled.

The hotel wasn't bad, under the circumstances. It was generic, but it had enough amenities for survival—attached bathroom, satellite TV, room service, internet port. Here she could hide out for a while, scanning the internet for stories about herself while catching up on the movies she missed.

Except for lunch near the Coliseum, she'd been inside all day. During that brief outdoor excursion, she's worn her big dark glasses and tucked her hair under a scarf. An American tourist at the next table struck up a conversation with her in bad Italian, and Diane, recognizing the accent, responded in English. She told the American woman she was a cancer patient, just getting her hair back after the chemo, and her friends at the animal shelter where she worked had raised the money for her to fulfill her life-long wish to see Italy while she waited to hear if they'd found a bone marrow donor. If they failed to find one, the prognosis wasn't good.

The American woman felt terrible, and even offered that she and her sister, with whom she was traveling, were type A positive and perhaps they could volunteer . . .

"I have a very rare blood type," Diane said. "But thank you for thinking of me."

She felt rather bad now for bringing the kind American down, so she tried to make up for it by saying lots of life-affirming stuff about how she knew she'd beat it, she wouldn't allow thoughts of defeat for a moment, and in the meantime she was just enjoying every minute of her life to the fullest. The woman left, all lit up with the joy of life.

I am such a wonderful liar, Diane thought, before retreating back to her mid-range hotel cocoon.

At night it was hard to stay inside. Across and just down the street from her hotel was a tempting nightclub. She could not only hear the music, she could feel it pulsate if she put the palms of her hands to her windows. It's too dangerous to go down there, she kept reminding herself, and tried to tune the club out by turning on MTV Europe and listening to it on headsets. After scanning it for about an hour, hoping to see Woy and his band, she did another line of coke and went online. There was a lot of e-mail waiting for her, but she didn't reply to any of it, scared the gobbledygook letters and numbers in the message header would give away her location somehow. The most she would risk was checking her supersecret e-mail address, the one only she and Woy knew, to see if he'd e-mailed her.

They'd agreed to keep communication to a minimum, until the heat was off, but she was hoping he couldn't resist the bit of risk in a quick "I worship you" e-mail. But there was nothing in her inbox except porno, "Make Money at Home," and "Friend, your dog could be smarter" spams.

In Britain, the papers were having quite a lot of fun with her. Naturally, they had puffed up her and her family in order to make the story even juicier. Her father, a long-time Tory, was suddenly bumped up to be a political hopeful. "Would-be MP's daughter flees rehab," said one paper. What a laugh.

Her drug use was analyzed by a TV psychologist for one of the splashy tabloids. The psychologist thought this was Diane's way to punish her father. She was acting out in a cry for attention and, most important, discipline, and she represented all Britain's troubled youth, victims of progressive times, who wanted their elders to impose strict boundaries and controls on their immature behavior. And so on. She confidently summed up Diane's problem and the cure in one short paragraph, then went on to analyze the Jude Law–Sadie Frost and Russell Crowe–Danielle Spencer marriages with the same smug economy.

There were now two reported sightings of Diane, one in Nice, where that wanker Ian Darius claimed to have seen her, and another en route to Corsica. The source wasn't named on that one, but it did sound more credible.

Both times she had been sighted she had reportedly been in the company of a dark-haired Canadian girl. This she found very puzzling. She stopped to think if she even knew any Canadians.

She'd had a Canadian penpal once.

With MTV blaring through her head, she read about herself through the night, until dawn came and the growing light shocked her away from the computer screen. She took off her headsets. The nightclub was quiet.

There was something about early mornings after all-nighters that always depressed her. She didn't like the quality of light. After she closed all the curtains, she tried to sleep, exhausted but still mentally wired. Buzzing softly in her chain hotel bed, she tried to envision her boyfriend's face, tried to fix him in her mind so they could perhaps connect telepathically. *Are you there?*, she thought, and imagined him saying, *Yes, I'm here, I hear you, I love you.* They conversed in her head a while, until she dropped off to a restless sleep.

PART FOUR

HE FALLS IN WITH BAD COMPANIONS

When Blackie and Chloe got to the hostel in Grasse, Eddie wasn't there. He hadn't checked out yet, though. The girl behind the desk said he had gone busking in Place aux Aires at the top of the old town.

They checked in and went to their separate rooms. While Chloe was unpacking, there was a knock on the door.

Standing there was a lanky man, mid-to-late twenties, with sandy hair that was too long and too unruly, giving him a Mad Mozart look. He was carrying a video camera and had a small black backpack slung over one shoulder.

"You were looking for Eddie?" he said. Sounded like an Australian accent.

"My friend was looking for him. You are?"

"Cameron. I'm a friend of Eddie's. You're who?"

"Chloe. Blackie's next door."

He leaned over and knocked on Blackie's door but kept his eyes on Chloe. When Blackie came out, he said, "Hi, I'm a friend of Eddie's. I'm on my way to meet him for dinner at the top of the hill. You want to come?"

"Yeah," Blackie said.

"Hey, great Ganesh."

Blackie looked behind at the statue, sitting in a pile of clothes on her bed.

"Thanks."

"Can we bring that statue?" he asked.

"You want to bring the statue?"

"Yeah. I want to bring it to dinner."

"If you carry it," Blackie said.

Cameron was not, it turned out, Australian, but from New Zealand, a "Kiwi," and he'd come to Grasse to shoot a digital film segment at the School for Noses. It was part of a longer film about his search for a proper career. Already, he'd worked as a fruit picker, tried to break into Bollywood as a leading man, taken lessons on their respective crafts from sandalmakers, sidewalk dentists, professional ear cleaners, and Venetian gondoliers. In America, he had jumped freight trains and sold maps to the homes of Hollywood stars.

In Grasse, Cameron planned to take the admission test at the School for Noses. It and the many perfume factories were here because of the town's pure, clear air and proximity to fields and fields of flowers. His guidebook said the School was open every day Monday through Friday, no appointment necessary. You just walk in and they'll schedule the test for you. This turned out to be wrong, and the School was closed for vacation.

"There are a thousand perfumers in the world, but less than fifty of them are professional Noses," Cameron said.

"Do you have any natural talent at ... smelling things?" Blackie asked.

"I don't think I have 'The Gift.' I'm just taking the test to add to my film. To be considered for admission, you have to be able to correctly identify something like 500 different smells in the test."

"That's a strange gift to have. The gift of overly sensitive smell."

"You know what gets me, very few people who go through the School for Noses will become professional Noses. Imagine dreaming of becoming a Nose, thinking you have the Gift, and flunking out. Where do you go from there?"

Cameron stopped and put Ganesh, whom he'd been cradling in his arm like a baby, on the cobblestones. He turned his camera on.

"Hey, move it a couple feet up the hill, will you?" he asked.

Blackie moved it.

"Again."

They repeated this for the next twenty or so meters.

"Great. I'll cut that together so it looks like he's climbing up the hill," Cameron said. "Whoa. I'm seeing a film here."

"What do you mean?'

"Look at the prodigious nose on this guy. If you have a nose like this, where do you go? Here's the plot: An innocent, elephant-headed God comes to Grasse to fulfill his lifelong dream of being a Nose—"

"—But he falls in with bad companions who corrupt him—that would be us—setting him on a path of wantonness and ruin," Blackie said.

"Right. And there's a girl he's in love with, like Esmeralda."

"Loves her from afar, too ashamed of his freakish appearance to actually approach her. Dreams that when he is an acclaimed Nose, she will see past his appearance and fall in love with his Gift."

Behind them, Chloe walked silently, annoyed about something. Even she wasn't sure what it was. Maybe it was that Blackie and Cameron had hit it off so effortlessly and seemed not to even notice she was there. Maybe it was just the overcast sky and the twisted cobblestone lanes and old stone steps leading up to the Old Town of Grasse. It made her think for some reason about medieval penitents carrying crosses to atone for their sins and emulate Jesus. The narrow passages seemed gray and ghostly.

The main square at the top of the hill was a little lighter, an airy place lined with flower stalls and cafes and a three-tiered fountain in the center. Eddie was in a cafe on the north side of the square, sketching.

"Whoa, hey!" he said to Blackie. "You made it."

"Yeah."

"And you met Cameron."

"How's business?" Cameron asked.

"So-so."

They all sat down, ordered beers, and exchanged a few more biographical details, that Blackie had just graduated college with a B.A. and was interested in film, but her parents wanted her to go to law school. Chloe was going to grad school in September for her Masters in English Lit, though she had no idea what she'd do with it once she got it.

After completing a diploma course in commercial art at the Ontario Institute of Technology in Toronto, Eddie had worked for three years in a series of jobs, including a stint as a freelance courtroom artist. He'd had the travel bug since he was a kid, on account of two girls he'd known back home, "the Hersh sisters," who traveled a lot. It wasn't until much later, after "a few things happened," he wouldn't go into "the boring details," that he decided to leave home and see the world. He'd been on the road for two years, and he and Cameron met in India.

Cameron had left New Zealand after his second year of college and started backpacking. He'd planned to take a year off to travel then return to school, but he hadn't gone back. It had been three years. His parents wanted him to come home and finish school, find a career—"anything but filmmaker"—thus inspiring the film he had been making. Using his laptop and a program called Final Cut, he edited as he went, and every now and then uploaded new videos to his websites, www.camerongetarealjob.com and www.cameronbakerly.com. While he was in the South of France, he hoped to videotape some Mithra archeological sites for yet another one of his projects, a short mockumentary on the life of Mithra, à la Spinal Tap.

"Mithra?"

"Persian fire god—" Cameron began when Chloe cut him off.

"How do you finance all this travel and filmmaking?" Chloe asked, using the same slightly mocking tone she used when playing Bad Cop to cheating husbands on the Riviera.

"Living cheap and busking."

"What kind of busking?"

"I play the guitar, sing a little, sell a little hash to other travelers. I make jewelry and do face-painting too."

"You should check out Cam's films on his website," Eddie said.

"I wanna do a new film here," Cameron said. "Blackie and I were brainstorming on the way up. It's like twisted Disney."

"If Disney remade *The Elephant Man*," Blackie said.

"And if I then remade the Disney remake," Cameron said, with a note of what sounded to Chloe like arrogance.

Cameron and Blackie described the idea to Eddie, and then the three of them shot ideas around.

"The other aspiring noses are envious of his Gift. They sabotage him before exams, get him drunk, turn him on to brothels, lie about test time, punch him in the nose, impairing his ability to sniff," Cameron offered.

"He flunks out of Nose school, gets laughed at on the street in front of The Love Interest," Eddie said.

"Or the other way around. She laughs at him in front of other people, like in the Toulouse Lautrec movie where the prostitute ridicules him," Blackie said.

"Oh, that's harsh. But I like it. She seems like a simple, good-hearted beauty who will see beyond his deformity, but she turns out to be shallow and cruel. He didn't notice, because he only ever admired her from a distance—"

"—so after flunking out of Nose school, he is humiliated in public by the woman he loves—"

"—jeered by children, subject to suspicious glowering from Christian wives and the sophomoric phallic humor of college boys—"

"—hits the skids, hangs out with low-lifes—that would be us—drinking with sharpies and burned-out prostitutes given over to the Green Fairy."

"The Green Fairy?"

"Absinthe."

"We have a video camera too," Blackie said.

"Great! We can do two-camera shoots."

Chloe watched, unable or unwilling to contribute at the moment, feeling the circle of their intimacy tighten and exclude her.

Cameron jumped up with his camera and put Ganesh in a chair.

"This is the scene where Ganesh arrives in town and meets up with some other students from the School for Noses. That's you guys. Look like students. Sniff something. Subtly. Scholarly."

Eddie and Blackie began to sniff their coffee, the sugar, each other, while Chloe turned her head to look out in the square. When Cameron had finished shooting, Chloe said, "Are we going to eat? We missed lunch because we were on the bus to Grasse. It's almost six now."

"Not here," Eddie said. "Too expensive. There's a bistro halfway down toward the hotel that's good and cheap."

"We'll buy you dinner here," Blackie said.

"If we eat at the cheap place, you can buy us wine," Eddie said.

Cameron had only arrived the day before, delayed by a hitch-hiking contest. "This crazy Brit I traveled with from Prague proposed the contest. The deal was, we'd split up, and see who could get to Nice first. We both had cameras, so we'd videotape each pick-up and drop-off and anything interesting in between, to show we'd actually hitchhiked the whole way and hadn't cheated."

"Isn't that dangerous?"

"Not for us, not in Europe. But it is hard for single guys to get rides. Some people probably thought we were dangerous, or nuts."

"How long did it take you to get to Nice from Prague?"

"Two weeks for me. It took Paul about five days. But then he got tired of waiting for me in Nice and took off for Marseille."

Over dinner, Eddie and Cameron told some of their shared and separate road stories at a table for five—including, of course, Ganesh. There were mutual friends to be discussed, people they'd run into at youth hostels, in Fair Trade rallies or at anti-war marches. Someone named Millman came up a lot, a "crazy Californian" with whom the guys had traveled a while in India and who was the reason they had crossed a river on a raft made of inflated goat stomachs in the Himalayas.

Blackie didn't find their joking overly exclusive, but Chloe found it obnoxious. Attempts to draw Chloe into the conversation seemed insincere to her, and she answered with single sentences. Yeah, she liked France, but she preferred the coast to being inland.

In the group, Eddie talked just a little but seemed to be always listening and observing, and when he spoke he usually said something meaningful. Chloe couldn't tell yet if this was consistent and genuine or if it was a carefully modulated pose to hide an absolute madman. Some of the stories he and Cameron told lent themselves to the madman theory. Cameron seemed like a madman, with his wild hair and excited way of talking.

Cameron was freakishly smart but insecure about it, so he showed off and talked too much. He was perfect for Chloe, Blackie thought, because she was the same way except for the part about talking too much. And that was one area where being different could only help the relationship. He was a talker, she was a listener—or knew how to appear she was listening anyway. Often her mind wandered away from the conversation to her own thoughts.

Chloe didn't seem to see any affinity though. Nor did Cameron. When Chloe said, "I'm tired. I'm going back to the hotel," Cameron said, "See you tomorrow," and remained at the table.

Eddie jabbed Cameron and motioned toward Chloe's receding back.

"She shouldn't walk back alone after dark," he said.

"Oh," Cameron said. "Wait up, Chloe, I'll walk back with you."

"Chloe is still in relationship rehab?" Eddie said, opening his sketchbook.

"Sorry, yes."

"How long has it been since she and whoever split up?" He started to sketch Ganesh.

"Over three months. You know what her problem is? Her parents—"

"Divorced?"

"No, still together, still in love, the most in love married couple you'll ever meet. They set a very unrealistic example for Chloe. She keeps looking for that, and getting burned. But usually she rebounds within six weeks."

"Is this guy worth it?"

"No. No. No."

"Love makes people crazy."

"It doesn't have to."

Without Cameron and Chloe there, Eddie talked a lot more. Blackie asked him how long he planned to keep traveling, and he told her he wasn't sure. He was happiest on the road for the time being. Sometimes the need to do some work determined a destination and how long he'd be there. He had no work papers for anywhere but Canada, but some jobs were easy to get without papers, like backroom restaurant help, English lessons, and fruit-picking. In Mumbai, he and Cameron had played London night club–goers in a Bollywood movie and been paid about 20 bucks, plus Cameron got an episode for his Career Exploration film. He saw no reason "at the moment" to live any other way.

"But what I plan and what happens could be two different things. I know that," Eddie said.

Blackie talked vaguely about going home and working for one of her parents until she could get into grad school. She preferred her mother as a boss, but couldn't see herself selling Pink Think cosmetics and still didn't know what she wanted to study in grad school. Or maybe she'd travel some more . . . maybe Paradise was an ever-changing landscape . . .

"It's not for everyone," Eddie said.

"What do you mean?"

"It's risky on the road. What happens when the money runs out and there's no work to be had?"

"What did you do?"

"I'm young and male, so it's safer for me to sleep on a beach or in a train station. It's tougher for girls—period, and it's harder as you get older."

He'd met a lot of people who had set off on an endless adventure, and then found themselves stopped in some foreign place, in love, raising children, or just plain out of gas and stuck. There was Mickey, for example, whom Eddie met at a Tokyo bar. An Irish guy, in his early fifties, Mickey had planned to travel the world till he died. Then Mickey met a Rhodesian woman in Sri Lanka, fell in love, and moved with her to London, where he lived five years . . . until he met a Japanese woman, fell in love, and moved with her to Tokyo. They had a child but had since divorced. After four years with his Japanese wife and child, he'd fallen in love with an English woman living in Tokyo. She had since dumped him and the Japanese wife wouldn't take him back.

"Now, he lives alone in Tokyo, working his ass off to support his Japanese wife and child. And he hates Tokyo, really hates it. He has to stay because the child is there. He carries a card in his wallet that says just 'I'm sorry,' which he whips out to explain how he feels about the course of his life."

"C'est la vie."

"Then you meet people who have been abroad so long, they can't go home. I met a guy in Pakistan who hasn't been home since 1989. He went back then, and it felt so foreign to him, he's never gone back again, he just keeps moving to other foreign countries."

"Gone native?"

"No! He's Mr. America. He lives like an American wherever he goes. He works for the U.S. government as a cultural attaché and every few years he moves to some other place. He lives in the

U.S.A. compound, which looks like the home he left, with lawns and barbecues and white people, mainly. He shops at the U.S. commissary and hangs out most of the time at the American club."

"Like a wildlife preserve for Americans."

"I guess. He likes other Americans, but only when they're an overseas minority."

While they were talking, people walked by, looking puzzled, or charmed, by the gold elephant-headed statue. A couple of tourists took pictures. One asked Blackie in Scottish-accented English where she got the statue, and she told him she'd won it off a guy in Monte Carlo, which was not a lie, really.

They drank some more wine before they went back to the hotel. About halfway there, Eddie kissed her and then they held hands, stopping every ten meters or so to grope each other. In one particular dark stretch, under an old stone arch further shaded by ancient trees, she almost suggested they have sex right there, Henry-and-June-under-the-bridge style. But she didn't know him very well and didn't know what his shock threshold was when it came to sex. So she waited until they got back to his room at the hotel.

— — —

Chloe and Cameron had talked on the way back to the hotel, though for Chloe it was obligatory conversation and nothing more. Cameron asked her a few questions about herself and she answered them briefly, only child, parents still together, parents run a commercial photography and printing company, and so on. Then he started asking about Blackie and asked a few too many questions about Blackie, which Chloe pointed out to him.

"She's interesting. Hey, you want to smoke a joint?" he said, thinking maybe if she got high, she'd loosen up.

The joint was hash and tobacco, and it was good hash, much better than Chloe was used to. But it didn't loosen her up. It made the dark stone walls around them just seem darker and more sin-

ister, made her want to hunch into herself and hang her head.
Medieval architecture was definitely starting to lose its charm.

Cameron kept talking, more to fill the silence than anything,
his voice sounding to her like it was under water. By the time she
got back to the hotel, she felt completely alienated from him, and
when she went alone to her room she felt the creeping paranoia
that comes when you get too stoned with a complete stranger in a
strange place.

She didn't like being here with these guys, and she didn't like
herself for not being able to get into this, to be one of the group,
to like Cameron and have him like her so everything would be
balanced.

Typical of Blackie to hook up with a guy like Eddie, she thought.
Blackie always went for the rebels who refused to "sell out" to the
system and so were always poor. Then she dumped them. Chloe
could hear John's voice in her head, describing Blackie's type:
"guys who move sideways, like crabs, never forward in life. Too
pure, too self-righteous, too unrealistic. Yeah, they're cute when
they're young, but wait until they're 50 with a ponytail, still sleeping on a futon, marching for peace while quietly hating almost
everyone, like the guy who worked the day shift at the vegetarian
grocery on campus."

Relatively early the next morning (9 A.M.), Blackie came to
Chloe's door to rouse her for breakfast.

"They only serve in the hotel until ten and it's included with
the price of the room."

"We can have coffee and croissants in a cafe until noon."

"Yeah, I suggested that to Eddie, but he and Cameron don't
have much money, and they don't want us to pay."

"I'll meet up with you later. Did you sleep with him?"

"Yes. Come now for breakfast. We're going to go straight from
there to Fragonard for the perfume factory tour. We need you for
the film."

"You don't need me."

"Yes we do. I can't play all the female parts."

Chloe was too tired to argue. She told Blackie she'd meet them down in the hotel's breakfast room, then dawdled getting ready.

By the time she got to breakfast, the others had finished. She had a cup of coffee while Blackie and Cameron discussed shots.

At the Fragonard factory, they saw how perfume was made. The Nose there was indulgent enough to let them shoot Ganesh on his stool, in front of an array of vials and lab equipment that looked like it was right out of the eighteenth century.

After the tour, they shot some scenes of the "Remote Beauty," played by Chloe. It seemed appropriate since the RB had no lines. All she had to do was look chilly and pretty, which was very easy, except for one scene where she had to laugh at Ganesh and his proposal. Blackie played one of the student-tormentors, and then, with her hair up and a lot of makeup, she played one of the prostitutes.

Chloe went along with it, but she wasn't having fun. At dinner, when Blackie, Eddie, and Cameron talked about everyone going to Avignon together the next day, she thought, *I've got to get us back to the beach somehow.*

CHAPTER 13

For four days, Diane didn't leave her Rome hotel room. All day she was online, checking for an e-mail from Woy and reading the latest on her whereabouts until, starved for some sort of human connection beyond the room service waiter, she'd cruise into a chatroom for a while.

Tonight, after she'd read her current press, she checked into a movie trivia chatroom on a UK website, this one "guess the movie from the cast." Before she logged on, she had to pick a chatroom handle, and she picked "MissingHeiressInCorsica," just to fuck with people.

```
[MissingHeiressInCorsica enters room]
MissingHeiressInCorsica:     Hi.
InedibleHulk:                Hi and bye. Exam tomorrow.
                             Fucking summer school.
                             'Night.
[InedibleHulk exits room]
MilesMonroe:                 Tony Curtis . . .
PovertyRowPictures:          Spartacus
SpearsBritney:               Hi Missing. Good night
                             Inedible.
MilesMonroe:                 Burt Lancaster
MissingHeiressinCorsica:     Sweet Smell of Success
MilesMonroe:                 Y. Go, Missing.
SpearsBritney:               WTG Missing!
PovertyRowPictures:          VG screenname, Missing. Run,
                             young fucked-up girl, run!
```

MissingHeiressinCorsica: Humphrey Bogart,
                            Edward G. Robinson
MilesMonroe: Dead End
MissingHeiressinCorsica: Barbara Stanwyck,
                            James Cagney
MilesMonroe: Need more
MissingHeiressinCorsica: Peter Lorre,
                            Sidney Greenstreet . . .
PovertyRowPictures: Speaking of heiresses,
                            have you heard the latest?
MilesMonroe: All in the same movie?
SpearsBritney: What heiress? This heiress?
MissingHeiressInCorsica: Ward Bond, Rachel Ward . . .
MilesMonroe: Rachel Ward? That can't be
                            right. She started acting
                            after Bogey died.
PovertyRowPictures: Diane Benham, stinking
                            rich Brit bad-girl. She
                            escaped from rehab in
                            Switzerland, supposedly to
                            chase after the frontman
                            for the Bean Counters who
                            dumped her ass.
MissingHeiressInCorsica: Steve Martin, Carl
                            Reiner . . .
MilesMonroe: Dead Men Don't Wear Plaid
PovertyRowPictures: Dead Men Don't Wear Plaid
MissingHeiressInCorsica: Y. Go, Miles.
MilesMonroe: I don't think Ward Bond
                            was in Dead Men.
SpearsBritney: WTG, Miles!
MissingHeiressInCorsica: Poverty, what is the
                            latest on that heiress
                            chick?

PovertyRowPictures:	She's not in Corsica at all.
MilesMonroe:	Dan Hedaya, Amanda Plummer . . .
MissingHeiressInCorsica:	Where is she then?
MilesMonroe:	Brooke Shields, Brittany Murphy . . .
PovertyRowPictures:	Freeway, starring Reese Witherspoon and Keifer Sutherland.
MilesMonroe:	Y. Go, Poverty.
SpearsBritney:	WTG, Poverty.
PovertyRowPictures:	Missing, I hear she's in Paris, hiding out in plain view.
MilesMonroe:	Are we gonna get some cast??? Go, Poverty!
MissingHeiressInCorsica:	Where did you hear this?
PovertyRowPictures:	OK OK, I'm going Miles . . . Earl Holliman, Walter Pidgeon . . .
SpearsBritney:	Is this another old movie? I can never guess those.
MilesMonroe:	Forbidden Planet.
Poverty:	Y. Go, Miles.
SpearsBritney:	WTG, Miles.
MissingHeiressInCorsica:	Where did you hear this about the heiress?
Poverty:	vomitintheshrubbery.co.uk.
MilesMonroe:	Madeline Kahn, Fred Gwynne . . .

Diane left the chat immediately and went to vomitinthe-
shrubbery.co.uk, a new website she hadn't heard of. It was de-

voted to the lives, loves, and larger-than-life fuckups of jetsetting
heiresses, royals, and Presidential daughters, with the occasional
groupie celebocrat or model thrown in. On the homepage, it featured a collage of images of young, rich bad-girls, drunk, screaming, and so on. Diane was represented with a mugshot, her
mascara and lipstick smeared, her then-blonde hair sticking up
all over the place, frowning. She hated that picture. It didn't look
anything like her.

Underneath the collage was a caption that said, "A site de-
voted to rudegirls with too much money, too much time, too little
taste, and no morals . . ." followed by a list of links:

How to be a Rupee
(Rich Urban Princess)

Spend Daddy's Money

Drink (and Drug!) with the Rich, Royal, and Famous

Dirty Dance with Your Swarthy Bodyguard

Flash for the Cameras!

Bitch-Slap a Rival or Social Inferior

Resist Arrest

Vomit in the Shrubbery

Each line was a link to another part of the site. Spend Daddy's
Money, for instance, was a link to a page with photos and stories
about extravagant shopping sprees. Diane was oddly pleased to
realize she had fulfilled all the requirements except for the swarthy
bodyguard one and the bitch-slapping, and not necessarily in that
order.

A site search for her name brought up two new listings since
her escape. Under Drink and Drug, there was a story that mentioned her:

WE CALL IT . . . RETROVICE

Listen up, Lady Thora Simpson and Diane Benham . . . you are using woefully unfashionable methods of glamorous self-destruction. Coke is so 20th century. In the Uh-Oh years, truly chic and decadent Rupees have gone back to the 19th century and palliatives like absinthe and good, old-fashioned opium, the sort their forebears traded along with tea to fund their own fortunes and finance the British Empire.

Classicists smoke it in a traditional way, in a long, jewelled wood pipe in a den, reclining on brocade cushions while a server softens the earthy-smelling brown ball by hand, massaging it gently until it is the consistency of soft taffy.

The post-post-mods "hot knife" it by plunging a white-hot knife into the opium, creating a funky white smoke which is immediately inhaled through white plastic or paper cones.

For those who prefer *de boire*, there is absinthe, not the denuded version now made in France, but the real deal with oil of wormwood that drove Van Gogh to raving genius and scores of can-can girls, grandes horizontales and shop assistants to the fetid gutters. This original recipe version is bottled in eastern Europe, and smuggled over from Amsterdam.

At one titled beauty's London apartment, the "Green Fairy" is served in custom-made glasses, the base of which contains a realistic replica of a human ear meant to evoke the mad sacrifice of Van Gogh, but which makes one think instead of Damien Hirst.

Diane clicked back to the search page. In the Latest Whispers section she saw the rumor about her finding refuge in Paris. Someone had fed off a report that she was in Nice and had gone from there to Paris.

She couldn't have people looking for her in Paris. That's where she was headed.

To steer them away, she posted a sighting of her own in Corsica, where, she typed, Diane Benham had been seen on the terrace of a cafe in Porto-Vecchio, drinking a margarita, no ice, no salt, with extra triple sec. She was overheard talking about going to Tunisia.

It wasn't long before someone posted that this sounded legit, because—"little-known fact"—Benham's favorite drink was a margarita, no ice, no salt, extra triple sec.

Little-known fact my ass, Benham thought. Every bartender in every club with a red velvet rope knew her drink. Someone was showing off, trying to create the impression they knew her well. Whatever. She wasn't going to contradict it.

This ruse bought her some freedom. With all eyes focused elsewhere, it was safe to leave Rome and head to France. She was bored with Rome anyway. She could drive north to Milan then head down to France through Turin, coming into Provence on her way to Paris.

Why wait. She wanted to go now. She did a line of coke to help her pack up, then checked out and hit the highway.

CHAPTER 14

There was a man named Harold Carpenter who matched the description of the Harold Carpenter/Doo McGarrigle in Monte Carlo. But he wasn't Australian. He was American. According to the Interpol report received by the French police, Harold Carpenter was believed to have been dead for quite a long time.

His bones, it was thought, had been found on a mountain ledge in northwestern Pakistan in 1989 where he had been smuggling drugs, guns, and Afghan antiquities through the tribal territories. He had last been seen in Peshawar in March of 1988, though the body wasn't found until late the following summer, and by then the flesh and clothes had been ravaged by vultures, wild dogs, and decomposition, the skull and several finger and toe bones carried away by animals or the spring melt, leaving an incomplete skeleton and an intact, but weathered, vinyl money pouch hung over his left shoulder. In it was Harry Carpenter's passport and some Pakistani rupees.

The local authorities didn't do an autopsy. The body had Harry's ID, and it was the kind of thing everyone expected to happen to Harry sooner or later. The bones were shipped to New York for cremation. The case was closed.

The bones, of course, were those of the real Doo McGarrigle. Poor Doo McGarrigle, last seen checking out of Green's hotel, was a friendly guy who ran into Carpenter in the dining room of Green's, which had a popular and cheap western and Pakistani buffet that featured a dozen different jello dishes and was well attended by smugglers, spies, tribal khans, tourists, and local shopkeepers. Carpenter had bummed a Dunhill from McGarrigle there and struck up a conversation. McGarrigle wanted to travel into the tribal territories, the Wild West of Pakistan, which were off-limits to foreigners, and then into Afghanistan. He hoped to write a few stories from there.

"This is your lucky day," Carpenter had said to him. "I can take you 'inside.' "

It was Harry's lucky day. He'd found a lone Quixote, a friendly, trusting type, just when Harry Carpenter's enemies were closing in on him and he needed a new identity.

— — —

Mike was still trying to work up the heiress story on his own when he heard that some dead American who had been passing as an Australian had been murdered in Monte Carlo—not just a dead American, but a dead New Yorker who had been thought dead since 1989. Harold Carpenter had been raised in Jamaica, Queens, and most of his family was still there.

Sharp had called Mike and offered him a chance to do the Monte Carlo angle on the story for the local reporter covering the Queens angle.

Yeah, now that they needed someone on the ground, Sharp was willing to let him work a little. Of course, Sharp made it seem like he was doing a big favor for Mike, letting him work the Monte Carlo angle on the story. And there were conditions. Mike would not be the lead reporter—that would be the New York reporter—but he could take the second byline on a combined story.

"I'm on vacation. If I'm going to interrupt this to go back to work, then I want the top byline," Mike said.

"No need for you to interrupt your vacation, Mike. I thought you'd like a chance to work a story happening right there, and maybe show management your willingness to cooperate. But we'll just use the AP reports from France on the murder. Forget I called. Enjoy your vacation—"

"Fuck. Okay. Second byline."

"Good. It's only a couple of days' work. Grab a train for Monte Carlo. You need a hotel there or can you commute?"

"Give me a hotel."

"Okay, Cassie will call you on your mobile with hotel info."

Train, hell. Mike called Buzzer's driver and told him he was going to need to go to Monte Carlo for a couple of days. After he loaded the car with beer and snacks, they drove off.

Carpenter was some sort of criminal adventurer. He'd been linked to a Bombay crime family, but he was nobody important, just a henchman, and India was still too "exotic" for his paper's readers. If the crime family had been involved in smuggling yellowcake uranium, anthrax, or underage girls, then the story would be sexy enough to play big in New York. Faking one's death by killing another guy and stealing his identity was juicy, could keep the story alive three, four days. Right now, it looked to Mike like a guy who had come to Monte Carlo to launder money and got himself killed in a robbery, a story that would fade with the next celebrity divorce scandal.

Still, there could be a book deal in it, if he could dredge up enough good info to use as leverage to get top byline.

To help him with the French, Mike brought Buzzer's driver, Alphonse, along on all the interviews in Monte Carlo. The two women seen with Carpenter the day he died were not yet official suspects in the murder and probable robbery. At this point, they were wanted as material witnesses. They were believed to be escorts, but police had turned up no one and nothing in the local escort population. Perhaps they had come from elsewhere, pros who traveled a circuit around the Riviera.

The night Carpenter died, there had been one call to the hotel, but it had come from a call box and that lead went nowhere.

"He was seen at the casino," Mike said to Alphonse. "You feel like going to the casino?"

Alphonse smiled.

The doorman who remembered the women, vaguely, was getting off for the day, so they gambled for a while before they went to meet him at a cafe overlooking the bay. He couldn't remember the blonde but he remembered the dark-haired woman. He was sure her name was Marsha, and that she and her friend were either Americans or high-class call girls. Maybe both.

The waiter, François Albert, heard the description and said, "I saw those women. But I believe the dark-haired woman was Canadian."

"Canadian?"

"Yes. She had a little red maple leaf pin on her purse. I thought it was a red version of a marijuana leaf at first, until I saw some elderly people with similar pins on their lapels a few days ago. Of course, it is the symbol of Canada."

François Albert regretted that he couldn't provide more information, but had only remembered as much as he did because he thought the dark-haired woman, the Canadian, was attractive.

"Thank you," Mike said, the word resounding in his ears—Canadian. A dark-haired Canadian traveling with a blonde woman nobody could quite describe, just like Diane Benham.

The story he was asked to do was twisting into the story Mike wanted to do. Sharp wasn't interested in the heiress beyond a few uncredited blips that made it into the paper's gossip section, as both she and her rock boyfriend were unknown in the U.S. But if the heiress was involved with the murder of the local boy . . .

Mike had to think about this. If he wrote a story for his paper suggesting any connection between the heiress and the murder, it would bring twice as many other reporters, at least, into it. It might not pan out at all, and if it did, the reporter in New York, not Mike, would get the first byline for it. He had to find a way to flush the heiress out, while leading everyone yet more astray about her AND about the Carpenter murder story. Then he had to catch the heiress himself.

Later that night, after he had filed his part of the Carpenter story for the paper, he checked for updates and saw a new rumor, this one running in the evening edition of a British tabloid, the *Daily Splash*. Diane Benham had been sighted in Grasse in the company of a dark-haired woman and two sandy-haired young men.

The only other new information was a post in a message board on www.vomitintheshrubbery.com, which had become Missing Heiress Central lately for its inside dish on Benham. EnemiesOfCarlotta had posted this:

> I'm told by a former schoolmate of hers that she met the Canadian friend years ago through a school overseas penpal exchange and they have written faithfully to each other for years. I haven't been able to find out her name. They are not in Grasse. They are still in Corsica. The villa is being rented pseudonymously by another friend from the UK who has been similarly blighted by scandal and overexposure in the last year.

It was so convincing, even Mike believed for a moment that she really was in Corsica, until he remembered that he was the one who started that story.

— — —

Diane, aka EnemiesOfCarlotta, had posted the information about the penpal because she had had a Canadian penpal when she was younger, and that was the only Canadian she knew at all. The penpal thing was part of a class project Diane thought was hopelessly outdated and silly—to "bridge the gap between cultures" by writing to their peers in foreign countries, followed by regular reports on what they learned about these strangers. Diane's friends all chose Americans, which pissed off the teacher, who'd been hoping they'd find penpals in places like Bangladesh and Soweto.

Diane, being even more contrary, had picked a Canadian and writ-ten to her under a false name, with a false biography and an in-vented life.

Nobody would ever be able to find the penpal, but old school-mates could confirm she had one, which would lend credence to the Corsica story. The Grasse sighting had scared her a little, as it was in the same general area as Sisteron, where she was now. She'd taken the Route Napoléon through the Alps and stopped here for a few days because she liked the name and it seemed re-mote. The road had taken her through the barren, rocky plateau of northern Provence, terrain that made her think of Tibet, or the moon. She'd gotten out at one point to stretch her legs and cut a line on a pale gray rock, then sat there chain-smoking and imag-ining that she was some space explorer 300 years from now and had just landed on a now-desolate planet Earth, where she would soon meet up with her true love and others of their kind to start a new colony here. The Canadian friend would be one of the colonists.

She liked the idea of a Canadian friend, the loyal penpal, who nobly came to her English mate's assistance when the rest of the world was against her. The mysterious Canadian. When she got to Sisteron and found a hotel, she logged on and posted the new tid-bit about the Canadian friend before she ordered room service and scanned the online papers for news of herself.

At the news conference called in her Knightsbridge apart-ment, Diane's mother Prudence told reporters Diane's father was to blame, just before she abruptly got up and walked out of the room, where she was found moments later asleep on a sofa.

Stepmom Lily Sue, commenting on the whole "Diane prob-lem" in *Splendor* magazine, took her digs. "As the French say, pi-geons can't give birth to chickens. Heredity has its destiny, and she has her mother in her. I can only hope the half of her she got from her father will kick in and she'll save herself. Her dad and I have done everything we can."

She said this to remind everyone of the trauma of having a mother like Diane's, while giving credit for whatever good there was in Diane to her father and foisting responsibility on the outcome totally on Diane.

Lily Sue was an American genius and one of those people who seemed to have taken a course to learn the exact proper thing to say in every public circumstance, in the most sincere-seeming way possible, without giving anything real away or touching any genuine controversy. Always quick to take a stand against child abuse and hunger, but truly, more interested in the politics of her husband's businesses and bank accounts.

Oh, if only Diane had had a hidden camera the day, two years before, when Lily got Diane alone at her father's house and, as chill as a warrior queen, said, not so graciously, "You can't win against me so don't even try. Save yourself a lot of time and grief, and just give up."

"If wishes were horses, Lily Sue."

In the beginning, Lily Sue had tried to do the "let's be friends" gambit, but it was hard for her, seeing as she couldn't hide her complete dislike and disapproval of Diane. Being Diane's friend for Lily Sue seemed to mean criticizing and instructing her on how to improve her sorry self. She even tried to get Diane to give her power-of-attorney over her financial affairs. (One of the reasons Diane and Woy had cooked up the scheme to transfer her money to him was to keep Lily Sue and her father from going to court, having Diane declared incompetent and taking control against her will.)

When "friendship" failed, Lily Sue tried being business-like, only dealing with Diane when she had to, and otherwise ignoring her.

But then it became war.

"I can make your life so much easier," Lily said. "But in return I want you to behave yourself, lose 15 pounds, see my psychiatrist, and come to work in my training program."

"I don't want to work for you, I don't want to be in business, and I'd never go see your shrink. You don't want my life to be easier, you want *your* life to be easier."

This whole episode was inspired by Diane's public revelation—in, of all places, the 5 A.M. Party column—that her father and Lily were about to launch a hostile and, until then, secret takeover attempt of Flume Media Group, because Lily wanted into TV, radio, and films. (The item also included a description of Diane's outfit, a pale pink dress with tiny black polka dots and a small black bow at the center of the bodice. "A sexy and sweet 199 £ at Harvey Nichols.") The news sent Flume stock soaring, thwarting the takeover.

"When I was your age, I'd already graduated high school, was about to enter college, and had made 47,000 dollars in the market. Ten years later, I'm president of your father's business and I'm his wife," Lily Sue had said. "Why? Because I'm smart, much smarter than you. I'm not someone who likes to lose, or will allow it."

"Everyone has to lose sometimes."

"Not me. I'm not only smart, I'm lucky in ways you'll never be, Diane. The wedding for instance. Thought you had mucked that up good, didn't ya?"

"Well, that day you were lucky," Diane said, quoting an IRA communiqué after a bombing in Brighton that failed to take out Margaret Thatcher and her cabinet. "I only have to be lucky once. You have to be lucky always."

"This campaign of terror is going to end. You have the 'only child' versus new wife advantage," Lily conceded. "But—"

"You have the 'I fuck the old guy now' advantage. He hasn't slept with me in ages."

"Wha—?"

"Just kidding—."

Lily stared at her.

Diane continued. "I still do him."

"No!" Lily said, but as if she was considering the possibility.

"Look at you. That's how much you care about, know and trust my father. You thought for a second I was telling the truth."

"I'd never think that of you, Diane. Don't think I don't know you were behind those stories about the Jamaican jockey and how I got rid of your father's previous girlfriend," Lily said. "And you're going to lose your only child advantage. I'm pregnant."

"You're going to be a mother?"

That Lily was smart. There was not a maternal urge in this woman, but she'd suddenly decided to breed? A canny PR move to soften her image and make her impervious to attack. Anything Diane did to her now would be an attack on a pregnant woman, a mother-to-be.

When the baby was born and Diane saw the rosy, soft-focus photos in *Hello* and *OK* of mother and child, she almost lost her lunch. Lily looked like the mother of Jesus, with the subtlest touch of halo from the diffuse back light. She was holding the baby in her arms, a little stiffly, her head bowed down slightly toward it. Lily's face was just an inch from the child, and she was smiling. She couldn't quite pull off that beneficent maternal smile. It looked more like the smile of a gleeful predator before it ate its own young, whole and raw.

It would never happen though. Lily didn't eat meat and in any event there were three full-time nannies in the wings to make sure little Lawrencia (vomit!) Carmichael Benham had round-the-clock care and protection.

Of course, Lily still controlled everything, and worked as much as she did before, with three nannies and assorted others to replace her at home, until such time as the child was ready to enter her mother's management training program. In the *Splendor* magazine piece, she affected the tone and troubles of your typical working mom, trying to balance work and career, work guilt, mother guilt, all the things regular working moms felt, which she had probably read about somewhere. There were pictures of her, bringing in a cake for Carmichael's second birthday.

(Mercifully, she was not known as Lawrencia.) Lily and Lord Larry and Carmichael were shown relaxing with a picnic in the country-side, en famille, Larry in tasteful casual American sportswear, not his usual attire. There was even a shot of Little Carmichael in her mother's lap at her mother's office.

It was an insult to motherhood, to working moms, stay-at-home moms, and children everywhere! This phony pastiche of happy family photos only did credit to Joan Crawford!

True, Diane's mother was a loon, who—after her own difficult 47-hour labor—became averse to human touch. But hey, Diane's mum couldn't help it. She was insane. Lily was hypersane. That made her worse—and much more dangerous.

But—joy!—there was a new e-mail from Woy, at last, from an anonymous e-mail address, Redkiss@yahoo.com, one she hadn't seen before and a private joke between the two of them: *Red Kiss* was one of her favorite French films.

"Am safe. Miss you. Hold on. CU soon beautiful. XX Me," he wrote.

She sent an e-mail to him: "Am safe too. I love you. Me Two."

PART FIVE

BOY, THOSE BUDDISTS ARE QUITE THE BUSINESS PEOPLE

Avignon, medieval city of popes, was crowded because of the annual arts festival. There wasn't a hotel room to be had. Even the private Camping Bagatelle and the municipal camping park were filled. But two acrobats from Wales told Eddie a camping squat had formed in a park across the Rhone on Ile de la Barthelasse and there was still space to be had there, as long as the police didn't chase them away.

"We don't have a tent," Chloe said.

"We'll sleep under the stars," Blackie said.

"What if it rains?"

"We'll figure something out."

The camping squat looked like a cross between an outdoor concert and Cirque du Soleil. Jugglers, clowns, and strolling minstrels meandered among the motley collection of tents and the tentless. There was hashish smoke in the air, and a few people selling food and drinks at makeshift stands or out of the side of VW buses.

After they staked out a spot next to some artisan weavers, Eddie and Cameron went to check their backpacks at a left luggage truck run by a Buddhist collective called Artery from Paris.

"We're going to trust a bunch of people we don't know with our stuff?" Chloe asked.

"They're Buddhists."

"So they say. You've got your money on you, right?"

"In my bra-safe," Blackie said, patting one breast. Some of their spoils had been sent home in money orders to their bank accounts. To hide the rest, the girls had made secret velcro pockets in the cups and bands of their bras. As Chloe noted, you don't always know when someone is picking your pocket but you wouldn't miss someone picking your bra.

Chloe looked around. "So where do we fit in shantytown?"

"Oh God, Chloe, quit complaining."

"Blackie, less than a week ago, we were staying in the Negresco. In Nice. Now we're camping out with a bunch of vagabonds on the cold ground, no tent or anything. And it looks like rain."

"Just a few clouds. Get into it! It's like Woodstock or something."

"It's different for you. You're fucking a guy, so yeah, it's Woodstock for you. For me, this is a bore."

"You could fuck Cameron."

"I'm not interested in him," she said.

"Maybe you'll meet someone here."

"I doubt it. I'm going into town"

"So are we, in about an hour."

"I'm going now. If I don't find you there, I'll meet you back here later."

She got up, dusted the dirt off her jeans, and walked until she found a taxi to take her to the Palace of the Popes, a massive fourteenth-century fortress with towers, battlements, and "sluices for dousing attackers with boiling oil," according to her guidebook.

The streets were thronged. It took her over an hour to work her way through and around the perimeter of the Palace, then another hour to find a space in one of the cafes near there.

To her left, a man dressed as a harlequin strummed a mandolin, while in a corner of the square a theatrical troupe performed a scene from something by Shakespeare, judging by the period dress.

The clouds above were thickening and cast the scene of medieval merriment in a day-for-night shadow. This made Chloe think of the side shows and festive crowds that might appear at a

public execution or bear-baiting in the middle ages. Bring a picnic, watch a heretic burned or a traitor disemboweled alive. Only
the belled lepers and papal concubines were missing from the
tableau.

Medieval architecture had definitely lost its appeal.

And it definitely looked like rain was coming. She drank her
wine and thought about how miserable it was going to be, sleeping soaking wet in the rain or, if lucky, invited to squeeze into
some smelly stranger's tent or van. All so Blackie could be with
some guy.

A local drunk sat down at the table next to hers, asked the
man at the table for money, then turned to Chloe.

"May I have one of those," he asked in slurred French, trying to
point at the cigarettes but nearly falling off his chair.

She didn't understand his drunken French.

"He says he would like a cigarette," said the other man, in
English, and smiled at her like the British man in the restaurant
in Nice, with both contempt and desire. Chloe immediately smelled
a rat.

Chloe handed the drunken man a cigarette while she took a
measure of the other man.

She wasn't quite sure what to do. Blackie was better at being
friendly, at playing along while a mark initiated his con. Without
Blackie, she couldn't pull the missing money scam to confuse him
while she sized him up. Chloe was on her own as she tried to do
a quick assessment.

His tailored casual style wasn't really casual at all. The clothes
were designer, and carefully put together. It was like a disguise,
designed to appear relaxed and democratic, but revealing him
as an anal poser by the gentle, perfectly aligned crease in the
trousers, the spotless light cashmere pullover, the subtle glow—
never a tacky shine—of the dark brown Italian shoes.

He reminded her so much of someone, and it took her a moment to realize who—John Carey, a recognition that suddenly

eddied a tidepool of emotions. She had to look away to steady herself before turning back to the man.

"You are here alone?" he asked her.

"No, I'm here surrounded by thousands of people," she said, looking around.

His smile tightened slightly.

"Where are you from?" he asked.

Judging by his slight accent he was either Swiss or German. He had no ring or ring line, but he smelled married.

"The Faroe Islands," she lied. "You?"

"I am European, born in Germany, schooled in Switzerland," he said, carefully avoiding any mention of where he lived now.

"Where do you live now?" Chloe asked.

"A small city to the northeast of here," he weaseled.

Chloe decided against pressing him. He was a mark, she wanted to play him, but not alienate him.

"How long are you in Avignon?" she asked.

"I leave early this evening for Marseille."

"Oh, that's too bad."

The waiter came by to collect, and Euroman took out his wallet, and pulled out a ten-euro note, carefully exposing the tips of two five hundreds. He insisted on paying for her drink, too. Then he slipped the wallet back into his front left pocket.

"I have to return to my hotel but I would like to continue this conversation. Would you care to walk with me?" he asked.

It took her a moment to catch on to this subtle Euro-smut offer, but, yes, he was inviting her back to his hotel. *He must think I'm a "working girl" here at the festival,* she thought, wondering what it was that gave that impression. Was it that she was alone? Had she mistakenly selected a cafe known for a certain clientele?

"Sure," she said.

Chloe could see the edge of his wallet sticking out of his

pants pocket. By now, she had become pretty good at picking pockets but she'd always had Blackie there to serve as a distraction.

She fell back of him a step. The road was thick with festival-goers, most heading in the other direction. Deliberately, Chloe moved into the path of two husky women, feigned tripping into Euroman, and dropped her purse on the ground. When he bent down to pick it up, she bumped him again, and handily slipped his wallet out as she did, and put it in her jeans.

"Your handbag," he said.

"Thank you," she said.

She walked with him until a band of unicyclists came through the pedestrians, and in the resulting confusion, she was able to give Euroman the slip.

— — —

Cameron had worked the crowd around the Place de l'Horloge near the Opera and was heading with his guitar to the Palace of the Popes when he saw Chloe. He'd split off from Eddie, not wanting to be a third wheel, trying to give Eddie and Blackie some space for whatever was developing between them. He didn't think it would last the summer. He was a little disappointed because he thought he and Eddie would be hanging out. All the same, he was trying to do the noble thing, because Eddie was an old road friend, and he liked Blackie.

Chloe he couldn't get a handle on at all.

Funny, just a second after this thought went through his head, he saw Chloe. She was standing with her back to the stone wall, behind a crowded circle of people watching a fire-eater. She pulled a black wallet out of her purse and tapped the shoulder of the man in front of her. When he turned, she showed him the wallet and said something to him. The man opened the wallet, nodded and shoved it into his left pocket.

Then she just stood there. Cameron was about to call out to her when the crowd in front of her pressed back from the fire, and he saw Chloe's hand slip the wallet out of the man's pocket. The crowd pressed back farther, and she slipped another wallet out of the man's other pocket.

When the crowd moved forward, she moved sideways into a passing stream of people and left the scene of her peculiar crime. Cameron followed, well behind her, until she took up position on the other side of the Palace where a large circle of people was watching a group on stilts. They were dancers, all painted chalk-white and wearing diaphanous white robes that flowed to the ground. They moved so smoothly, Cameron couldn't believe they were really on stilts—they seemed to be on wheels. But a breeze blew up the robes of two of the dancers as they skirted the circle of viewers, revealing ordinary wooden stilts.

Chloe tapped a man on the shoulder, and showed him the same black wallet. He looked at it, and put his hand on his front pocket, to check his own wallet was there. He shook his head "no." As soon as he turned his back, Chloe put the original wallet back in her purse, and started walking away.

Cameron looked at Chloe with a great new interest. He followed now, weaving through the currents of colorful people to catch up with her.

"Hey," he said.

"Cameron. Where are you going?"

"Wherever. You?"

"I think I'll go to one of the museums before it rains."

He glanced at her purse, and then at her, in such a knowing way that she self-consciously pulled her purse closer.

"I'll walk with you part way," he said. "What did you do this afternoon?"

"Walked around," she said.

Walked around and played judge and jury, looking for an honest man. She'd nicked the wallet of a German man from the cafe first. Then she offered the German's wallet to a Dutch guy. The Dutch guy opened the wallet, saw all the money in it, and nodded. Crook. She waited until he put it in his other pocket, then she picked it again, and took his own wallet, too. The last guy, nationality unknown, had been honest, and so she let him keep his wallet.

"What did you do? Another film?" she asked.

"I played guitar and sang, made 11 euros," he said.

"What did you sing?"

"A couple of songs a friend of mine wrote."

It started raining, big slow drops that smashed and splattered on the cobblestones around them, quickening within moments to a full-fledged storm.

"It's a monsoon," he said.

They ducked into an Algerian bar in the Place du Change with a mob of similarly soaked people. Cameron was quick enough to get them two places at the bar.

"What do you want?" he asked.

"Just a coffee. Wow, it is coming down. Do we really have to sleep at that squat camp?"

"No choice. There's no room anywhere else. The rain will pass. It can't rain like this forever."

"Even if it does stop, the ground will be soaked."

"No, we rented plastic sheets from the Buddhist collective. That should keep the ground from getting too wet. Tonight, we can jig 'em up to form a kind of lean-to-slash-tent. If it's still 'sooning, we can maybe get a space in the Buddhist dinner tent after the vegetarian dinner and dance tonight."

"Oh that sounds like fun. Lentils and Kumbaya."

"We all bought tickets for the dinner. We bought one for you, too."

"Boy, those Buddhists are quite the businesspeople. They're renting tarps, they're checking luggage, they're feeding the masses. They have their hands in everything," Chloe said.

"Their prices are dirt cheap. They also have high-speed internet in a van. Tonight I'm going to upload the first episode of the Ganesh film we made. By tomorrow you and Blackie could be stars."

"Thrilled."

"Chilled did you say?"

"Thrilled."

"I don't think much thrills you, Chloe."

"Well, you don't know me."

"I saw you in the Place, offering a guy a wallet that wasn't his."

She flinched. *He'd seen her with the last one,* she thought, *the honest one.* "I found it on the ground and thought it was his. He was the only guy in the vicinity."

"He took it, and then you took it back, along with his wallet."

"Where—" Shit. He'd seen her with the Dutch guy whose pocket she had picked. Twice.

"It's cool. I don't care. I just wonder why," he said.

"Don't tell anyone."

"Right."

"I was bored. I wanted to see if I could find an honest man. That first guy you saw, the Dutch one, wasn't honest."

"And then you found an honest man. The next one."

"Yes. End of game. Don't—"

"I won't tell anyone," he said.

It was too late now to meet Blackie and Eddie in town, so when the rain stopped Cameron and Chloe went back to the squat camp. Because of the downpour, there were fewer people outside. Most were inside tents or old refurbished campers, just starting to drift toward a large open-air tent set up for the Buddhist supper. Eddie and Blackie returned, laughing at some had-to-be-there joke they couldn't seem to explain. They didn't stop talking as they led the way to the Buddhist barbecue. It flashed Chloe back to the early days of her relationship with John, when they had just started building a history together.

The dinner was held in a big open-air festival tent with tarps on the ground in lieu of tables and chairs. Each tarp was divided into eight "virtual tables" bearing a flower in a jar as a centerpiece.

After their dinner tickets were taken, they were given a reusable plastic plate with a red flower pattern. Pour-your-own wine, beer, soft drinks, and goat milk were on a separate table with a large cardboard box full of real glasses, all mismatched, some recycled jam and yogurt jars. An equally diverse collection of silverware was set out in three bowls under a handwritten sign that said,

Please return plates and silverware. Or save silverware by eating with your hands and your bread. There are buckets of rainwater for handwashing at the north end of the tent. Free breakfast or lunch will be provided to anyone who helps with dishes and cleanup.

Thanks

Artery

"Using our evil for good,* instead of for evil since 1998"
*mostly

"Eat with our hands!" Eddie and Blackie both said at the same time. They found this hilarious and ran off together to the row of buckets, some full of water, some empty, some with about an inch or two of soapy water.

A sign above the buckets said,

Please soap up your hands using a teaspoon of the eco-friendly squirt soap.* Scoop water out of the bucket marked "Fresh" with a bowl and pour it over your hands above the bucket marked "Discard." Do not dip your hands into the Fresh bucket! People are washing after you. We recommend two to three full bowls of water for the job.

Thanks.

*We make this natural antibiotic soap from herbs, spices, vegetable fat, and organic alcohol we distill ourselves. If

you want to take some home, we sell it for one euro a liter.
Buy the recipe for 5 euros. See Bruno or Tim in the tarp
van.

The food was set out buffet style, vegetarian lasagna, vegan
couscous, grilled vegetables, a curried potato and cheese dish, a
fish stew, rice pilaf, chocolate mousse, some kind of cake, fruit
salad, and four kinds of bread.

During dinner, a guy with wild dark brown hair sat in one corner and played the violin. The place filled up quickly. Blackie recognized Nickels and Jones, two of the Artery Buddhists they'd
seen in town, and after they ate she and Eddie went over to talk to
them. Cameron went to the computer van to plug in his laptop
and finish editing the first episode of "Requiem for a Nose," which
he planned to upload to his websites that night.

Chloe was left, alone on the tarp. Two tarps away, Blackie and
Eddie were laughing with strangers. She tried to ignore them, but
out of the corner of her eye she saw Blackie wave her over. She
continued pretending not to see until Blackie came over and said,
"Hey, we're going to help with dishes. We'll save money on breakfast tomorrow and, you know, be helpful."

"We don't need to save money."

"It's a nice thing to do, and it'll be fun. At nine there are performances and at midnight they serve free coffee and cocoa. A DJ
spins and everyone dances."

"I think I'll go read while there's still light," Chloe said.

"Okay, fine. Listen, some of this group are heading back to
Paris with this guy Nickels, and some are going down to Arles
with Jones so there'll be room for us in one of the vans. Eddie
wants to go to Arles anyway—"

Blackie watched Chloe wander off and went back to Eddie and
the Buddhists.

"God, she's a large and bitter pill these days," Blackie said.

"Has your friend always been like that?" asked Jones.

"She always had a streak, but this summer that streak got real wide and took over," Blackie said, thinking how easily Chloe had taken to the bad cop role with the men they'd robbed.

"Chloe was in love with a guy who dumped her," Eddie explained to the Buddhists. "She's in relationship rehab now."

"Ah," said Jones.

"What she needs is relationship electroshock," Blackie said. "Or some deep trepanning."

"You're too hard on her," Eddie said. "It's painful to get dumped by someone you love."

"Her parents are still in love. Her paternal grandparents were like that, too. She comes from long lines of faithful, in-love-to-the-end people," Blackie said. "She's unable to find that and it fucks with her."

"For such a white girl, she seems really dark," Jones said. "Really, she looks like she was carved out of ice, she's so white, but I sense some deep magma below that glacier."

"Her parents used to tell her she was 'heavy for her weight,'" Blackie said.

"Was she ever fat?"

"No. She's always been thin. She just always seemed heavy in her parents' arms. Her mom told me that even when awake Chloe had the dead weight of a sleeping child."

"I knew a girl whose parents were madly in love," Nickels said. "So in love there was no room for her."

"Blackie, you had any trouble being American over here?" Jones asked.

"People think I'm a Canadian. You? Anyone spit in your soup or piss in your beer?"

"No trouble, maybe because I'm black. It's much better to be a black American over here than an American, or an African black man."

"Hey Hiro!" Jones called to a Japanese man passing with his cleared plates. "Hiro is a Japanese Buddhist monk we picked up in Dijon. He doesn't speak English, but he speaks French. You speak French, Blackie?"

"No, a little Spanish. Chloe speaks a little French—"

"Hiro, Permets-moi d'introduire Blackie des Etats Unis et Eddie du Canada—" Jones said. He, Eddie, Hiro, and Nickels spoke French, with Eddie and Jones taking turns translating for Blackie. Jones rolled a joint and they passed it.

These Artery Buddhists were fairly casual Buddhists, some vegetarian, some fish-eaters, a couple carnivores, and they didn't chant or anything. It was more like a philosophical guideline for them. *If Chloe couldn't get along with these Buddhists for a few days,* Blackie thought, *maybe she couldn't get along with anyone right now.*

Later, during the outdoor performances at the camp, she saw Chloe on the other side of the audience watching unhappily, and she wondered how Chloe could fail to enjoy all this. The stilt dancers glided around in the dark, lit by different colored floodlights. An ethereal-looking woman with an otherworldly voice sang flamenco. A juggler who was painted pale fluorescent blue glowed in the dark as he juggled three glowing golden balls.

After Cameron finished his computer work, he joined Eddie and the others, and they smoked another joint. Hiro the Japanese Buddhist monk smoked with them, and spent the rest of the night trying to teach himself how to play Beethoven's "Ode to Joy" on his pocket computer. A Buddhist came out and called everyone in to coffee and cocoa. During cocoa, Cameron played and sang his cover of "Alice's Restaurant," the 18-minute version, and got everyone to sing along, then a DJ from Marseille spun and everyone danced, except for Chloe. Chloe went to the internet van and checked her e-mail.

— — —

To: <Chloe>Chloebower@apu.edu
From: <Ma and Pa>MomandDad@customartphoto.com
Subject: Dearest Chloe

How is your trip so far? Did you get to the Chateau
Grimaldi in Antibes?

Went to Hamilton township yesterday where we
photographed the Wilson family reunion, 187 Wilsons
from all over the world. Mom met a girl she knew from
Girl Scouts years (!) ago, who is now married to a
Wilson who works in Japan. They hadn't seen each other
in over 30 years. Small world.

Got back just in time to change and go to the banquet
at Grandad's club, where he was given a plaque for
leading the Benevolent Committee. During the dance Mom
was coaxed to sing, which everyone enjoyed.
Write soon. Much love and a hug to Blackie,
Mom and Dad

They always did this, spoke to her as if they were a unit. She
could never tell who wrote the e-mail, since they were always referred to in third person, Dad and Mom, he and she, as if an invisible "secret" parent had written to tell about them.

— — —

The second day in Avignon the weather was beautiful. They went
into town in the morning, Blackie, Eddie, and Cameron together,
Chloe on her own, Ganesh stashed with the Buddhist luggage
check.

They sat under a tree with low, spreading branches, Eddie with
his fold-up stool and easel and Cameron with his guitar, the case
open at his feet with a few seed coins scattered on the black felt

lining. While Eddie finished a partial sketch of Blackie and waited for a customer, Cameron played and sang in five-song sets after which he'd take long breaks to drink beer.

"I wish I could busk. I don't know what I could do though. I don't have any talents I can perform in public," Blackie said. " 'Guess your weight,' maybe."

"But people don't pay to have you guess their weight," Eddie said. "They pay for you to be wrong so they win some cheap prize."

"Can't sing?" Cameron asked.

"No. Chloe sings."

"Really?"

"She's good, but she's too shy to do it in public."

"Chloe has a lot of hidden talents," Cameron said.

Nickels and a guy named Loudon saw them and stopped to hang out for a while to drink beer and talk about their squat in Paris. Their collective, Artery, shared the space with four other artist groups and some individual artists. Their squat was in a building that had been abandoned for nine years, and was owned by a bank that had a lot of vacant properties. The bank had been unable to evict them because they were "providing a community service" and the bank had not filed plans to use the building, so the police wouldn't act.

"You robbed a bank ... by taking one of their buildings?" Blackie said. "You *are* the balls."

"Heh, well, we didn't steal the building. We're just borrowing it."

"It's not the image most people have of a squat," said Nickels, an Asian-American who sculpted and worked on Artery's internet TV project, which interested Cameron and Blackie. "A lot of people think of junkies and rats when they hear *squat*. We're an art space, no hard drugs, no rats."

"Every three months we have to do a massive cockroach extermination however," said Loudon, an English actor. "We wait until the vegans are out of town. Then we flush out the cockroaches with a blowtorch and suck them up with an industrial vacuum cleaner. It's barbaric, but effective."

"We have only cold water except on the sixth floor where the shower is. We have 12-minute intervals of hot water there every two hours. It's rough and industrial, it's no palace—"

"It is homey in its way."

"But it's fairly clean and there's always something interesting going on."

"I stayed in an art squat in Amsterdam two years ago," Cameron said. "It's in a bank, too, near Rembrandtsplein. Kind of sterile on the outside but it was cool. The guys I stayed with were doing some bizarre things with blue-screen animation."

"What's that?" Blackie asked.

"It's filmed in front of a blue screen, then you use a computer program to blip out all the blue and replace it with the background of your choice. You've seen it in cheesy movies. But they were doing something stylized with it."

"How long have you been in the squat?" Eddie asked Loudon and Nickels.

"Three years."

"You've survived as a collective *three years* in the same space without any homicides?" Cameron said, laughing.

"It hasn't been easy. We had to compromise our ideals, sometimes a lot. We started out sharing everything, and without any hierarchy, but that broke down at the refrigerator over a package of tofu sausages."

"Within six months of start-up people were labeling their food and marking the liquid levels in their beverage bottles," Loudon said.

"We had problems when it was just guys there. Then women moved in, and we had all different problems."

"We have to sit down and spill our shit about once a month."

"It helps if people leave for a while when they're tense and come back when they've chilled."

"Some don't come back. But most do, and new people arrive to replace those who move on. You should come visit us in Paris."

"You're sure you're not a cult. We won't have to wear robes and sell daisies for the reverend, will we?" Blackie asked.

"We may make you wash dishes, like everyone. If you stick around you'll be expected to pay your share of groceries either with cash or by working the bar at one of our shows."

"Hey Jones!" Eddie yelled out as Jones walked toward them.

"Hi," Jones said. "I just saw your friend. What's her name?"

"Chloe."

"She found a wallet on the ground and asked if it was mine. It wasn't."

"Where was Chloe?" Blackie asked.

"That way, around the corner, next to the wall."

"Thanks. I'll see you guys later," she said, and took off.

Fucking Chloe. She just had to mess things up.

This was turning into a big problem.

She found Chloe casing the crowd, carefully situating herself near a group of women and one man. Just as Blackie was about to walk over and yank her away, she noticed someone else watching her, another man. He looked like a tourist.

Before Chloe could tap her intended mark on the shoulder, the tourist snapped her picture, then snapped some more. As he did it, he said, "Gotcha."

Then he turned and ran.

"Chloe," Blackie called.

Chloe turned.

"Who was that?"

"I don't know."

"Whatcha doing?"

"Wandering, thinking—"

"Picking pockets."

"What?"

"I know."

"How do you know?" Chloe said, thinking that damned Cameron was a rat.

"One of the Buddhists, from Artery. You played your wallet scam on him."

"Did he take the wallet?"

"No," Blackie said.

"I didn't recognize him. There are so damned many Buddhists around here."

"I thought we were going to give it up."

"Take a break from it. That's what we agreed. I took a break. It's over now."

"Chloe, this is insane. And risky. You're going to get into trouble, and you're going to get me into trouble, too. A lark is a lark, but you've got an addiction. You steal, then you get moody and weird, like a drug crash, then you want to steal again. That's addict behavior."

"I'm not addicted to it—"

"I do not want to get arrested. I do not want to spend my whole vacation as perv-prey. You're turning into a klepto, Chloe—"

"I'll give up crime. But let's go to the beach. I want to go to Cannes and Ste-Marguerite—"

"And I want to hang out with Eddie."

"You're making too much of this guy. He's a penniless drifter."

"Fuck you. Just because you keep fucking it up doesn't mean I have to be a nun."

"I keep fucking it up? You haven't had a relationship longer than two months."

"Bill Stock. Five months. And I try not to drag my friends down when I'm getting over guys."

"You don't need to get over them, Blackie, because they're interchangeable for you, this one or that one, a generic guy. That one's gone? Oh well. There's another one."

"Bullshit. I liked them all for different reasons. And I was in love with Bill. That one hurt. But what can you do? You can cry for a couple of weeks, and then you have to move on. C'est la vie!" Blackie screamed at Chloe.

"Two weeks exactly? You have a timetable for this?"

"Your mileage may vary, Princess Chloe. But it has been almost four months of you as a pale, weepy Brontë character, except when you're ripping people off. It's even worse than your breakup with Will, who was a far better catch than John Carey."

"You didn't like Will, either."

"I liked him, I just didn't think he was right for you. In retrospect, next to John Carey, Will was Prince fucking William. We're staying with Eddie and Cameron."

Suddenly, that British tourist jumped from around the corner and pointed his camera at them again.

"Fuck off!" Chloe screamed at him. Then she turned to Blackie. "You too."

Chloe ran off. The British tourist tried to follow her, but Blackie blocked him.

"Get out of my way," she said. They tried to dodge each other but only moved to block each other again, and again, until finally Blackie pushed him aside and stomped away.

The tourist looked for Chloe, but she had disappeared into the crowd. When he turned to look for the dark-haired Canadian girl, she was gone too.

Without any idea where she was going, Chloe walked the streets away from the festival epicenter, past a techno-rave club in a sixteenth-century stone building where her guidebook said Huguenots were sheltered during the Inquisition, a Sony store in an eighteenth-century building, a modern McDonald's next to a Roman ruin, before she swung into a bar called Max and ordered a glass of whiskey. She didn't usually drink whiskey, and she'd never had one this early in the day before, but it was France and she was in a mood.

Princess. Blackie hadn't called her that in a long time. Blackie thought Chloe felt a sense of entitlement, but she was the one, Blackie was. Blackie looked like the working-class girl and played the part well. She liked to tell people she was the daughter of a carpenter and the granddaughter of itinerant farmers. "Strivin' White Trash" was how she described her social strata: poor, hard-working people who never got a break and had to push to stay alive. She had aunts and uncles in trailer parks with cars on blocks in the front yard and big cans of lard in the pantry.

It was all true, but Blackie tended to leave out the part where her father started his own construction business when she was in ninth grade and became much richer than Chloe's dad, who with his wife ran a commercial photography business and specialized in weddings and school photos. For a couple of years, Blackie's dad was a real millionaire, until he lost a bunch of money in the stock market, then got divorced and had to split the remainder with Blackie's mom, who used it to start a successful cosmetics dealership. Even after the family's reversal of fortune, they were still much richer than Chloe's family.

Yet, Blackie always acted as if Chloe owed her something because Chloe's family had started out upper-middle class and hadn't had to build a fortune from the ground up.

Chloe gave into it, all through junior high. When her allowance was 20 bucks a week and Blackie's just ten, she gave Blackie five so they'd be equal. Even now Chloe picked up the tab for more than Blackie, or if they went Dutch, Blackie would say, right away, just split it down the middle, even though she always ate the most expensive things and had an appetizer and dessert.

Then there was junior year, after Blackie blew six months' spending money on a motorcycle, and Chloe had to buy her dinner whenever one of Blackie's boyfriends wasn't around. When Blackie was back in the green, she offered to pay Chloe back by taking her to dinner, using a Visa card that set off alarms. So Chloe paid again. When it happened with the same Visa card the next time Blackie invited her to dinner, Chloe thought, well, people make mistakes and Blackie has never been great at balancing her checkbook. Then it happened a third time, and the third time the card set off alarms, Chloe paid but forever resented it. Blackie protested she was sure there was money on her credit card. She didn't know where it had gone. She sounded so innocent, Chloe had to let it go. Blackie was her friend, after all.

But now she wasn't feeling so indulgent. Such a user and a schmoozer, that Blackie. It was freakish the way Blackie could be friendly with just about anyone. It was socially slutty, borderline sociopathic, it meant nobody was special.

She sipped her whiskey. This bar, Max, had a player piano playing romantic songs, like Mantovani's "Moulin Rouge." The keys went down with each note, as if an invisible man were playing the piano.

John played the piano. Not often, but on occasion.

Oh fuck. She knew she should be over him by now. To hell with it. She'd go to Cannes. She'd meet someone, a guy, a real guy, not a perv, and not one of those watery philosophers Blackie had fallen in with.

— — —

Chloe had left a note with the Buddhists at the squat camp's message center: "I've gone to Cannes. You've got your money, I've got mine. See you later. Chloe."

"Shit," Blackie said, reading the note.

"If she wants to go, let her go."

"She's not in a good frame of mind. She'll get into trouble."

"You think she'll be back?" Cameron asked.

"Maybe we should go after her," Eddie said.

"No. I think that's what she wants. And I'm sick of her schtick. My dad always warned me not to let people push me around for too long, because when you stop letting them, they act like they're the victims. I am not giving in to her." Blackie had decided.

"I'll go after her," Cameron said.

"You're not her type, Cam. She makes fun of guys like you."

"A challenge. Good. I'll win her over and lure her back, catch up with you guys in Arles."

"Give her a day to come back before you set off behind her, okay?" Blackie said, thinking Cameron had no idea what he was getting into. The way Chloe was these days, she'd eat him alive, leaving nothing but a desiccated pit.

"She can't get into too much trouble in a day," Eddie said.

CHAPTER 16

Finally, Veena consented to see Papa, inviting him for lunch on set. When she said *lunch*, he didn't think, you know, *lunch*— that they'd sit and eat a hurried meal while the pedicurist trimmed her toenails. But she explained this was all the time she had, regrettably, and she had absolutely no time alone these days.

Amit had come to see her the day before, and she was very grateful for his visit and to Papa for his offer to lighten her workload. She said she was declining his kind offer, but that as soon as these three pictures were finished, she was taking a break, and they could go off together to their special place in Simla, just the two of them. Oh how she missed him. For now, she was channeling her passions into her work.

Papa didn't think he could wait until she was finished shooting.

"Then we shall have to try to arrange a rendezvous, carefully," she said, smiling, her eyes twinkling in a way that made his loins and heart ache equally. "These are dangerous times, Papa, as Amit reminded me."

"And what is this about an American director?"

"It's a small part, but a very good one. Filming would start in October. But I won't do it if you don't want me to."

"I don't want you to."

"Fine. I won't do it, because of my devotion to you," she said, and then a makeup artist came by to touch up her face, so that all she would allow when Papa said good-bye was an air-kiss, lest he mess her cosmetics.

He was a dervish of dammed-up energy when he returned to

the house and set to multitasking, paying his daily visit to his wife while dictating memos into his microcassette recorder. His wife blinked what he took for encouragement, though she was really saying, "You old fool, don't you see what is going on around you?"

She was getting better and faster at Morse code. The frustrations of two strokes and of not being "heard" when she now "spoke," was making her even nastier than she had been before, when she was healthy and in full force as the matriarch of a powerful crime family.

Lately, she'd found a measure of freedom in her silence. No longer did she have to couch her criticism in the guise of concern. She could insult freely, spill secrets, whatever she wanted.

When Papa told the story of his father the humble washerman's lifelong plan to rob the richest family in their town, the Gadi family, she could contradict him with, "You ass, that's not the way it happened. You have always denied me my due."

And when he talked about how he had lovingly educated and raised her, his simple scullery-maid wife, to a state of dignity despite her coarse village ways, she could blink out, "I had such longings for other men every minute I was under you."

Farha came in with Baby Ganesh, who drooled on Mama. Mama blinked, "Good luck, kid, you are going to need it." Then Papa cooed and nuzzled the baby, whom he had affectionately and narcissistically nicknamed "Little Me."

Amit came in, and she blinked, "Weasel."

"Papa," Amit said. "Come with me to the computer. I've found Ganesh."

In Aligarh, India, a young Hindu nationalist was searching for good drawings and photos of the popular god Ganesh for his website when he stumbled across the Ganesh film and some digital "behind the scenes with our stars" photos that accompanied it.

Sacrilege, the nationalist thought, using Ganesh as a player, a prop, in a sordid spoof about perfume sniffers! Who was this "I am a Camera" person who did this? "I am a Camera" gave no name, just an e-mail for contact. But the pictures has been taken in France, which was full of Muslims, and certainly, a Muslim was behind this insult.

The young nationalist copied down the e-mail address and immediately sent it out to his mailing list along with a link to the offensive video. In Varanasi, one of the recipients sent an angry e-mail to "I am a Camera" and then also sent the link to his mailing list.

It took about three days for the link to be forwarded to Amit.

— — —

Sanjay and Chunky had slept with every high-priced escort they could find in Monte Carlo, and had learned nothing about the women with Doo, or whatever his name was. To them, he was still Doo. It was hard to think of him now as a guy named Harry Carpenter, an American. Jeez, Sanjay and Chunky could remember all "Doo's" stories about Australia, about Mollywat, about his parents, his sisters and brothers, his aunties and uncles.

"He must have stolen all those stories from the real Doo McGarrigle," Sanjay said, as he lay in the sun at a beachside cafe, reading the latest on the McGarrigle/Carpenter case, plotting their next move and waiting for the waitress to come take their drink order.

"Some were his," Chunky said. "The one about him playing that game with the headless goat in Afghanistan is true I think, and playing Russian roulette during sex."

"But the story about his uncle who buried all his money in tobacco tins in the back yard, then the rains came and flooded it and washed all the tins into the river, I think he stole that story from the real Australian."

Chunky was distracted. He was reading a text message on his Nokia from his wife in Mumbai.

"Oh no. The Mumbai police got Raj Ghosh!"

"Where?"

"Shot him dead in the fishermen colony on Kamarajar Salai."

"This is bad, Chunky."

"Acha—wait. Another text message. From Amit. He wants us to get to the computer immediately. Papa has found Ganesh!"

— — —

That doesn't even look like me, Diane thought, as she studied the photo on the front page of the *Daily Splash*. Taken in Avignon the day before by British holidaymaker Dexter Mills, it purported to show her in a classic pose, her face contorted in anger, screaming at a camera. Inside, a series of other photos showed the young blonde woman: in profile holding a wallet up; with the "dark-haired Canadian woman"; and in another version of the screaming face shot.

The woman was blonde and had the same build as Diane, but other than that, Diane could see no resemblance.

She read the paper while sitting in a cafe in Grenoble. For a moment, she toyed with the idea of going back to her hotel to post something on the internet that would discredit all this, but she didn't for two reasons. The first was that it was obviously useful for everyone to be led astray, the second was that she honestly felt this woman was slightly better looking than she was, if that was possible, or at least more photogenic.

In other news, her schoolmate Kate was furious with her, claimed Diane had stolen her car and "other valuable property." Coke. There was also some "new" gossip about Diane's family . . . that her mother's mother was quite the scandal. Rumor was, her three children had three different fathers, none of whom was the esteemed man Granny was married to.

This was old news. Grandmother was a tramp, in the classic sense of the old Frank Sinatra song, at least as far as Diane was concerned. Yes, she slept around—a lot—but she had to. Grandfather was far too busy with his hobbies, pink gin, and being tied up by young male ballet dancers. Nobody knew who

Prudence's father was. There were legends, of course. One suggested a Mecca bookmaker, one an American Kodak executive named Big Bill, another a bar owner in the West End known as Charlie the Champ because he'd briefly been the Lightweight Boxing Champion of Great Britain until an inner ear infection destroyed his equilibrium.

Diane was sure her mother's father was Charlie the Champ. It just made sense: bars, pugilism, lack of balance.

Next to that musty nut of gossip in the newspaper was the same old tired rehash of Diane's misdeeds, assault with a deadly weapon, drugs possession, resisting arrest . . . Yes, she had smacked the model Jenna with her stiletto shoe, but not with the spike, despite what the newspapers and witnesses (two of Jenna's friends) said. Diane had taken the shoe off to wiggle her toes and was holding it by the spike heel when Jenna shoved her and whispered, "I fucked Woy last night." Instinctively, Diane had hit her with the toe of the shoe, not even hard enough to cause a small bruise— though she meant to hit her much harder.

Right away, Jenna screamed, and one of her friends got a cop. The police arrived to see Diane screaming at Jenna and found the coke on her. It wasn't even Diane's coke.

What else could she have done? Maybe she shouldn't have hit Jenna. She knew Jenna was lying, because Diane had been with Woy the night before. She could have just walked away.

But everything was okay, Diane reasoned. In fact, things were pretty good. There was a "Free Diane" movement building. Soon she'd see Woy. She'd get her money and she'd buy Kate a new car and lots of coke.

Avignon was a bit too close to Grenoble though. She needed to steer all eyes away from the north and Paris, and down to . . . where? She checked a map. From Avignon, the press would probably head to Arles or Nîmes. When she got back to her discount hotel, she posted something credible-sounding to this effect in the message boards on vomitintheshrubbery.co.uk. Then she packed up her stuff and checked out.

With her dyed hair, scarves, and dark glasses, nobody had recognized her so far on the trip, so she was confident about being safe when she got to Paris, especially with her unwitting decoy being hunted in her place. She was almost out of coke and had been cutting herself thinner and thinner lines. But she had a good connection in Paris.

She did a half line. She plugged in a CD. She hit the highway. If she drove the rest of the day and through the night, she might make it to Paris by morning. She could call up her connection Aye-Aye, pick up some coke by lunchtime and then disappear into Paris. Would Aye-Aye give her away? No, she decided. If he did, he knew she'd rat him out.

The coke wore off quickly. She was trying to make the rest last so she gritted her teeth and tried to hold off the urge by thinking happy thoughts, her fourth birthday party, her first puppy Bloosie—she'd never forgive her mother for what happened to Bloosie—her first love Geoff—she'd never forgive her father for what happened with Geoff—her school production of *Stage Door*, the first time she did coke with Woy—

Coke. Just one more line ... No. She'd need what she had to get her to Paris and through the morning until she could hook up with Aye-Aye. Think about something else. Think about Woy.

She thought of his body—what she could remember of it— piece by piece, traveling up his legs to his cock, his abs, his chest, his mouth, his eyes ...

Physically and emotionally tired, distracted by her visualization, Diane missed a turn just north of Dijon, lost control of the car and ran off the road into a field, where she fought to regain control before crashing through the side of an old abandoned barn. A large wooden support beam stopped the car, crumpling the whole front and activating the air bag. This likely saved her life but pushed her with such force her neck snapped back slightly.

When she got out, her neck was sore and the car was hissing steam and smoking. Her suitcase was stuck between the dashboard and the front seat, impossible to extricate. She managed to grab her purse and laptop, and get out of the barn as flames leapt from the car. As she crossed the fallow field and was approaching the road, the car blew up in the barn behind her, which lit the short fuse of her fear and sent her running as if rocket-propelled, arms flailing, purse flapping, to the highway.

It was a disaster! How was she going to get to Paris now? She could get a train from Dijon, but she was afraid she'd have to show ID to buy a ticket. There was no choice. She'd have to hitchhike. But first, she had to get well clear of the scene of the explosion, get to an alternate road, and do a line of coke. She'd earned it. Her nerves were shot.

— — —

Avignon? It sure looked like her, and there was a dark-haired woman with her, so Mike figured the British tabloid, the *Daily Splash*, was right. As far as he could see, nobody but him had made the connection between the missing heiress and the dead guy in Monte Carlo, but it was just a matter of time before someone else put the two stories together. Mike had to get there before the hordes of British snoops descended. He'd finished with the Doo McGarrigle/Harry Carpenter story—as far as his newspaper was concerned, that is. Officially, he was back on vacation.

CHAPTER 17

A good night's sleep in a proper hotel bed in Cannes, and Chloe still couldn't stop fuming about Blackie. If Chloe hadn't invited Blackie to Europe, she wouldn't even be here. Blackie was here because of Chloe's broken heart. They had pockets full of money because of Chloe's broken heart. Blackie met Eddie because of Chloe's broken heart . . .

But then, Blackie was always like that, a member of what one of Blackie's college roommates called, "The Better Offer Club." If something more fun, more interesting, came along, Blackie would cavalierly cancel her previous plans.

She always knew best, she was so selfish, so pushy, so condescending, so conformist, yes, conformist, a charge she herself had often leveled against John Carey and Chloe. Blackie was the one who could seamlessly fit into any new group. She dropped some things and picked up others in order to conform. For example, she hadn't read one of those gossip rags since she hooked up with Eddie the Earth Father in Grasse, and suddenly she was a socially aware recycling nonconsumer.

And she probably didn't miss Chloe as much as Chloe missed her right now.

The room service waiter brought her breakfast, looking at her strangely as he set up her place setting on the balcony overlooking the Promenade de la Croisette.

"What is your name?' he asked in English.

"Chloe."

He untucked the newspapers, which were complimentary

with breakfast, and opened up the *Azure Coast Chronicle* to a story inside.

"Is this you?" he asked, pointing to the picture.

Chloe grabbed the paper. There was a picture of her scream-ing at a camera, next to a smaller picture of her and Blackie argu-ing. She was identified as "Runaway Heiress Diane Benham."

"Are you the runaway heiress?" the waiter asked.

"God no!" she said, and laughed.

"You look very much like her."

"Do you think so? I'm not her. Here, see, my passport."

"Ah."

Busy either committing crimes or reading sad books from the past like *Bonjour Tristesse*, *The Conscience of Love* and *Anna Karenina*, Chloe had been in a near news blackout. Most of the local press had been in Italian or French, she'd stayed in places without television or hadn't turned the TV on in the more upscale hotels. Once or twice a week, she'd pick up the *Herald Tribune* to catch up on the major news, scan the op-eds and read *Doonesbury*.

But this she had missed completely.

She tipped the waiter well and drank her coffee without look-ing up from the story.

Missing Heiress in Avignon, said the headline.

The pictures and story were reprinted from a British tabloid. Evidently, quite a lot of people thought she was a bad-girl British heiress named Diane Benham, and Blackie her "mysterious Canadian friend."

After her coffee, she went down to the hotel business center and read up on the story further on the internet.

God, she had a wicked idea.

She sent an e-mail to a few of the newspapers and posted to some of the online forums that the heiress was hiding out in a squat camp in Avignon and heading to Arles with her Canadian friend, two young men, and possibly some Buddhists. The Canadian and the heiress, she said, would be traveling separately to avoid drawing attention to themselves and would likely be in an old white van or a white VW bus with a picture of a human heart on the side.

Now that she had encouraged some nosy photographers to annoy Blackie and her new best friends, she felt better.

Blackie thought she was a klepto? She'd show her. She wasn't a criminal, after all. It was justice, stealing from the rich, giving to the poor. Like Blackie always said . . . it's a sin to be too generous with the greedy.

Though . . . she hadn't given to the poor lately, and guilt began to creep through her. She dropped a few hundred euros in a donation box at a museum, but after that she was at a loss. There didn't seem to be a lot of poor in Cannes. Instead, there were a lot of fat wallets and Louis Vuitton purses. At the moment her guilt was such that Chloe found them easy to resist. It wasn't until she passed a wall bearing a poster for the "Godsmacked" religious media festival that the Devil got her attention.

She stopped. Cannes was hosting a religious TV, radio, and film festival, set to start the next day, sponsored by the Christian youth group Godsmacked. All sorts of Christian celebrities and businessmen sponsors would be attending as well as a thousand young "Jesus Groupies." Oh how she wished Blackie was here. Playing her pickpocket game might be interesting with this bunch, but she suspected these were the kind of guys who would not take another man's wallet as their own. The contents, yes, but only if donated through a 1-800 number.

But they also struck her as the kind of guys who would take another man's wife in a sleazy motel room off the interstate after they'd both been protesting for Christ outside a same-sex wedding reception.

This was not a hypothetical example. Her favorite prof at college, Professor Joe, had married his boyfriend Craig in Canada and his students and colleagues had thrown a reception for them when they returned to school. The Godsmacked chapter on campus was part of a religious protest outside the reception. Several organizations were involved and, to their credit, Godsmacked was not the noisiest or crudest contingent there. One group chanted, "marriage is for men and women," and "Adam and Eve, not Adam and Steve," and a handful of extreme-extremos shouted and held signs that said, "God hates fagots."

The Godsmacked group, which the other right wing Christians considered soft on the gay issue, simply prayed quietly while holding a banner that said, "Hate the sin, but love the sinner." It was decorated with pictures of crosses, doves, flowers, and hearts. In its way, this was much more offensive than "God hates fagots," in crude black marker on a piece of cardboard.

"Good lord, they misspelled fagots," Professor Joe observed.

He and Craig tried to shrug it off, cranking up the music to drown out the shouts. The guests defiantly celebrated but it cast a shadow over what was otherwise a very happy day. Everyone danced and ate cake. Chloe caught the bouquet. As the couple left, their guests showered them with confetti and environmentally friendly bird seed, weaving their way between the protest signs without ever acknowledging them.

Later that night, after a hit-and-run incident at the Blue Moon motel in a neighboring county, the cops picked up a couple of the protesters, a married man and a married woman, not married to each other. The man had hit another car when he was pulling out of the motel, where he and the woman had rented a room for an hour. Professor Joe felt bad for the couple. He thought they shouted down the "sinful" urges of others in order to shout down their own, but all that thinking about other people's urges just aroused their own more.

Chloe was not so forgiving and her urge now to rip off a few of these folks was getting aroused, but it'd be hard to pull it off without Blackie. She thought for a moment about e-mailing Blackie, but she just couldn't bring herself to talk to Blackie first. Within a day, she figured, Blackie would e-mail her instead, and then she could tell her about the convention. Until then, she would resist temptation, just to show Blackie she could.

If she couldn't commit crimes, she could at least have some fun playing the runaway heiress for a day, slyly. She kind of got off on being mistaken for someone so wild, so bad, and so spoiled.

At a cafe where she stopped for a lemonade, she was trying to behave heiress-like, when temptation found her. A famous man and his entourage sat down at the next table. It was Peter Thorogood—that was his stage name—a popular religious media figure in America, star of Christian movies and a popular Christian talk show, and now with a gold-selling CD of Christian pop songs. Chloe recognized him from late-night commercials hawking his products. Around him was a gaggle of fluttery young acolytes wearing identical T-shirts that said "True Love Waits" on the front and "Godsmacked" on the back.

Thorogood had co-opted the trappings of rebellion—jeans, loose shirt, a scruffy five o'clock shadow even though it was early afternoon. His stage name was said to be an homage to George Thorogood and his song "Bad to the Bone," which Peter Thorogood interpreted as a primal, rock-out way of saying, "I am a sinner, we are all sinners." In his live act, he often used a sample of this to segue into his own song about salvation, "Sinners' Stomp."

The waiter came, and everyone ordered soft drinks and ice cream. Peter Thorogood was treating. When he pulled out his wallet, Chloe noticed it was black, like the one she'd taken from the first victim in Avignon and had in her purse now.

Chloe leaned over and said, "You look familiar. You're on TV, right? You do those teeth-whitening commercials?"

"No, he's Peter Thorogood," said a young woman at his side.

"I'm sorry, I don't know who you are," Chloe said to him, ignoring the Godsmacked groupie.

"I'm a Christian entertainer," Thorogood said.

"Oh, Christianity," she said. "I didn't grow up with that."

"You were raised in another religion?"

"My parents are atheists and vegetarians," she lied.

"What's your name?" he asked.

"Diane Benham."

"Diane, did you ever believe in a higher power, in a Creator?" Thorogood asked.

"When I was little, I dreamed a fairy lived in the wall and listened to all my wishes."

He laughed.

"Tell me about Jesus," Chloe said.

"Why don't you tell me what you know and I'll build on it or correct it," Peter said.

"I know all the PR stuff. Son of God and the Virgin Mary, became a carpenter, 12 disciples, speech from the mount . . ."

"*Sermon*," one of the groupies said, very pleased with herself.

"Excuse me?"

"*Sermon* on the mount. Not speech."

"Okay, sermon."

The other groupies ate their ice cream sullenly, annoyed at this outsider's intrusion on their time with their idol, yet not wanting to interfere with the saving of a soul.

They had, it turned out, won a Christian rock radio contest to come here and hang with Peter. At home in their rooms, these girls were probably having impure thoughts while looking at pictures of Peter Thorogood and listening to him rap the Song of Solomon on his latest CD. Peter was clearly a safe-seeming born-again icon young girls could invest with their sexual longing with no danger of return on their investment, ensuring continued chastity before marriage.

Chloe pointed to T-shirts the groupies were all wearing.

"What does true love wait for?" she asked.

"Marriage," he said.

"Gee, I'd have an awful hard time giving up sex," she said. "Are you married?"

"No, not yet."

"Are you a virgin?"

"Well, I wasn't always a Christian. The Devil had me for a while. I was drinking, I did drugs, I don't even remember what I did because I was blacked out most of the time." Changing the subject, Peter moved in closer to Chloe. "My crew and I are taking the ferry to the little islands today. Would you like to join us?" he asked.

"Will you tell me more about Christianity?"

"Of course."

"Great." Chloe wanted to go to the island called Ste-Marguerite anyway.

When they got up, the groupies quickly surrounded Peter to create a barrier between him and Chloe. They were obviously worried, and resentful too. They were good girls, but the bad girl was being rewarded with Peter's attention. It seemed unjust.

They walked to the Gare Maritime ferry terminal in the old port, where they left for Ste-Marguerite and St-Honorat, the Iles de Lérins off Cannes. It was hot, but the movement of the ferry on the sea produced a cooling wind, and the sound of the ship's engines and the chatter of the groupies and other passengers made it easy for Chloe to avoid conversing with Peter.

While he was leaning over to listen to one of his young admirers, Chloe bumped him, pushing him into the young woman so she could slip his wallet out of his pocket. She switched it with the empty black wallet in her purse. Then she let it slip to deck and pushed it surreptitiously with her foot to the end of the boat railing, right next to his foot. It was half perched off the boat now, so when she yelled, "Peter, is that your wallet on deck?" and he turned around, his foot knocked it into the sea.

"Oh shit," he said, as he watched it toss in the foam churned up by the ferry, then disappear under water.

"Oh damn," he said, and dialed his cellphone, sticking one finger in his ear to block the outside noise. He hit a key, paused, then another. "American Express? I just lost my platinum card. It's at the bottom of the Mediterranean. I need a cash advance and a re-placement card delivered to my hotel."

Chloe turned to the sun and smiled. When they got to Ste-Marguerite, she proclaimed her desire to be born again. Then, as if they were in some cheesy technicolor musical, the group spontaneously burst into a chanting sort of song—a Peter Thorogood song, of course—"Rejoice, yeah yeah yeah, rejoice," sung to a derivative pop-rock melody. Godsmacked members did this whenever a soul was saved.

After she got the song, the prayer, and the group hug, she snuck away from them and wandered around Ste-Margeuerite, where her parents had always told her she was conceived. She didn't know why this fact should matter to her. She strained to feel some spiritual connection here but came up with very little. It was a charming and pretty place, but it didn't feel like "home" in any way.

It didn't matter though; she felt great after robbing the Christian rock star. She'd been Good Cop and Bad Cop rolled into one. She didn't even need Blackie. On her own, she got almost 1000 euros and 500 U.S. dollars from that fake.

— — —

Later, as Chloe was celebrating over dinner back in Cannes, she saw a face from her past, Bob Parker, the spam king, sitting with a group of religious entrepreneurs, probably trying to sell them Mailflooder 8.1, or perhaps a custom program for spreading their fire and thunder, Apocalypse 1.2 or Horsemen 4.0.

He hadn't seen her.

Maybe it was time for her to get out of town after all, meet up with Blackie and Eddie and Cameron in Arles.

But more temptation was conveniently at hand. When Chloe was about to check out of her hotel, she was shocked to see the rich Arab woman from Ventimiglia and her little Filipino maid walking toward the elevator.

"I will pay you when you do your job properly," the rich woman scolded.

Chloe followed them up. She had no opportunity to steal anything from the boss woman, who went into her room with her servant and came out about a half hour later, firmly clutching her purse.

Well, she could steal her maid.

This would alleviate any future guilt she might feel for the day's thieving, or future thieving. She took the money from Peter Thorogood, added some of her own stash, and knocked on the hotel room door.

The maid answered. She'd been crying.

"What's your name?"

"Maria."

"Maria, I'm Diane, runaway heiress. Do you want to go home?" Chloe asked.

The maid nodded.

"Get your things, and come with me," Chloe said.

They took a cab to the nearest airport, where Chloe bought the woman a one-way ticket back to Manila, putting it on her credit card. She then handed the young woman 3000 euros and said, "When you get home, put this money in the bank, and use it to go to school, okay?"

"Yes."

"Promise me you will."

"I promise. Thank you, Diane."

Chloe asked another tourist in line to take her picture with Maria.

Maria would go home, get a new start, the Arab woman would come back to her hotel room to find she had nobody to berate. She'd be victimless and maidless in Cannes.

After that grand gesture, Chloe felt fantastic. She had freed a sister. Later, she'd worry about the good-intention-slicked road to hell, and hope the woman didn't go back and use the money to start a brothel or become a heroin addict. But for now, Chloe felt good and purposeful. And powerful.

And Cannes was crawling with Christians, the best kind for her purposes—the rich, really annoying kind. But the spam king was here too, and she wasn't keen on running into him, or being mistaken any more for that heiress. She figured she'd better leave Cannes on the next train, in case the Godsmacked Christians got wise.

She got a train for Toulon, where she'd dye her hair to avoid further confusion with the heiress, spend the night, and a have a full crime-free day before she went on to Arles to wait for Blackie.

— — —

"Look for her on the Promenade, probably in a very, very nice hotel," Blackie had said before Cameron left for Cannes. Then she had said, for the third time, "Are you sure you want to do this?" with worry and warning in her voice.

"You make it sound like I'm about to embark on some terrible, heroic quest," he said.

"You are," she said. "Now, go fetch the ring from the mouth of the dragon."

"You are so hard on Chloe," Eddie said.

"I know her better than you do."

"I'll meet you in Arles," Cameron said.

After he checked into the hostel, he took his guitar out to the Promenade to make some money, figuring Chloe was sure to pass sooner or later. When he arrived, the place was fairly quiet, but by the time he got down to the shore the town was starting to fill up with clumps of tourists. He sang for a while, made almost nothing, though many people stopped and smiled. Finally, a young American woman asked him if he knew any songs about Jesus and when he said no, she helpfully suggested he learn some, as a convention of religious youth was starting that day and it would be worth his while.

"You'll make a killing," she said. "Are you a Christian?"

"No," he said. "But I do admire that guy, the one born on December 25th in a stable to a virgin mother . . ."

"Oh, you're teasing me. You have a cute accent. Where are you from?"

"New Zealand."

She sat down beside him. Her name was Wendy and she was here with a show on Christian Rock radio called XGRRRL, "not as in ex-girl," she felt compelled to explain to ward off rude transsexual jokes. "The X is a Christian symbol, so it means Christian Girl, with a little growl."

She was also a founding member of Godsmacked, who were sponsoring the convention, about which Cameron knew precious little before he read her brochure. They believed God is fun, which they spell *phun*, and that he is also phat, and that if they could spread this message, people would respond all over the world. Fun, or rather, *phun*, for them, however, meant no homosexual, pre-, or extramarital sex, no drinking or drugs, no swearing, and a long list of other things that were poorly compensated for by Christian rock parties, prayer groups, and rounds of seven-minute dating presided over by the local pastor. Godsmacked also organized Christian flash mobs, spontaneous mobs activated by e-mail and cellphone alerts that showed up at designated locations and shouted slogans like "Jesus Saves" and "Abortion Kills."

"Can I interview you?' she asked.

"Can I interview you first?"

"Okay. About what?"

He turned on his camera. "About that guy, born on December 25th in a stable to a virgin mother, worshipped on Sunday . . . you love him?"

"I love Him more than life itself, of course," she said.

"What has he brought to your life?"

"He has brought light and wisdom and discipline to my life. And purpose. I consider myself a media missionary for Him."

"Thanks."

"That's it?"

"For now," he said.

"Okay, my turn," she said, and clicked on her recorder. "What's your name, where are you from, and what do you do?"

"Cameron Waverly. I am an itinerant artist from New Zealand."

"So, you told me you admire 'that guy born on December 25th in a stable'—"

"That's right. Mithra."

"Mithra?"

"Persian fire god, said to be born December 25th to a virgin mother in a stable. Worshipful shepherds brought gifts—"

She snapped the recorder off.

"You know very well I was talking about Jesus," she said. "Okay, I'm going to turn my recorder on again, if you'll behave."

"I'll behave."

"So we're here at the Godsmacked convention in glamorous Cannes, France, talking Jesus with Cameron Waverly, an artist from New Zealand," she said. "You've got crazy hair, Cameron, what do you call that style?"

"Forgot to comb it."

"Are you a Christian, Cam?"

"I'm a questioning deist, I guess. I believe Jesus was a brilliant and foresighted philosopher. Clarify something for me, Wendy. Your group, Godsmacked, doesn't believe in premarital sex?"

"No."

"You know the joke about the rabbi and the priest?"

"Do they walk into a bar?"

"No. Well, maybe. Yeah, let's say that's where this conversation takes place. A priest and a rabbi walk into a bar. The priest says, 'Rabbi Schumer, tell me, is it true you can't eat pork?' The rabbi says, 'That's right, Father Gordon.' 'What a shame,' the priest says. 'You should try it sometime. There's nothing like the taste of bacon.'

"And the rabbi says, 'Is it true you can't have sex, father?' and the priest says, 'Yes that's true.' 'You ought to try it, father. It's better than bacon.' "

Wendy shut off her recorder with an assured snap and smirked. "You're a smart ass, aren't you?"

"Are you allowed to say ass?"

"Of course. It's in the Bible. Mary rode to Nazareth on an ass."

"So when you say it, you think of donkey, you don't think of my bum," he said.

"Uh huh," she said, nodding, a knowing look in her beautiful green eyes. "You promised you'd behave."

"I said I'd behave. Should I have specified how I was going to behave?"

"Oh you," she said, smiling, shaking her pretty head. "I have to run and interview some celebs. But there's a Christian Rock barbecue tonight on the beach. Would you like to come?"

"Will you give me a lesson in being a Christian missionary?"

"Sure. I'm at the Majestic. Room 421. Pick me up at 7?"

"Okay."

She blew him a kiss and ran off.

The sun had been shining down on him for a while, so he picked up his guitar and camera and walked off to find a soft drink. The cafes near the Promenade seemed inviting. He would have loved to have sat down in a real chair under a beach umbrella sipping a coca or a cold beer. But a coca went for 5 euros at the first cafe he checked. Five bucks for a coke. He could have a coke and a modest dinner for that price, once he got away from the tourist part of town and found a falafel place. As he was crossing the esplanade in front of the Majestic hotel, he saw Chloe in a group of Godsmacked girls led by a handsome man. What was she up to now?

He tried to follow but lost her somehow. No matter for now, she was here and he felt confident enough about catching up with her that he e-mailed Eddie that afternoon, "Found Chloe. More later."

After he read the rest of his e-mail and deleted the hate mail from raging Hindu nationalists, he uploaded another episode of "Requiem for a Nose" and some "behind the scenes with our stars" photos of Blackie and Ganesh from Avignon.

PART SIX

AN UNLIKELY PLACE TO FIND RELIGIOUS NUTS

Though Diane knew the basics of hitchhiking—stick your thumb in the air, wait for a car to stop, don't ride with men alone—she hadn't done it before. Sometimes the girls from school would do it to get from the campus to the nearest village pub, but they never invited her, perhaps because they didn't think she'd be game for it. She always traveled alone, in a taxi or her own car, and sometimes even with her father's chauffeur.

Right away, she got a ride with two elderly Germans, a husband and wife, the husband driving while the wife criticized his driving and conversed with Diane in English. The husband kept turning around to talk to Diane too, taking his eyes off the road. At one point, the wife unfurled a large map to show him where he had taken a wrong turn, in order to win her point in their argument. The map blocked his view, the wife's, and Diane's.

Diane pretended she didn't speak English very well, and spoke to them in a combination of French, English, and a made-up language she insisted was the language of Madagascar, where she claimed she grew up because her parents were missionaries. She once did a school report on Madagascar and could speak credibly about it for fifteen minutes, at which point she spoke jibberish and the elderly Germans stopped asking questions.

A businesswoman with a tight face picked her up next. Diane didn't even try to start a conversation with her. She just knew it wouldn't be appreciated. The only time the woman spoke was when a song came on the radio. After hearing just a few bars, the woman said, "Non!" and shut it off. Her eyes looked wet, slightly hypnotized, not by the road but by some recent gashing memory.

She stared straight ahead at the road, but didn't seem like she was seeing it.

Just outside of Auxerre, about a hundred kilometers outside of Paris, the woman dropped Diane. There Diane lingered for about half an hour before she was picked up by a man giving a woman a driving lesson. As if that wasn't bad enough, the man auto-locked the doors and wouldn't let her out in Paris until she paid him 100 euros.

She was getting low on cash, and she needed to buy coke and then find a hotel room. Aye-Aye was not around. When she called, she got his "messagerie," saying he was "en vacances" and would return end of August. But she wasn't completely at a loss. On a trip to Paris the year before with her friend Kate, they'd been able to score through a guy Kate knew at a bar in Barbès.

The bar was called the Nuit Violette, tucked into a little street between Barbès and Château Rouge, not the kind of neighborhood Diane would normally venture into. It was a hard-core neighborhood for Paris, crowded with overworked immigrants, druggies, their dealers, and poor artists. As the immigrants prospered, the area improved slightly, but it was still a place of drugs, crime, cheap markets, and boxy discount stores where you could buy women's panties from a bin piled high with them out on the sidewalk, right next to the bin of bras and the bin of tube socks.

And after dark, it was still a place most parisiens didn't go without a good reason.

Diane tried to look casual, at home, completely unlike the runaway heiress/fish out of water that she was. The bar was pretty empty. Aside from the bartender, there were two men at the bar. One was an African so dark his skin glowed blue in the bar lights.

"What do you want?" the bartender asked, and he wiped a glass with a white towel.

"I'm looking for Luc le Lion," she said. "I am a friend of English Kate."

"He is not here."

"Do you know where he is?"

"No."

"Do you have a telephone number? It is an emergency."

"It is always an emergency. I have no number."

"What you are looking for, I can find for you," said one of the men at the bar.

Diane sized him up. His nationality wasn't clear. He could have been a pale North African or a dark Frenchman, or some combination thereof. His clothes were fraying and faded but clean and pressed. He looked like the kind of guy who would know where to find cocaine, but also like someone concerned with appearances, someone who would return with the drugs.

"I want a coca," she said, the short term for coca-cola.

"En poudre," he said, nodding.

"You can find it for me?"

"Yes."

He wanted 300 euros.

"Okay, but I want something from you too, a token of faith," she said.

He opened his wallet and took out the picture of a woman, "my wife," and his two children, a boy and a girl.

"I leave my heart with you," he said, so genuinely that she felt kind of bad asking him for something more tangible.

"My phone," he said, handing her his mobile.

She gave him 300 euros. That left her with about 150. She could get a hotel room for a first night's deposit of about 50 to 75 euros. She'd spend the rest on street food and cigarettes until Woy arrived.

She sloshed back her wine and ordered another to keep her calm until the guy came back. Soon she'd have cocaine. That would make her feel better, give her some perspective. Jesus Christ, where was that guy?

Another hour passed. She drank two more glasses of wine and ate a ham and cheese baguette, while she stared at the photo of the man's alleged wife and children. Were they his wife and children? She shoved it into her purse.

The bartender claimed not to know who the guy was, nor did the only other guy at the bar.

"Some addict," he said, and shrugged.

When the bar closed, she finally had to accept the man wasn't coming back. She checked his cellphone to see if there was anything on it that would identify him, but the thing flickered on for a few seconds, and then died out. It was probably stolen, too.

A taxi took her to the Left Bank to the Hotel Bottecœur, a modest little hotel near St. Michel where she and Woy had stayed during a romantic week the year before. The owner, Monsieur Bottecœur, didn't ask a lot of questions, and because there was a discrete entrance into a tiny street with a single dim lamp, it was a favorite for romantic trysts.

Nine precious euros later, the taxi dropped her off and she checked into a first-floor corner room with windows looking out at the Seine on one side and onto the tiny street, Rue du Chat qui Pêche (Street of the Fishing Cat) on the other. She began crying the minute she got to her room.

Relax, she thought. *In a few days, Woy will be here. It'll be romantic. He'll be able to get my money, and we'll get coke and take off to the Islands, where we'll hide out, while Woy writes songs for his next CD.*

Before she tried to sleep, she e-mailed him: I'm in the place in our city. Counting the minutes. Dreadful journey. CU soon. All my Love, Me.

— — —

"It's blasphemous. It's insulting," Sanjay said, as he looked at the computer screen, where the further adventures of Ganesh were chronicled. In addition to another episode of "Requiem for a Nose," there was a thumbnail in the corner of the dark-haired woman with Ganesh in Avignon, both of them wearing sunglasses, the woman in a tight half-tee that exposed a tattoo around her navel. The tattoo looked like a flower. Below it was a link that said, "Our stars off the set . . ."

When clicked on, it brought up a page of photos of the dark-haired woman, called here, "Italian screen star Francesca Tuttimilti," with "Bollywood legend Ganesh," lounging around in cafes, smoking cigarettes, reading a script, window shopping at Gucci. At the bottom was teaser text, "Next!" at the bullfights in Arles.

"Well, we're going to Arles. You want to drive?" Sanjay asked.

Chunky was more concerned with the news from Bombay.

"Four goondas killed in the last two days, Sanjay."

"Four?"

"All in Mumbai. They took down Asran Kumar. He was very tough. Tougher than Tiger Memon. But the police got him—"

"Asran was always a little crazy. As Doo said, he had a head full of wasps."

"Hah," Chunky said, reading on. "Oh no. One of them was ours. Rishi Rashta. Poor Rishi."

"Rishi kya? Tall or fat?"

"Tall."

Tall Rishi was 18, a kid from the slums near Sahar airport who became an errand boy for the Dajgits. He was a cheerful fellow who thought his life was a movie. Once in a while, Chunky would take him to pick up protection money on Bollywood sets or to deliver movie financing to producers in Bollywood film hangouts, just to give the kid a thrill. The last time, they delivered the money to a producer at a party after the Filmfare awards, and Rishi got to see a galaxy of his favorite stars in one Malabar Hill penthouse, including Twinkle Khanna. The producer introduced Chunky and Rishi to Twinkle as "aspiring actors." Rishi walked on clouds for a month.

"Rishi could act all the scenes from *Joru Ka Gulam*—Govinda, Kader Khan, Johnny Lever, Ashok Saraf, even Twinkle," Chunky said. "He was funny. He could have been the next Johnny Lever."

"You can pray for Rishi on our way to Arles," Sanjay said.

When they got to Arles in their rented Renault, they plotted their rounds, splitting up so they could patrol the fringes of the old Roman arena more effectively. If one sighted this dark-haired woman, he'd immediately beep the other with an urgent text message.

They were in Arles two days before Chunky saw the dark-haired woman, moving in the middle of a crowd of people coming toward the arena from the town gates.

CHAPTER 19

One of Eddie's travel buddies in India, the "crazy Californian" Millman, had run with the bulls in Spain once. That was nuts, he said, because they let any asshole run with the bulls, even him. Millman ran with a hospital administrator from Derbyshire and a literary agent from New York, the three of them in provocative red scarves and white Nikes. The man from Derbyshire got gored in the calf as he was scrambling over the barricades and required twenty-some stitches, which was not nearly as bad as a dessert chef from Oslo, who ended up with a punctured lung.

This running through the old stone streets of Arles would be different. The bulls were trained to run forward, would be led by an old neutered leader bull with a bell around his neck. They'd be herded by galloping camarguais cowboys in white shirts and black hats. Amateurs would not be allowed to run with angry bulls because that would be, well, stupid in the opinion of the manadiers, the bull managers. Spectators were herded, in turn, behind sawhorse barricades lining the route around the side of the old Roman arena, where the bulls would be moved into holding stalls for the course camarguaise, the animal-friendly French bullfight Eddie wanted to see.

After the run, the Buddhists were leaving. They didn't have time to stay for the actual course because they had to pick up a Buddhist guy in Aigues-Mortes before heading to Cap d'Agde to pick up two Buddhist girls on their way to Carcassonne. Nickels and Loudon had gone back to Paris.

The crowd was four and five deep at the barricades and growing, pressing Blackie and Eddie toward the front. It was a bright sunny day, and hot. Blackie put on her sunglasses and held Ganesh in her arms as Eddie took pictures and Jones took in the crowd.

"Millman from California, that sounds familiar," Jones said.

"If you'd met him, you'd remember," Eddie said. "He's about six four for starters."

"He's on a quest to travel around the world by as many means of transportation as possible," Blackie said.

"You've met him?"

"No, but I feel I kind of know him from the stories Eddie and Cameron have told. He's the reason they crossed a river in the Himalayas on a raft made of inflated goat stomachs."

"Yeah, I've heard Nickels talk about him," Jones said. "Nickels met him in Amsterdam. He was working on a freighter heading down to the west coast of Africa."

"Sounds like him."

"He told Nickels he was broke so he signed on to this freighter as kitchen help. He said there was a tough winter coming and he had to get his mules moving now because it's a long way up the hill in winter."

"He says that a lot, gotta get my mules moving."

"The world is getting smaller."

"Or Millman is getting bigger," Eddie said, but Jones didn't hear him. The crowd jostled, and Jones was pushed back, away from Eddie and Blackie.

— — —

Chunky held his gun in his pocket as he pushed his way through the crowd. He was wearing sunglasses too, so as to confuse any potential eyewitnesses, and he was wearing the straw bolero hat popular at bull spectacles, sold for three euros each by hawkers who moved through the crowds holding five-foot stacks of hats that shrunk down to inches in minutes.

He had hoped to get close to grab the statue and run, but it would be impossible to run in this pack of people. The only other option he could see was to kidnap the girl and ease her out of the crowd to Rue Voltaire, where Sanjay was waiting with their rental car. There he'd let her go, and he and Sanjay could take off with Ganesh.

— — —

Mike saw the mysterious Canadian on the other side of the Place, holding some weird statue and posing for pictures. He pulled out his camera and zoomed in. It was her all right. Through the zoomed-in viewfinder, he scanned the crowd next to the Canadian, but saw no sign of the heiress.

Wait. He scanned back. It wasn't the heiress, it was another reporter, Ian Darius, working his way through the crowd to get to the Canadian. He was about 20 feet away. To get to her before Darius, Mike would have to charge over the barricade and cross the road. But it was too late for that. The bulls were running.

— — —

The bulls had just started charging when Blackie felt something hard in her back and a man with very spicy breath put his cheek close to hers and said, "Come with me quietly and bring Ganesh or I will shoot you here."

Blackie didn't have time to react before one of the bulls brushed up against the barricade, causing the crowd to push backward. A large man fell against Chunky, knocking him to the ground. Chunky rolled over on top of him, and when the man pushed Chunky off him, Chunky went flying, tumbling over the barricade into the bull run.

"That guy threatened to kill me," Blackie said.

Eddie took her hand. "Let's get out of here."

With the two Buddhists, they pushed their way out into an uncrowded street, leaving Ian Darius stuck in the middle of a group of Chinese tourists, and one French woman who thought he was trying to rub up against her. She gave him an appreciative look. He didn't notice.

—   —   —

Mike got pictures of it all, and then pushed his way out and followed the Canadian's trail as she escaped from the bull run. Through his viewfinder, he was able to follow her as far as the gates of the town, where she and her friends hopped into a white van with a human heart on it, just as one internet report had said.

He didn't have time to get his car, which was parked on the other side of town, illegally, and was now being ticketed by a young parking officer. Mike flagged down a taxi and said, in bad French, "My friends are in that van. I must follow them."

"How far?" asked the driver.

"As far as they go. I'll pay double."

—   —   —

Sanjay saw the Canadian girl run by with Ganesh in her arms. She was about 50 feet away. He tried catching up to her, but he wasn't in great shape and then he got bodychecked by some guy with a camera yelling in English, "outta the way."

He got to the city gates, huffing and puffing, leaning up against one of the ancient stone barriers for support, just in time to see the girl with Ganesh get into a white van with a human heart on its side.

By the time Chunky found him, the van was out of sight.

Chunky looked terrible. He had a black eye that was swelling up in a black and yellow lump and one side of his face was covered in scratches. He was limping.

"I was pushed into the street, where the bulls were running. I was almost killed."

"But you weren't. We've got to go," Sanjay said.

"Where?"

"They went that way. We go that way, and we look for a white van with a heart on it."

Chunky was pretty sore. He could have been killed by those bulls and horses, had he not been pulled aside by a man on a horse who threw him free. Sanjay seemed shockingly unconcerned about it. As Doo liked to say, Sanjay truly was a "company man." Doo used to say it as if it were a compliment, but in light of everything that had passed, Chunky now thought maybe it was an insult.

— — —

"He told me to come quietly and bring Ganesh or he'd shoot me right there."

"Was he trying to kidnap you or rob you, Blackie?" one of the Buddhists asked. He was driving the van.

"Both."

"Why would he want Ganesh?" Jones asked.

"Cameron has been getting hate mail from extremist fundamentalist Hindus," Eddie said. "For making satirical films and photo essays of the Ganesh statue."

"You think they were trying to kill Blackie for sacrilege?"

"Rushdie had a fatwa put on his head by Muslims."

"Gandhi was killed by a hardline Hindu," the other Buddhist said.

"Rabin, killed by a hardline right-wing Jew. Hindus and Muslims in blood feuds in Uttar Pradesh, Christians and Muslims in Chechnya—"

"Look at the Taliban, or Northern Ireland—"

"It's ridiculous. I mean, you can buy Ganesh ashtrays and creamers in the bazaars of India. Milk comes out of Ganesh's nose with the creamers. That is a pretty disrespectful take on a widely believed miracle, that in 1995 the Ganesh statues all over India started drinking milk from silver spoons. None of the guys selling that stuff has any trouble."

"We should go to the cops—" Eddie said.

"No!" Blackie said. "No, I don't want to go to the police."

"This is what cops are good for."

"No. I—I don't want to get in the papers, let every nut know what's going on. There could be a hundred of them tomorrow. I'll call the cops, anonymously, and describe this guy. Other people must have seen him anyway. If the bulls didn't trample him, the cops probably already have him."

"Blackie—" Eddie stammered.

"I can't handle cops."

"Just as well if we don't have to go to the cops," Jones said. "Since we're all in France illegally and we've got a kilo of premier African pot stashed in this van."

Blackie turned and smiled at him, gratefully.

"We were supposed to stay in Arles until Cameron got here with Chloe."

"E-mail Cameron when we get somewhere," Blackie said. "And ask him to take me and Ganesh off the website."

About halfway to Aigues-Mortes, Jones said, "I don't want to sound paranoid, but that taxi has been following us since Arles."

"Are you sure?"

"Yeah."

"Is it that crazy Hindu?" Blackie asked.

"I don't know. I can't see into the back seat from here."

"Maybe we should dump the statue," the other Buddhist said.

"No, I like him," Blackie said. "I've earned him."

"Pull over, see if he pulls over."

The taxi didn't pull over. It went on by.

"Okay, I was being paranoid," Jones said. But they waited 15 minutes before he got back on the road.

— — —

Mike had the taxi driver pull into a gas station ahead of the van and wait. When they saw the white van with the heart on it, they fell in behind again, but not directly behind, allowing a blue Renault Twingo and a delivery van to come between them and the van. Just outside Aigues-Mortes, the delivery van turned off and the Twingo pulled over, leaving Mike's taxi directly behind his target.

They must have seen the taxi, because suddenly they pulled a U-turn and barreled onto a secondary road. Mike had a hard time convincing the driver to do the same, and in the hesitation and negotiation for more money, he lost them.

— — —

Sanjay and Chunky had driven for miles before they got a break. They saw the van, parked off the shoulder of the road, just pulling back into traffic. They followed it almost to Aigues-Mortes, when their rented Twingo ran out of gas.

"You forgot to get petrol?" Sanjay shouted.

"I didn't know how far we were going," Chunky said.

"We have to get that statue, Chunky. You must use your head!"

Chunky had never seen Sanjay lose his temper before, and it scared him. Of the two, Chunky was considered the scary one, the obedient ruthless enforcer. But he himself was scared now by the expression on Sanjay's face, his eyes as hard, black, and opaque as obsidian rock.

"We must return with the statue, you understand? How have you managed to live this long, Chunky? Do you think you'll survive long back in Mumbai if you don't use your head, think before you act?"

It was then that Chunky began to think ahead, and, though he hadn't yet formulated a real plan of action, he began to wonder, in a vague way, if he could succeed where Doo had failed.

— — —

After the Buddhists picked up the Artery guy in Aigues-Mortes, they left town, making sure they weren't being followed. The plan now was for the Buddhists to drop Eddie, Blackie, and Ganesh in

Cap d'Agde, at the nudist town called Port d'Agde. Blackie figured a whole town of naked people was an unlikely place to find religious nuts, and they could chill for a while and wait for Cameron and Chloe to catch up with them there. The idea of a naturist paradise had a lot of appeal for Eddie, who envisioned a place of smiling, nonjudgmental purity amid trees, sand, and sea—right up his alley.

Blackie got a kick out of the whole settlement. "Look, a nude supermarket, a nude apartment building, A NUDE POST OFFICE!" Eddie found the nude town disappointing. Instead of naked people in some bucolic French fishing village drinking organic orange juice, it was a hypermodern settlement with three major malls and too many shops selling tourist trash and cafes serving five euro cokes, just like so many other tourist traps.

The people they were picking up there, an Indian novelist and an American painter, were away from the commercial part of the naturist quarter. They had been staying in a trailer between the main nude beaches and the nudist campground. This area, Eddie fell in love with. It was a sliver of private beach and camp space surrounded on three sides by shady trees. There was some privacy, but at the same time, easy access to the nude town.

"Who's staying here now?" he asked.

"Nobody. We'll be back in two weeks, " the novelist said.

"Can we stay here?" Eddie asked.

The Indian woman looked at Jones. Jones nodded. Eddie and Blackie had been vouched for.

"Yes, okay. It's got two bedrooms but not a lot of amenities—sink, organic outhouse. No kitchen, no phone, no TV, but there's a barbecue pit over there."

"This is perfect," Eddie said.

"If you leave before we return, drop the keys off with Omi, the bartender at the Sea Breeze in Port Nature. You should go by and see him anyway. Otherwise, he might see you here and think you're trespassers. He'll look out for you here."

"Tell Omi hello and I'll see him on the way back from Carcassonne," Jones said. "Come to Paris before you leave Europe. You can stay at our squat as long as we're not in lockdown."

"Lockdown?"

"Yeah, every fall, the corporation who owns the building where we squat makes an attempt to expel us with hired thugs, so we have to lock down. No one but long-term residents can come and go except in emergencies. Last year it started in September and lasted until November 15th, when they gave up for the winter."

Their convoy had to go. Jones gave Eddie and Blackie some pot, and everyone kissed cheeks three times, a sign of extra affection in France.

"This is Paradise," Eddie said.

"With big mosquitoes," Blackie said, slapping her arm.

"If Paradise was perfect, it would gradually dull the senses and become a kind of hell."

After they stripped down to their flip flops, they went to the mall and stopped by the Sea Breeze to meet Omi. The Sea Breeze was pretty standard—it had modern fixtures, generic lamps, pinball games, and video off-track betting, which was advertised on the bar's glass windows with a garish green racing courses sticker two feet high, just down from the bright orange lotto sign.

Behind the bar, a big, frenetic Senegalese guy with neat dreads to his shoulder was multitasking. He was dressed, wearing blue shorts and a white T-shirt with the word *Omiscience* in green, red, and black rasta colors. With one hand on the blender lid to steady it, he whirred a strawberry margarita, while kicking open a bar fridge door with his foot and talking rapidly in French to a nude blonde at the bar who was jabbing the air with a menthol cigarette to make her point.

"What are they talking about?" Blackie asked.

"He wants to buy into this bar and remodel it with a New Africa theme, minimalist, done with shapes, colors, and lighting. She owns the bar and doesn't like the idea."

The Frenchwoman ended the discussion with a fervent pfft, waving him away as she slid off her chair and walked away.

"You'll see, Yvonne," he said in English, smiling, "You are being short-sighted and ignorant."

Evidently, she didn't speak English, because she turned, smiled at him appreciatively, as if she had just been complimented.

"Fool," Omi said, and she smiled again as she waved good-bye and walked out the door.

"Omi?" Eddie said.

"Yes."

"We're staying in that trailer and we were told to—"

"Are you with the Artery group?"

"We've been traveling with Jones and—"

"Jones! Is he here?"

"No, he and the rest had to get to Carcassonne. He's going to stop by to see you on his way back. He and the women from the trailer said you'd look out for us here."

"Looking out" for them meant, to begin, free beers as long as the boss lady wasn't around, endless cocktail peanuts, and an answering service. They could give Omi's number to anyone who might need to contact them out at the trailer. Omi could zip over there on his Vespa in five minutes.

— — —

"I think we should go Luddite," Eddie said. "Lay low here for a while, just to be on the safe side."

"What do you mean?"

"Limit our excursions into town, hang out here, on our private beach."

"My parents will worry if I don't e-mail them. And what about Cam and Chloe?" Blackie said.

"We'll give them all Omi's number. If there's an emergency, they can contact him, or he can contact them. I'll e-mail Cameron to grab Chloe and join us."

They sent e-mail from the clothing-optional internet cafe and, as the sun just started to set, shopped naked in the supermarket, taking back two big bags of groceries.

Blackie didn't e-mail Chloe. She was still angry. Instead, Eddie e-mailed Cameron. Since Cameron and Chloe were together, it would have the same end result, right? Cameron would tell Chloe where they were, and this way Blackie didn't have to give an inch.

— — —

```
   To:  Godslefthand@earthlink.net
 From:  mail@strangecode.com
Subject:  MAILER-DAEMON: Undeliverable message
```

The original message was received at Tue, XX Aug 200X 08:26:00-0500(from mail.strangecode.com [65.61.149.253] (—The following addresses had permanent fatal errors— (<cameron@getareqljobcameron.com>((reason: 550 Host unknown)(—Transcript of session follows—(550 5.1.2 <cameron@getareqljobcameron.com> . . . Host unknown (Name server: camerongetareqljob.com: host not found)

Cam,
Can you take the Ganesh and Blackie material down from the website? A Hindu nationalist tried to kidnap Blackie and Ganesh at gunpoint during the bull run in Arles, then we think he followed us in a taxi to Aigues-Mortes. We lost him there and escaped with Jones and his bunch from Artery to Cap d'Agde's naturist quarter. It's an all nude village of over 20,000 people, with nude shops, post office, and so on. Google it. We're laying low here just off the public beach, in a camper, incommunicado. We have a private beach, surrounded by trees, and a view of the sea with

two giant black rocks jutting out of it about 100 meters from shore.

We're going Luddite for a week or two. If there's an emergency, or you want to check up on us, call the Naked Lunch Bar in Cap d'Agde. The bartender Omi is an Artery "asset," used to live with them in their squat in Paris. He owns the trailer we're staying in and is the only one who knows where we are. He'll come over from the village center to give us a message.

Get Chloe and come and join us. We've got this place for two weeks and the caravan has two bedrooms.

Eddie

After all the excitement of Cannes and her more peaceful day in Toulon, Chloe went to Arles, where Julius Caesar had fostered a favored city of the Roman empire, and Van Gogh and Gauguin had painted. She knew Eddie and Blackie were planning to see the bull run followed by the French-style bullfights. She arrived late, just saw the tail end of the run into the holding pen, and didn't see Blackie and Eddie in the crowd, which she followed into the arena.

In Toulon, she had gone brunette, leaving her brief foray into heiressdom behind, so she knew Blackie and the guys wouldn't be able to pick her out of a crowd now. Chloe would have to find them, in a crowd of about 15,000, most of them locals and brunettes.

When the stands were full, she walked around three times, looking for Blackie or Eddie or assorted Buddhists from that organization Artery. She didn't see anyone she recognized. She was going to make another round of the old arena when Spanish-style music blasted through loudspeakers, and ten young men in crisp white shirts and trousers paraded into the bullring and formed two rows. They marched forward, then split off and circled around the arena.

One in particular caught her eye, and she his—a dark-haired young man with the sweetest mouth she'd ever seen on a man. His shirt said *Gironde*.

Chloe squeezed herself into the walk space between seats, so she could be in the front row, and watched as the costumed men moved to opposite corners of the arena. After their show, they left the ring.

On the way in, the man who took her ticket had handed her brochures about the arena and about the course camarguaise, or "cocarde," which she now read with interest.

The young men were known as "raseteurs," and their job was to pluck the rosettes, tassels, and strings from the horns of the bulls, armed with just a hook-like gadget called a crochet. The bull's head was protected from the crochet's scratch by a thick nappy pile of hair on top of tough hide.

The bullpen opened and the first bull came in, trotting to the middle of the ring, standing proudly to survey the crowd, snorting, then pawing the ground. He was huge and black with long white horns that tapered into razor-sharp points. One by one, the raseteurs began to re-enter the ring. An older man, the "tourneur" according to the program, called and waved at the bull to get it into position. One of the young men then ran beside the bull, swiped its horns with his crochet, then ran past it. The bull charged after the young man, who was just inches from the horns when he leapt, as if his legs were spring-loaded, to the top of the bullring wall and then again to the metal fence fronting the first row in the stands.

Other raseteurs took their turns running past the bull, most coming up empty-handed but all escaping injury. They had no defense against the bulls but their agility, speed, and strong legs. It was hypnotic watching them dance around the bull before going for its horns. One held up his crochet, and the crowd roared. Evidently, he'd managed to snag something.

And then came Gironde, whipping past the bull, leaping to the bullring, where he perched on the ball of his left foot like Baryshnikov before he sprang up to the fence right in front of Chloe.

He looked at her. She looked at him. They stared for a moment. Then he jumped down, back into the ring.

After that, she could not take her eyes off of him. He was so beautiful and so brave. He was magnificent!

After fifteen minutes, the bullpen opened, the crowd cheered, and the bull trotted off. A few moments later, another bull trotted on and the game began again. One raseteur barely escaped the bull. It seemed he was safe, clinging to the fence, when the bull jumped over the bullring and tried to get him in the stands. Quickly, the raseteur jumped into the stands and pushed the crowd back while a bull handler prodded the bull from behind to distract him and push him toward an opened gate to re-enter the ring. The bull was tough, but the third was tougher, another ring-jumper, and more agile. This time, Gironde barely escaped, and Chloe could hardly breathe.

After every "course" past the bull, Gironde paraded past her place in the stands and looked up at her. He looked tough and earthy, but also sweet. Those eyes. That mouth. She'd never seen anything like him before.

The third bull didn't want to leave the ring. When his fifteen minutes were up and the raseteurs had retreated, he stood in the ring, looked around at the crowd, and snorted, before a bull handler prodded him toward the open gate.

After the third bull there was an interval, and a drink seller came around with a cooler of sodas and bottles of beer and Evian. She bought two bottles of Badoit, drank one right away, then lit a cigarette to calm her nerves. While she waited for the second act, she read about the arena, built in 90 A.D. when Arles was Julius Caesar's "little Rome." It seated 20,000 people. Gladiators had fought there, Christians probably pitted against lions, in this same arena where Gironde was daring bulls.

It was during the fifth bull that Gironde got the rosette, bringing a great cheer from the crowd as he held it up. And then he walked around the ring, leaned over, and presented it to Chloe, who, inspired, held it up for the crowd for a second cheer. Then he smiled at her and said something in French she couldn't understand.

She sat back, burning from the sun and the man, holding her rosette, her trophy, in her hand. It was unbelievable. Magic.

PART SEVEN

WELCOME, WANKER

Mike had looked for the heiress and her friend fruitlessly in Avignon, Nîmes, and Arles. The last tip he'd had, they were headed to the famous Stes. Maries de la Mer—Saints Marie of the Sea—in a white van.

So here he was in Stes. Maries, right in the middle of the Camargue, the land of gypsies, wild horses, and black madonnas, looking, waiting.

For all of one day, Mike had been front page again back in New York. Even then, he didn't get the main body of the front page, which was a big banner, "COWARDS KILL SELVES AND 43 OTHERS IN WEST BANK," above a picture of the twisted wreckage of a bus. Below that, "under the fold" as they say in the broadsheets, was Mike's story: "Double Life of Dead Adventurer." After that, the drift began, to page 2, 3, 4 . . .

The heiress story never made it farther forward than the gossip column on page 5. For him to advance further, the heiress needed to do something dramatic. The cops had to connect her with the murder, as he had in his mind, at which point he could file the story he had waiting.

He had no leads, he had no new angles or scams. He read the New York *Mail* online, seeing who was covering what, the parties he wasn't attending, especially the public relations parties he wasn't attending.

Reading the party reports caused a mild feeling of discomfort and thwarted desire, but nothing sapped the adrenaline he still had from the heiress story. Then he checked www.MediAmerica.-

com and saw, in the middle of the web page, a photo of his colleagues Masha and Smithy. They were at a birthday party for
Masha, thrown by Smithy at Loft, a new dinner club that had
opened in an old warehouse in the meatpacking district.

This was the equivalent of a thousand parties worth of bilious
envy. They were the hot new media couple now, gorgeous, under
30, with book *and* movie deals. Smithy's book on the Mr. Smile
case was now in galleys, and would be out in six weeks, when
there'd be another big party for him, then another when he and
Masha finished their instabook on Bonnie Parkavenue.

Masha looked absolutely gorgeous, red hair, alabaster skin,
those plump, Jolie lips and huge blue eyes, help-me-protect-me-
fuck-me eyes. She looked sweet, and the MediAmerica.com correspondent bought it, describing her as "very gracious and friendly."

Yeah, she'd been very friendly with Mike too, back when she
was starving for decent stories and under attack from her envious wannabe colleagues, in large part because she was too thin
and too pretty to be as smart and talented as she was. But pretty
wasn't the right word for her. Strikingly beautiful was more like it.
Or *strangely* beautiful, perhaps. When she walked into a room,
everyone noticed, and she noticed everyone noticing, but didn't
show it.

When she arrived in the newsroom, she needed help and protection, and Mike was there to provide it, to clue her in on the
back-room politics, to feed her sources and story ideas, support
her, comfort her, buy her meals, tag her onto his stories. Most important, he filled her in on the boss, Sharp, on his weaknesses and
blind spots. Eventually, he helped maneuver Masha into Sharp's
good books.

She was already in Mike's good books. When she slid her
hand under the table, the second time they had dinner, and un-
zipped him, the tablecloth concealing all but their knowing
smiles—well, he wanted to believe that a woman like her, beauti-

ful, smart, and kind too, was real. She wasn't just a possibility in this crappy world, but a reality for him, Mike Handel.

Then Smithy came along, the male Masha, handsome, tall, athletic, confidence-trumps-ability Smithy, and Masha became increasingly difficult and impossible.

The acid burn Mike felt thinking about that made him impatient. He couldn't wait for his moment in the sun. He wrote an anonymous letter to the French police, pointing out the similarities between the two women seen with Doo McGarrigle/Harry Carpenter in Monte Carlo and the heiress and her Canadian friend. He kept a photocopy for himself, careful to wear latex household gloves while he was doing all this. On his way to mail the letters he stopped at a phone booth and called the police in Nice. Using his best imitation of Tony Blair to disguise his voice, he reported the same thing and hung up.

On his way back to his hotel, he dawdled, stopped at a cafe for a leisurely lunch, read the *Herald Tribune*, struggled through the *La Provence* newspaper. Back at the hotel, he waited until just before 4 P.M., and then he called the French police to say he'd heard a report that there was a connection between that runaway heiress and that murdered American in Monte Carlo. The police had "No Comment," which he duly added to his pre-written story just before he filed it around 11 A.M. New York Time.

France was starting to really grow on Mike. Over here, Sharp couldn't check his facts, couldn't breathe down his neck, couldn't take the story away and give it to another reporter. The Heiress and the Dead Imposter were all his.

— — —

Diane saw the new twist in her story while she was holed up in her two-star hotel wedged into the pedestrian streets around Rue de la Huchette in the Latin Quarter on Paris's bohemian Left Bank.

The first site she went to, routinely now, was vomitinthe-shrubbery.com.

There it was, above a picture of her doppelgänger and the Canadian, a huge headline:

FLASH!
WANTED: MURDER.

She clicked on the link and went to the story. Police in Monaco and France were looking for her and "her Canadian friend" in connection with the murder of an American adventurer named Harry Carpenter, aka Doo McGarrigle, found dead in a Monte Carlo hotel room. The story had been posted just an hour earlier.

Her heart almost stopped. This was insane. She hadn't even been to Monte Carlo. But who would believe her, in light of all the other crazy rumors and, well, the truth?

— — —

By the next day there were already four more reporters in Stes. Maries de la Mer, all of them Brits. Then Sharp called.

"I'm sending a second reporter to assist you."

"Second reporter?"

"You'll have top byline, Mike, you broke the story. But you've got a lot of territory to cover there. You're going to need help. So I'm sending—"

"Who?"

"Masha."

Before Mike could object, Sharp said, " 'Nother call," and hung up.

What kind of sick joke was this, sending Masha over here to do *his* story? It was because of Masha he got into all that trouble. Sharp had to know that, even though Mike and Masha had tried to keep their affair secret. The fist fight at Elaine's, the incident with the two call girls, the rest that landed him on "vacation," it was because of Masha's betrayal.

Masha was probably sleeping with Sharp, too. Mike always suspected Sharp and Masha had something going on back when Mike and Masha were involved.

So why would Sharp send Masha? To punish Mike? Or to sow discord between Masha and Smithy, and maintain his power over all. Sharp was so Machiavellian.

All he needed was one big book deal (or movie deal with book tie-in), and Mike would no longer have to be at Sharp's mercy.

He wasn't giving this story up to anyone. He was just going to have to work a little harder to lead the others astray. That was pretty easy. He just downloaded some pictures of the heiress and her Canadian friend, and with some Photoshop magic he reversed them, changed the color of their clothes, moved the Canadian's arm up, then put them against a different background, in Marseille. The last touch was to blur the picture a little to take out the rough edges and make it look like it was taken with a telephoto lens.

But that wouldn't help him find the heiress himself. He needed to provoke her somehow. Then he had a brilliant idea . . .

— — —

Masha arrived and Mike picked her up at the airport, took her bags, then promptly sent her to Nîmes to check out a false lead. Since she was only going for a day, two at most, she left most of her clothes behind. Perfect.

It was relatively easy to make the suicide note. There was a copy of a note Diane had written to an ex-boyfriend online. He printed a copy. By cutting and pasting the letters of her real note together, scanning it, and futzing with it on Photoshop, he was able to create a quality forgery, using her own words and letters.

This he printed out, then painstakingly traced over, millimeter by millimeter, throwing out one tracing before coming up with a satisfactory one. He made photocopies to send to other journalists. These he handled very carefully, holding them from him to avoid leaving any DNA evidence. Each was sprayed with Benham's favorite perfume, which Mike had learned was Shalimar by Guerlain. He carefully placed almost all of these in pre-stamped envelopes with computer-generated address labels.

The original he would mail to himself, but not just yet.

Masha was about the same size as the heiress, and she loved some of the same designers. She came to the South of France with four suitcases and a plan to stay on after the story and take two weeks' vacation here with Smithy. While she was in Nîmes, Masha stashed her suitcases with Mike at his hotel in Stes. Maries de la Mer.

He picked out a little cream number, prêt à porter by Stella McCartney, the kind of thing Mike figured a chick like Diane Benham would wear if she were drowning herself in the sea.

He then placed one of the photocopies in an emptied Krug champagne bottle, because he'd read Benham liked Krug. The contents went down the sink drain, and when the bottle was dry, the copy of the letter was placed in it, the cork replaced and sealed with melted wax.

The dress he tore raggedly. The next day, he mailed the letters. The day after that, he took the dress and the bottle down to the water after midnight. He pushed the dress into the sea with a stick, forcing it down into the sand and dirt to rough it up a bit more. Then, making sure nobody was watching, he pulled it out with the stick and flung it about 10 feet into the sea.

The bottle he scuffed up on a rock, dirtied up and lodged next to another rock about 25 feet away, just in front of a now-dark cafe.

Conveniently, he was the first to file the (pre-written) story when the bottle and the dress were found. He got the scoop, but he expressed some healthy skepticism in his story. When the police team working the case for Monte Carlo, France, and Interpol arrived, he even said to them, "I can't buy that girl killing herself, can you? Where's the body?"

But as he hoped, his tabloid competitors jumped all over it.

There were pictures of the Canadian in Arles, but without the heiress. There were stories of previous suicide attempts and threats, even a photo of a suicide note Diane wrote in lipstick on a hotel mirror in Ibiza 18 months earlier, when she and Woy, the frontman for the Bean Counters, broke up for the first time. That time, she threw herself into a hotel pool (to be fished out by security guards before she could drown).

Mike, of course, knew all this beforehand.

Her parents, interviewed separately, said, that yes, she'd always had this morbid fear and fascination with water and drowning, that she was a troubled, troubled girl, and oh they hoped this was a terrible mistake but feared it was true.

The notes started showing up in newsrooms, and experts determined it was indeed her handwriting, though it reflected a great deal more stress than usual.

Then Mike mailed the letter to himself, c/o poste restante in Stes. Maries de la Mer.

— — —

Chloe didn't know quite what to think about her first bull "fight" and the young raseteur Gironde. Maybe he did this every time, picked a girl out of the crowd for a one-night stand. Well, she didn't care. She decided she was ready for a one-nighter, Vitamin XXX, as Blackie liked to call it. But she didn't want to hang around as the Roman arena emptied, looking desperate or foolish, so she lingered, dawdled on her way out, and then took up position at a cafe across from the arena's steps. About a half hour after the match ended, he came out with two of his fellows, and he saw her right away. He stood at the top of the steps with his buddies, looking at her, and she looked at him. Neither moved.

She wanted to invite him but wasn't sure what to do. He was about a hundred feet away. So she lifted her drink glass to him and then cocked her head sideways and subtly motioned with her free hand to the empty chair at her table.

One of his friends poked him in the side. He turned, said something to him, then began to walk down the steps to join her.

Immediately, they discovered their language problem, but it didn't matter. Neither one was really listening to what the other said anyway. It was all heat and hormones, eyes and the movement of lips. He walked her back to her little hotel and she took him upstairs with her. Two days later, Gironde invited her to come stay at his apartment in Arles.

CHAPTER 22

At first, Diane was distressed to learn someone had faked her death. She was distressed because she was a) out of cocaine and forced to survive on an alternating diet of caffeine pills, cheap table wine, and old Valium, which brought on moods that were not the blues, not the blacks, more like the creeping blue-grays, a deepening, low-energy depression; b) a virtual prisoner in her cheap hotel room because she had not paid, and dared not pass the front desk and the increasingly hostile Monsieur Bottecœur; and c) considered dead by her own hand by people who should have known better.

Did her parents really think she'd kill herself? She'd faked her suicide attempts before to get attention. Her father had even accused her of that in the past, though she had denied it, and her then-psychiatrist had confirmed that Diane was suicidal. (The psychiatrist was an earnest woman who had wanted to save Diane and then write a book about "girls like her," as Diane discovered when she read her doctor's notes, just before she fired the woman. She was probably making a deal now to write a book dissecting Diane's short sad life.)

But now that she was a suspect in murder, she wasn't too anxious to disprove the theory. She felt bad for her parents but figured they wouldn't really miss her, and if they did, well, it served them right.

In fact, there was a jolly Tom Sawyeresque thrill in reading the tributes to her now that she was, you know, dead. In Cannes, a religious entertainer named Peter Thorogood claimed to have met her and, seeing her distress, tried to bring her to Christ. She had said she wanted to be born again, but he lost her in a crowd before he had a chance to sit down with her alone and complete that process. He and his youth group, Godsmacked, were praying for her soul and its ultimate rest in the Kingdom of God.

(Before this was all over, there would also be a report of a Filipino maid rescued from an abusive employer by Diane Benham, who gave the woman airfare home and money to go to school. "A Change of Heart?" asked the *Daily Splash*, when it obtained a copy of a photo a tourist at the airport had allegedly taken of Diane and the Filipino maid.)

Death vastly improved her reputation. Suddenly, people were telling good stories about her. Guys she'd barely acknowledged, guys she wasn't sure she'd met, guys she knew with certainty were total strangers, were claiming to have had sex with her. This was not new. However, in the past, they had boasted about it as if it were some dance with danger only a few good men dare attempt, like rasslin' a gator or defusing an intricate bomb.

Now, they were full of sentimental eloquence. "She always had a haunted, faraway look," said a guy named Timothy Farhquar. Him she remembered from a private rave at her ex-friend Lady Daphne Trott's manor in Warwickshire. She and Daphne had a huge falling-out that night, and Diane was invited to leave before being forcibly ejected. Outside, she saw a drunken Timothy Farhquar preparing to unzip for a casual piss in the bushes, and Diane saw an opportunity and paid him 50 pounds to piss on the driver's seat of Daphne's classic Jaguar roadster.

The guy was so drunk she had to help him aim his urine stream in order to hit the target, so how he managed to read her complicated emotions and determine "haunting" in her eyes during their meeting was a bit baffling to her.

Yes, death was all good fun afterall. And soon she and Woy's plan would come to its romantic conclusion. Then she got an e-mail alert from vomitintheshrubbery.co.uk.

New news on Diane Benham.

She clicked.

Up came a picture of Woy. Below it the story said:

Bean Counter frontman Woy Simpson is "deeply, deeply" saddened
by the alleged death of his ex-girlfriend Diane Benham and "very
surprised" that she had transferred all her assets into his name
before she died. In effect, she has made him her heir, which lends
even more credence to the suicide theory.

Woy told us through choked voice in a late night phone call that his
very troubled ex-girlfriend was shattered when they split up, and he
feels very guilty about that, because in retrospect he thinks he
should have seen all this coming. But he could not continue the
relationship, he says—Diane was too young, too crazy, and she
refused to give up cocaine. Once he cleaned up, his own recovery
was threatened by his relationship with her. Of course, it made him
feel terrible to break up with her right after her court appearance, but
he felt like it was the best time, as she was going into an esteemed
care facility in the "disciplined beauty of the Swiss countryside,"
where she would have professional help to deal with it.

Cleaned up? The last time they managed a phone call, after
their "breakup" and two days before Diane went off to Switzerland,
he was doing coke the entire time. She could hear him snorting it
up. She was pretty sure he hadn't cleaned up since. And he wasn't
clean when he met her either. She'd never done more than a half
line of coke maybe three times, just to be sociable, before she met
Woy. He had musical ambitions and a coke habit, she had money
and connections and, soon, a coke habit. To be fair though, she had
to admit, he didn't go to any trouble to hook her. He didn't need
coke to control her, he held her heart by its trailing veins, and

there were nights when they almost ran out of coke while looking for a dealer and he probably would have been happier if he was the only one using.

No, that she chose to do. She wanted to share his addiction with him. She saw how good it made Woy feel, and she wanted to feel that way too: confident, unconquerable, walking through the world half an inch off the ground on a cushion of air. A sick feeling came over her, the truth sickness, as she continued reading.

> How is this tragic series of events affecting his recovery now? Woy admits it's been very difficult, and says he wouldn't have had the strength at all if it wasn't for his fiancée Jenna, who has been "strong, rational, and empathic" when he could not be. "I should not have broken up with her to be with Diane in the first place," he said. "Jenna has forgiven me, and she has forgiven Diane too. She's as upset as I am about all this."

> Woy and Jenna have not been seen recently. Woy told us they have both been in seclusion at an unnamed place, grieving and trying to digest events. To memorialize Diane, Woy is writing a song dedicated to her for his next CD, a song called "Bad Girl Heaven." Proceeds will go to a program to educate school children about the dangers of drug use, and he says he plans to contribute the greater part of Diane's fortune, anonymously, over the years to causes that honor her memory.

Woy and Jenna—O my God, no! She read it again, and again, looking for anything that would negate what she thought the text said. That rat, she thought, as sobs rose from her gullet in huge waves. Pretending he didn't know she'd transferred her money to him before they faked their breakup to mislead everyone, and before she was carted off to rehab.

Their plan was they were going to reunite secretly at his Paris concert. She'd be in disguise, moving among the crowd, going backstage later so they could sneak off to a hidden car and run away to an island paradise in the Caribbean, and there she'd be his muse and he'd finish writing the songs for his new CD and they'd get married, and when the heat was off they'd come out in the sun. When people heard the songs, they'd love them both again, and admire the lengths they went to to "live their love" away from the "hypocrisy and pollution of modern society."

Or so Woy had said.

And she'd believed him. That sort of magic seemed entirely possible when she was with him.

But that hadn't been his plan at all, had it? He must have wanted her to come to his show in Paris to reveal her. No doubt someone—Jenna—would tip off the cops and she'd be nabbed there. What great publicity for Woy and the band.

He can't get away with this, she thought. But what could she do? If she reappeared, she might be charged with murder. She could probably prove she wasn't in Monte Carlo at the time of the murder, but she'd certainly be sued, jailed, made to look foolish, and forced back into rehab. But if she didn't reappear, who could she go to? Where could she hide? What would she do for money? How would—

There was a knock at the hotel room door.

"Mademoiselle?" said the male voice.

She peered through the door peephole. It was ancient Monsieur Bottecœur, a yellow Gitane cigarette hanging from his mouth, dreadful cigarettes, meant to approximate the rough corn cigarettes smoked during the Nazi occupation of World War II. The only reason she could see for anyone wanting to smoke them was nostalgia for that time. The old Collaborator.

"I can hear you in there. I'm afraid we must have payment immediately."

"I just came out of the shower," Diane said. "I will bring the money to the desk in one half-hour."

She waited until she heard his bootsteps fade away. She was about to be evicted, like some out-of-work 1930s Montmartre chorus girl, set out on the sidewalk in a pile of hatboxes and feather boas, or the equivalent, her laptop and purse.

Shit. She had no money left. Why was everything happening at once, and why was it happening to her, she wondered as she climbed the stairs to the roof.

At first, she'd planned to escape through her front window via the demi-balcony, but that would take her past the hotel's ground floor window, in view of the Monsieur. So she went instead to the roof, stepping over to the roof of the next building, which had a steel ladder riveted to its side, opening into the Rue du Chat qui Pêche, Paris's tiniest street.

She jumped the last seven or so feet, landing awkwardly on the ground, a bit bruised but otherwise unharmed.

Now where?

She had nowhere to go. In a milky blur of tears, she headed down the Quai des Tournelles fronting the Seine on the Left Bank, going nowhere, walking on auto-pilot and more swiftly than usual, as if she were in a big hurry to get nowhere. When she got to Pont Neuf, she burst into audible sobs. Woy had kissed her there one night almost a year ago, in one of the huge stone semicircles that jutted out from the bridge walls—there, on Pont Neuf, which means "new bridge" though, in fact, it's the oldest bridge in Paris. That had seemed so significant to her then. She was all coked up at the time, the Seine was a deep blue, almost black, reflecting the light of a crescent moon in its shivering waters. The old misted lamps were lit, the medieval Conciergerie on shore was dark, the Eiffel Tower glowed a coppery gold in the distance. She'd turned to Woy, who was also coked up, both of them with bright eyes, and said, "I love you. I want to marry you." He'd said nothing, but taken her face in his hands, and kissed her. And every time she tried to speak again that night, he kissed her.

At the time she thought it was frightfully romantic, like Bogie and Ingrid in *Casablanca,* or Lambert Wilson and the young chick in *Red Kiss.*

But now she realized it was one big fucking cop-out! He'd never said he loved her except when he was inside her, and even then only twice, though sometimes he got to I lo—before he came. He didn't love her. He loved the reflection of himself he saw not only in her eyes, but the eyes of the tabloid-reading public. And her money and connections, of course. Before Diane, he and his band had been a minor note in the press, a promising indie with a young, good-looking frontman, one of a hundred such frontmen in London. Before he met Diane at frozen potato heiress Emma Kendall's birthday party, he'd been in the papers three times, twice with then-aspiring-but-none-too-successful model Jenna, and once chugging pints at a World Cup party.

Before Diane, he was sleeping on his mum's couch and playing audiences of 200 in bars. Then he was her boyfriend, in the papers all the time, playing bigger clubs, signing a record deal. That deal came because Diane leaked a rumor that Prince William was a fan, which sold out their indie CD within days.

Now he and Jenna had everything, and she had nothing and nobody.

She sat down in one of the circular seats and looked down into the river, crying, the tears running down her face on to the abutment below. The dark water looked so inviting then, and she wondered if maybe it was time she did it, flung herself into the Seine . . .

"Bonsoir," said a voice.

Diane looked up and saw an Asian man, about her age, looking down at her.

"Bonsoir," she said.

"Are you okay?"

"No."

"You have an accent. Are you English?" he asked. He sounded American.

"Yes. Who are you?"

"Sam," he said. "What's wrong?"

"I'm homeless," she said. "And broke and—" she started to cry again.

"Don't get upset."

"What will I do?"

"You want to come home with me? It's not a palace but I can find you a bed."

"What for?" she asked.

"Nothing bad. I'm not a perv or anything. I have roommates, both sexes, so we won't even be alone."

"You have any cocaine?"

"No. I don't do it. There might be some hash and some beer."

"You aren't going to hurt me?"

"I promise."

He looked trustworthy, but then what did she know?

Then again, what choice did she have?

CHAPTER 23

Chloe hadn't checked her e-mail for days. For three nights she had been holed up with Gironde. For three days she had been at bullrings, watching him practice this bull running thing.

She'd almost missed out on this because of her inferior French. When he spoke to her that first time in the stands, quickly and with the crowd roaring around them, she had no idea what he said. Was it "Meet me after the show," or "You have nice tits," or "You're cute, you gotta brother?"

Because Chloe didn't speak French well, and he didn't speak English beyond a few sentences, they seemed more mysterious to each other, more exotic, and more physical. He was busy all day training or competing. She watched him, or read and walked around. She began keeping a journal. After he was finished, he went to the cafe with a few of his colleagues and friends. She instinctively knew to let him stay there for an hour at least before she showed up, so he could have his guy time. They'd have a drink, the group would disperse, and then she and Gironde would eat there or go back to his apartment in Arles and he'd cook.

On the second day, she met some of his friends after a course in the town of Aimargues and a wide variety of his family after a course in St. Gilles. They'd had a big dinner with them and some of his neighbors, a sprawling affair with children and dogs weaving through the legs of grownups. The family looked on her with curiosity, but a few neighbor girls viewed her with suspicious resentment. Gironde, it turned out, was a guitarist too, and played a little, old Django Reinhardt songs for the older people and some more modern French stuff for everyone else. Chloe sang a little, when everyone else did.

The fourth day he had off, so he took her around the marshy Camargue, which was full of rice fields, wild white horses, black bulls, cowboys in crisp white shirts and black hats, mountains of white salt, and, in a startling contrast to the all black and white, flocks of pink flamingos.

She learned about Le Sanglier, the most famous of the course camarguaise bulls. (The bulls got top billing on all the posters, over the raseteurs.) Le Sanglier, from the "manade Granon," a herd designation, was born in 1916, died in 1933, and was buried at Cailar where a monument honored his old cow bones. She ate poutargue—camarguaise "caviar"—and learned to say a few things in Occitan, which one of Gironde's great-grandmothers spoke.

Meanwhile, she and Gironde were speaking in the language of children, in her basic French and his simplified so she could understand. The language problem was charming now, but it would certainly become a liability soon enough, and she didn't want this relationship to go badly. Chloe wanted to enjoy every minute of it and when it ended to end it amicably. It was a summer fling in her mind, it had an expiration date in the fall when she went back to grad school and he went back to university in the South of France. Somehow, knowing it would be over, and when, made it all so much easier, as did her newfound ability to forgive—and even be a little grateful to—John Carey. If John hadn't dumped her, she wouldn't have discovered her talent for crime, or freed a Filipino maid, or be sleeping with this handsome French bullfighter . . .

CHAPTER 24

Now that almost the whole world was convinced that Diane Benham had done herself in, Mike prepared to put the second part of his plan into action. He was among the suicide skeptics, cleverly enough, acknowledging the possibility she had killed herself while gently questioning a few details. The police were also skeptical but continued their investigation. There was no body, but then there was no body for months when the glamourous Contessa Agusta had thrown herself into the Mediterranean in the late 1990s following her implication in an Italian political scandal.

The investigation into Benham's suicide could get uncomfortable for Mike. It was time to bring it to an end and get himself another scoop.

Masha had been following false leads he'd planted for her since she arrived. Officially they were working together, but of course they weren't really, each trying to hoard their own information. Here, he definitely had the upper hand, though she tried to wrest it away with the bat of her lovely blue eyes. Her eyes promised sex, her words only alluded to it, a classic manipulation of hers that had worked on him before. It was easy for a smitten guy to interpret that low-lidded, pointed look of hers as, "do for me and I'll do for you," especially if her hand was on his mid-thigh under the restaurant tablecloth.

When she returned to Stes. Maries de la Mer, he told her they were relocating to Arles to get better access to trains and highways. But before they left, he stopped at the post office and picked up his mail at his rented box. There was only one letter, the

Benham suicide note he had mailed to himself. Mike was driving a rental (Buzzer had just returned and summoned Alphonse and his car), so he asked Masha to open the letter and read it to him.

"It's the same note she sent to all the reporters," Masha said.

"Shove it in my pocket," Mike said.

Masha did so, a little provocatively.

Later in Arles, in a hotel room at the Jules César hotel, Mike filed his story: The suicide may have been faked, he said. He had received a suicide note from Benham, mailed two days after she supposedly vanished into the sea. Either Benham mailed it as an afterthought, or her Canadian friend had done it. The Canadian was still missing. The *Daily Splash* had just offered a 5000-pound reward for information leading to her capture.

After he uploaded a scan of the envelope with its postmark, he called Masha to tell her, and they called the police.

"Either Benham didn't mail those letters herself," Mike said to the French police. "Or she faked the whole suicide. I have a postmark to show you . . ."

— — —

To: MikeHandel@NYMail.com
From: EnemiesOfCarlotta@yahoo.ca
Subject: Where in the world is Diane Benham?

Congratulations. You guessed right. Diane didn't kill herself. But she didn't fake her suicide either. Someone else did that.

Diane is fine. She's with me here at this very moment. She'd like to speak to you, exclusively, but only on her terms.

Don't bother trying to trace this e-mail. It was made through a call to the Cayman Islands, then rerouted to a number in Canada. It has been anonymized and detrailed.

E-mail us with a land line number where we may call
you tomorrow, August ▌▌, at 17H00 with further
instructions.

Attached is a digital photo of Diane holding today's
newspaper as well as a scan of a note to you in her
handwriting.

Don't tell anyone about this or the deal is off.

Enemies of Carlotta

P.S. We are excellent hackers and can blow you out of
the water with what we've learned about you.

— — —

To: EnemiesOfCarlotta@yahoo.ca
From: MikeHandel@NYMail.com
Subject : Okay

Call 04.XX.XX.XX.XX. It's a cafe. I'll be waiting.

— — —

He took the call at a payphone in a bar for toro aficionados in
Arles, at a payphone under the stuffed head of a black bull.

"Come to Dijon tomorrow, to a place called the Bonobo Beat.
Make sure nobody follows you. Be there at 21h30. Go to the bartender and say, 'I am a friend of the Enemies of Carlotta.' Your
contact will then drive you to see Diane. Do not bring a camera.
Photos will be taken there and provided to you for just the developing cost. The interview will be recorded so take care not to mis-
quote or quote Diane out of context."

"Okay. Can I speak with Diane?"

"When you get here. If we have any doubts to your integrity *in
this matter at least* the whole deal is off."

"If I could just speak to Diane to be sure—"

"You're a gambler, Mike, aren't you? Didn't you run through about 50 grand in Atlantic City about six months ago? This is much less of a gamble, and much more lucrative too. See you tomorrow," the caller said, and hung up.

The handwritten note looked authentic, and so did the photo. But then, the faked photos of the heiress and the Canadian and the suicide note he made up looked authentic too. These days, with computers, seeing isn't always believing.

Yet, he was convinced. He believed it, because he wanted it to be true—the same reason so many of his readers believed his stories.

At the Bonobo Beat, the bartender directed Mike out the back door, into an alley, where two women in a black masks grabbed Mike's arms and pulled them firmly behind his back. They gagged him.

After they loaded him into the back of a vehicle, they tied his legs and went through his pockets, taking his cellphone, wallet, and notebook, and drove off.

He was sitting on a surface that felt both soft and rough, like carpeting. He had plenty of head room and room to stretch his legs, and when the doors had closed in front of him, they'd sounded like the back doors on a van. Through his gag, he tried to ask what was going on, but only a few strangled, muffled noises emerged.

Who was behind this? Benham, maybe, though Mike's intuition told him it was something Smithy and Masha had cooked up to get him out of the picture. Smithy didn't want Mike near Masha, and he didn't want Mike getting the Big Scoop. And Masha wanted the story.

"Should we untie his gag?" asked a guy. Sounded like an American.

"Let's wait," said another guy, who spoke with an Indian accent.

"Hand me another of those sandwich halves," said America.

"Here. Will we be back in time for Bruno's opening?"

"If traffic is good. I saw it in his studio. I'm not sure about it."

"Why?"

"Well, I liked it, but I'm not sure—have you seen it?"

"No. He does nudes, right?"

"Yeah. I'm not sure if I like them because they're good mastur-bation photos, or if they're actually art. The women are all around 18, 19, the poses are sexually provocative, but the light quality, the texture, it looks cheesy, amateurish, like someone who photo-graphed other men's wives naked in their living room in the 1970s and then sent the photos in to a stroke mag."

"Maybe they're just stroke pictures. But if he was paying homage to the style of vintage amateur porn polaroids, it's art. Maybe it's art either way. I'd really like to see the exhibit. Besides, Vanessa is working the bar."

Mike listened, hoping to pick up some clue about where he was going, but their conversation was confusing. They discussed how good the sandwiches were, made by someone named Julie, and then bitched about another woman, Elle, who was evidently away in Spain for the summer. One of them had fucked her and wouldn't mind doing it again.

Were these guys freelance thugs? Thugs who talk about art? They were in France after all, where one's plumber or trash man may have read either Proust or a bestseller by the female journal-ist who had thousands of affairs with thousands of men—all with her husband's permission.

Where were they taking him and what were they going to do? They wouldn't kill him—he wasn't worth it, and if Smithy and Masha were behind it, they wouldn't want that on their rap sheet. Murder was too hard to conceal. These guys were clearly just underemployed artists hired to play a prank, humiliate him, break his spirit.

He had a terrible vision of bachelor party pranks he'd played on friends—putting one passed-out groom-to-be on a Greyhound bus to Chicago two nights before his wedding after taking his wal-let, for example. Another they stripped naked and dropped off at a New Jersey rest stop bathroom. The women's bathroom. In that case, the victim was a colleague at the paper. Maybe he got together with Smithy and Masha . . .

Stripped naked in France with one year of college French . . . well, it could be worse. He could be naked in Utah, or maybe Iran.

Worst of all, he was going to lose his story, the story he found, he built up, he worked . . . it wasn't fair.

Even if Masha and Smithy weren't behind it, they'd make sure it leaked to the newspapers, he'd end up once again in *Page Six, Rush & Malloy, The Observer,* and assorted snarky media watch columns in the States. If Benham was behind it, her purposes would be the same, to humiliate him in Fleet Street, and Smithy and Masha would naturally spread the good news to New York and points beyond.

They drove a long time it seemed. Hours. Then the van stopped.

"We're taking you in now," America said.

They helped him out of the van without untying his legs, so he had to hop between them. A door creaked open and a third man said, with an English accent, "Welcome, wanker."

Mike was pushed through a doorway and forced to hop another twenty yards or so, a journey that included a turn. He was trying to remember all this but he was blind and having trouble conceptualizing the geography.

They were all squeezed together, a door closed. It was an old elevator, which rattled slowly upwards. After they got off, he was put in a room, set down upon a chair, and told to wait.

A door closed. Silence. He was all alone.

When the door opened again, the steps were lighter than the heavy, unfocused steps of the guys who had hauled him in. The person walked around him slightly, then said, in a girlish English voice, "So, Mike, why did you do it? Why did you decide to kill me, resurrect me, then crucify me? Oh. You can't talk, can you?"

The hood came off.

Diane was there. She didn't remove his gag.

"I am going to give you an exclusive interview. You may not reveal my whereabouts. To ensure this, I will allow you to file your story, but after that, I want to keep you here for a week, under supervision, with no contact with the outside. Then I want you to do another story for me. But before we do anything else, I want you to come up with a good answer to my question: Why do you do this kind of work?"

She smiled, then left.

What could he say? His business is the shark pool, these are the rules, play by them or get eaten up—but that didn't fly out there with the *Mail*'s largely working-class readership, who were struggling to play by the "good" rules of society, despite the secret suspicion that they were getting screwed over by all the people breaking them.

Those were his readers. His job at the *Mail* was to expose and pillory the rule-breakers in the most sensational, humiliating way possible to satisfy the workers and confirm that they were right to follow the rules and do the right thing, marry the girl, give up the guitar, take the job in the insurance office or factory, put the child first, obey the law.

That's what he told himself, to give his shit life a noble veneer, but Mike was the son of working people, a plumber and a secretary, and he knew the working people broke the rules too, just differently and with fewer rewards and greater consequences. His mother brought home boxes of pens, printer ink, and other sundries to keep him supplied when he was in school, and both his parents had committed adultery. They plotted against and undermined their rivals at work, in the neighborhood, in their own family.

He looked around the big office-type room, with big windows looking into the hallway and two mattresses on the floor. When Diane returned, she ungagged him and he told her the truth.

"I'm a shark, I swim with sharks, we show no mercy."

"Well, I respect your honesty," she said. She seemed uncharacteristically calm. "Mike, did you really get caught with two hookers in a car on First Avenue in New York? I read that about you."

"I was going through a really bad time . . ."

"And did you really fall dead drunk asleep on a bench in a Central Park playground, and then vomit on your shoes when you woke up in front of a lot of mommies, nannies, and small children?"

"There weren't that many nannies and small children, maybe seven. I just got royally screwed over by this woman . . ."

"We'll start the interview tomorrow. Sam is going to be your keeper. He'll be sleeping here with you and will help you with everything tonight. You've had a crazy day, so why don't you get a nap."

CHAPTER 25

The first few days in their sanctuary were fun. Every morning when Blackie and Eddie got up, they showered with a garden hose, then ran into the sea—a better wake-me-up than caffeine, Eddie said, though Blackie insisted on having her coffee too when they got back from swimming, making it in an old tin pot in the barbecue pit, like they were hobos or something. They cooked all their meals in the pit, while naked, carefully dodging sparks, stray embers, smoke, and the ubiquitous mosquitoes.

Sunburn was a problem too. There was a reason people wore clothing on their most sensitive parts, Blackie discovered, as Eddie covered her with aloe vera, then applied calamine lotion in a targeted fashion for the mosquito bites.

"Have you been anywhere you'd like to stop?" she asked him the second night, after they'd had a big campfire-cooked dinner, smoked a blunt, and had sex on the beach. Now they lay on the still warm sand, looking up at the stars, his arm round her. He smoked a cigarette. He'd seemed distracted and distant that day, and she was trying now to reconnect with him.

"There were a few places where I thought I could stop here, open a little hotel or something," he said. "There's this guy in northern Pakistan, runs an eight-room inn and one-pump gas station out in the middle of nowhere. It's probably 50 miles to the next gas pump or bed, maybe more. He's never been farther south than Islamabad, and the only trip he wants to take now is to Mecca before he dies. The guy listens to BBC World Service, knows so much about the world, asks a lot of questions, but has no desire to go see it. 'The world comes to me,' he says, and then he shows you a thick guestbook, signed by backpackers from all over the planet. I could see living like him."

Eddie's road stories were interesting, she liked them, but she was already feeling the itch to get moving and create some more of her own. This would be one of hers: There was this Crazy Canadian named Eddie I met in Italy, liked to draw pictures of God. . . . We spent some time as nudists in a camper on the Mediterranean. In her mind, she was already writing him into memory.

"What about you, you must have had an adventure or two here in Europe, before you met up with me. Or was it all relationship rehab for Chloe?"

She would have loved to have told him a few of her adventures, but she wasn't sure he'd approve.

"Nothing too exciting."

"How did you and Chloe meet and become friends?" he asked.

"I used to smoke," Blackie said, recalling distant memories. "We were in a stop smoking program together."

"And her family?" Eddie asked. "Long lines of love forever people?"

"Legendary. Her parents have been married almost 30 years. Her father's parents were married 55 years, before her grandfather died a few years ago. Big Bill Bower and Little Sally Bower, that's what they called themselves. They were a cute couple. I went to her grandparents' 50th anniversary party with Chloe and even after all those years, the way Big Bill looked at Little Sally over the banquet table . . . It was something." She smiled. She was starting to forgive Chloe a little.

"And Chloe didn't get that gene?"

"Evidently not. She didn't get the photography gene either— the whole family is involved in photography. She did get the Europe bug from them though. Big Bill was a sales executive for Kodak and worked a lot with the European offices and Chloe's parents came to Europe every year before she was born. She was conceived somewhere over here."

"Only child?"

"Yeah," she said. "I guess I got the travel bug from Big Bill via Chloe. And you—you got yours from the Hersh sisters?"

"Yeah."

"Who were they?"

"That's a long story. From a bad time in my life," he said. "You sure you want to hear it?"

"Yeah."

He took a drag off his cigarette, inhaled, then exhaled.

"I've done all sorts of bad things," Eddie said. "Sorry to say."

"Really? Like what? Ever been arrested?"

"Yep. Went to reform school for a while," he said.

"No way. What for? Drugs?"

"B&Es, breaking and entering, starting when I was 12. I did it until I got caught when I was 16."

"What did you steal?"

"I didn't steal anything, except maybe a cup of coffee. I used to break into people's houses while they were on vacation, just to hang out, look through their photo albums, watch a little TV."

"Why?"

"At home . . . my parents were fighting a lot, my sister had become this nihilistic punk who hated everyone, and my grandfather was convinced I was gay and kept trying to get me into the army and make me do manly things."

"Manly things? Such as getting a mortgage, chopping wood?"

"I chop wood. I've chopped lots of wood. No, like hunting. 'Huntin' out in de bush dere.' That's how he talks. He's a funny old guy. He's 78 now."

"You went hunting?"

"I don't know if I would call it hunting. I don't hunt and Grandpa's in a wheelchair, so it was him with a rifle and me pushing him around trying to track deer spoor through the bush. He's barking orders at me so loud he scared away any deer in the vicinity. He's half-deaf too, so he shouts a lot."

"You just broke into other people's homes? How long did you stay in them?"

"A few hours at a time, usually late at night, after I got off work at the donut shop. I went to one house a lot, the Hersh family house. The parents were both teachers, and every summer vacation they went off with their daughters to teach for two months on Indian reservations or in other countries. I'd spend a lot of time in their house every summer."

"Nice house?"

"Yeah, not expensive or fancy. You know, they were teachers. But it was comfortable. They had great photo albums. The two daughters put together an album for each summer, with text, postcards, photos, little mementos, like pressed flowers and ticket stubs. I remember the India album had a ticket stub from the Jamuna Cinema on Chowringee Road, and a handwritten receipt from a place called Mohan's Drink Shop in Jaisalmer. That one was right beside a picture of the two of them on camels. There were some great photos of them, on top of elephants, on horses with native cowgirls, playing cards with old Chinese guys in cafes, taking tea with silk sellers or Nepali girl students in blue-and-white uniforms. I got the itch to travel from them."

"Are they the ones who busted you?"

"No, that was a family called Miller. The whole family was supposed to go skiing in Quebec for Christmas, but the oldest son stayed behind to see his girlfriend. He busted me. I knew the guy from school too, so that made it worse. I don't think the Hershes ever knew about me. For a while I entertained a fantasy of going back and introducing myself to them, maybe falling in love with one of the daughters."

He laughed.

"Think you'll do it?"

"If I went back now I'd have to confess everything—"

"Why?"

"I'd feel weird keeping it secret from them. But if I told them they'd think I was a nut."

"How long were you in reform school?"

"A year, then a year probation. I might have got off lighter but I had a record at school for fighting and a 'bad family environment at home.' So they sent me up the river. I got into a lot of fights at reform school. But I also got into something good there. This old guy, an ex-con, came by once a week to teach an art class and he taught me a lot. When I got out, I enrolled in graphic arts at the vocational high school and went to technical college and so on . . ."

"What was the trigger that pushed you to pack your bags?"

"Oh, just . . . it's not that interesting. If it hadn't been one thing it would have been another. Like I said, I've had the bug since I looked through Jessica and Sarah Hersh's photo albums."

"And you never stole anything from those people, other than a cup of coffee?"

"No. God no. I don't steal. They kind of felt like family. It's creepy I know, breaking into their house and peering into their lives. But I never meant them any harm. I liked them."

It was kind of creepy, but that wasn't what bothered Blackie later. It took her a while to name the feeling that was seeping through her, a kind of nausea and a mild, sick chill. At first she thought it was food poisoning, or maybe she was getting her period.

Then she identified it. Guilt. Somehow, what he'd done seemed more innocent and noble than ripping off pervs and pawning their Rolex watches. Well, the pervs deserved it. But she didn't know how to tell it to Eddie in a way that wouldn't lessen his respect or esteem for her.

God, she hated this feeling, this guilt.

She suddenly missed Chloe very much. Chloe's presence allowed her to be the Good Cop, to shine in contrast. She didn't feel like that with Eddie. For all his regret about his teenage forays into voyeurism, he was a proverbial Good Cop. It made her like him less for some reason, and that made her feel like even more of a shit.

After that, during those long stretches of the day when Eddie would draw or write in his notebook, Blackie would duck over to the nude town to hang out with Omi and play pinball with him. He had a computer with a DSL connection behind the bar, and he let her use it when things were quiet. She thought about e-mailing Chloe, but Chloe hadn't e-mailed her. Cameron had e-mailed: "All okay here, lost Chloe and have been detoured by strange girl who is trying to teach me how to be a missionary. We should all meet up soon. Pick a place? We're in Cassis, heart of the Calanques, the French fjords."

Blackie clicked to his websites to see if he had taken down the Ganesh stuff. He hadn't, so she e-mailed him: "Cam, PLEASE remove the Ganesh stuff from your sites. The Hindu extremists are after us. We're still on the nude beach. Eddie has gone old-school and hasn't checked e-mail lately."

Just after she sent the e-mail, she had one of what Eddie, quoting his friend Crazy Millman the Californian, called those "celestine road coincidences, those meant meetings that connect people randomly on the unseen byways of the world."

"Hey, I know you," said a man behind her.

She looked. It took a moment to place him.

"Doug Mason, commercial poet, how the hell are you?" she said.

"Good. What was your name again?"

"Michelle," she said, not sure if she had used her real name or an alias with him.

It didn't matter, he had forgotten her name "and that of your friend." He was topless but wearing Bermuda shorts and carrying his shopping bag full of poems. He wasn't yet used to being around a lot of naked people and very deliberately kept his eyes above her neck. Whenever they would start their natural drift downward, he'd yank them up quickly and self-consciously and stare above her head, as if to compensate for the downward pull.

"How's the poetry business?" she asked.

"It's okay. I got someone to do a French translation, to increase my market coverage. I only sold a single poem all day though. For some reason naked people don't buy a lot of poetry."

"Are you here with your bus tour?"

"Yeah, just here for the day."

"Any of you going naked?"

"Most of us swam naked today. That was fantastic! Naked in the sea. One of the gals got naked to go to the post office, just so she could mail postcards naked. That's all she wrote on her cards, 'I mailed this card in the post office while I was completely naked!' "

"Good one."

"Yeah, but the postcards were of doorways and fields of flowers in Provence. Her sister went with her but she wore a sundress over her bathing suit. But you know, when that sister started this tour, she was afraid of everything. She has a phobia about stairs, especially escalators. You ever heard of that?"

"No."

"Thank God for wheelchair ramps, because not every place has an elevator, you know?" he said. "Where are you staying? In one of the hotels here?"

"No, we're camping not far from here. Buy you a beer?"

"Yeah, I've about got time for a beer before the bus leaves," he said.

While they drank, Blackie told him about the Artery Buddhists, the private beach she was staying on with Eddie, and that Chloe had gone by herself to Cannes. She left out the craziness, the angry Hindu nationalist after the Ganesh statue, and the crime of course. Then she helped him sell a poem to a naked Swedish woman and her very hairy boyfriend.

"I didn't know hair could grow there," Doug Mason said after they'd left. "Think it itches when he sits down?"

He finished his beer. "I'd better go meet the bus. Nice running into you, Michelle. Small world, eh?"

"Quite a coincidence running into you here, in a nude bar."

"I've had some good ones on this trip. Coincidences, I mean, not nude bars."

There was another little one happening right then too, and Blackie was completely unaware of it. Denise DeMars, an accountant from the French city of Lille on vacation in Cap d'Agde, had just arrived that morning. She'd flown down to Montpellier and hopped a train from there, and on her train was a copy of *La Provence* newspaper, with a story about the murder, the heiress and the Canadian friend with the flower tattoo. The police were looking for tips.

And here, walking past her out the door was a dark-haired woman with a flower tattoo and a little red maple leaf on her purse. She took out her cellphone.

Denise DeMars knew nothing about the *Daily Splash* reward of 5000 pounds or, being a practical sort of person, she would have called them after she called the French police to report the Canadian friend was in the nudist quarter on Cap d'Agde.

PART EIGHT

USING OUR EVIL FOR GOOD, INSTEAD OF FOR EVIL (MOSTLY)

CHAPTER 26

It had been a hectic day at the Dajgit household. Papa was agitated because Sanjay and Chunky had not yet recovered the statue, and Papa had hoped it would be back home before the city's Ganesh festival.

Then Amit and Papa had argued all morning about business.

Since the baby was born, Amit had had quite a head on him, Mama thought, as her day nurse Rakha attended to her morning toilet.

In the afternoon, someone wheeled Mama and her rack of IV bags to the sunroom for lunch with the family. The nurse spoonfed her some strained okra.

Oh, what she would have given for a nice crispy samosa and a little ceramic cup of hot milk tea, like they sold at the train station. Or one of her favorite sweets, barfi, made by boiling sugar, milk, and crushed nuts until thick like fudge. She liked the barfi made by an old man on Chowpatty Beach. That she could still eat, if it was broken in small pieces so she could dissolve its creamy sweetness on her tongue. But nobody thought to get it for her anymore. Madhuri ordered sweets from an overpriced shop near the Taj Hotel, very fashionable, and they wrapped the sweets in a pale pink box tied with a silver ribbon—very classy—but the barfi was spongy, too sweet and not milky or nutty enough.

Madhuri had taken to widowhood very well, Mama observed. Only moments after she learned Doo was dead, she went to have the vermillion streak removed from the part in her hair, a clear decalaration that she was no longer a married woman.

Well, if Madhuri had listened to her in the first place . . .

But even when she could speak, nobody listened to her.

All the riches they had, and she could no longer enjoy them. She thought now she would give up every luxury she had if she could walk freely again on Chowpatty Beach at night and enjoy the simple pleasures like train station tea. Since she couldn't tell anyone if the tea was too hot, she was only allowed lukewarm tea now, served in a child-proof cup with a white plastic lid and little spout designed to minimize dribbling.

"If they do not find the statue this week, then Amit must go," Papa was saying.

"He can't leave me and the baby," Farha said, jiggling her squalling infant in the cradle beside her chair.

Amit said, "I can't leave the business either. We are in the middle of important work channelizing our resources—"

"I should have sent you in the first place," Papa said to Amit. "That's it. I've decided."

Amit said nothing, but as he lowered his head to eat, Mama saw the trace of a smile. *Why was he smiling?* she wondered. He saw her staring at him and he smiled openly now. It was a victorious smile. Mama had never liked him, and he was doing his best to prove her wrong, siring a son, trying to make the family business somewhat legal.

I still don't like you, she blinked at him.

The rest of the lunch was eaten in silence. Papa left the table early to take a call in the hallway. As they wheeled Mama Dajgit back to her room she overheard Papa talking—no, begging, "Please Veena, I must see you. You must make time. I will have Amit come by to arrange it."

The family was falling to pieces, its legendary treasure missing, its street soldiers gunned down, and he was still obsessed with that round-heeled flower-seller mistress of his. Fool.

She was the only one in this family who knew what was going on. Ironic. She was now the wise one and Papa was the Fool. When they'd first met, it had been the other way round. Papa was the street sharpie, the smart one. He read and wrote.

And she knew nothing when her mother said a washerman named Ganesh Dajgit from the house where she worked wanted to arrange a marriage with her. She was a 16-year-old unmarried girl. The boy she had been betrothed to had died in post-partition riots that had also taken her father and a brother, and she was sent to work to support the survivors. She was not very pretty and there were rumors about her chastity, but what poor woman didn't hike up her skirts when the man who gave out her wages demanded it.

But here was a man who wanted to marry her, and when she met him she could hardly believe her luck. He was so handsome and intelligent.

After she moved to the house Papa shared with his widowed mother and sisters, she learned of the master plan to rob the Gadi family. Over the years, Papa's father had put together a layout of the house, using what little information he got each time he came to drop off and pick up laundry. He couldn't wander freely about the house as could, say, a cleaning maid, so he got information by asking innocent-seeming questions of the other household help. How many rooms do you clean? Which family members are there? What part of the house are they in? How interesting. Do they have many beautiful things?

Bit by bit, Papa's father visualized the house, then put together the family's daily and seasonal schedules. After he died, Papa took over, adding new bits of information. There was a safe in the family patriarch's study. Off the study was a bathroom. And she herself had been the maid who cleaned the bathrooms.

It was years later before she realized that this was the reason she had been brought into the Dajgit family. At the time, she was distracted by a new family, the handsome husband, and the excitement of the lifelong plan. As she went over her father-in-law's maps and schedules, she was able to correct his mistakes and fill in many of the blanks.

Thinking of all this, she had a soft moment for Papa. If it wasn't for him, she never would have robbed the Gadi family and laid the foundation for the family empire.

— — —

Sanjay and Chunky got the jump on the hordes of reporters who would descend on Cap d'Agde because Sanjay had been faithfully reading the *Azure Coast Chronicle*, the first English-language newspaper to report the sighting of the dark-haired Canadian woman in the naturist colony. The other English papers wouldn't have the story until the next day.

It cost nine euros for them to enter the naturist quarter at Cap d'Agde with their vehicle. Once they parked, they had to walk to the main shopping and hotel areas, which were en route to the beach. Everywhere they looked, there were naked people, if not totally naked, then partially naked. Some had great magazine-photo bodies, but most were not so photogenic. As they were walking into town from the parking lot, they passed a raw paunchy dad with his bouncy but inert manhood, mom with pendulous breasts, C-section scar and unshaven pubic area, child, about 3, naked, swinging a yellow plastic sand pail with one hand.

Sanjay and Chunky kept their clothes on as long as they could, until they felt it was making them stand out, then they took their shirts off so as to better blend in as they wandered through Naked City, asking questions. Chunky had a hard time not staring at the women's breasts. They were everywhere.

In a seeming non sequitur, he asked Sanjay, "Do you ever miss your wife?"

"Hah, of course. But I've been married a long time. I enjoy missing her more than being with her. I miss my children."

"I don't miss my wife," Chunky said.

Chunky had been quiet lately, thoughtful, even morose. It was clear to Sanjay that he did miss his wife, very much, and he was trying to cover it up. Sanjay had been really annoyed with Chunky's witlessness and incompetence lately, but this sad observation made him soften toward his brother-in-law.

It took a special kind of man to be in love with a woman like Chunky's wife, and to still love and miss her after all these years. Chunky's wife had the temperament of a tiger, the looks of a water buffalo, and the "charm of a crusting rash," as Doo used to say. None of the Dajgit daughters was rich when it came to charm or temperament, except Tara, before Tara's husband was gunned down. But what they lacked in grace, they made up for with dowry.

Chunky had his own plan now: Get the statue, run out on Sanjay, and once he opened the thing to find out what it contained, sell it and start a whole new life here in the South of France, which was really growing on him.

That's how Papa got started after all, robbing a rich family, stealing the gold and gems that laid the foundation for his empire.

— — —

The French police had also arrived in the naturist quarter. They checked into the Heliopolis Hotel, remaining dressed—they were European, so staying with nudists didn't faze them, but they were on duty, so joining them was not an option. This made them stand out as they went around the scattered ports of the naturist quarter, asking questions.

Naturists, who were so uninhibited about their bodies normally, automatically covered themselves when police officers said they wanted to ask them a few questions. Only when they realized the police weren't investigating them did they relax.

A lot of people had seen the woman with a rose tattoo in town, once with an elephant statue, but nobody in the Port Soleil section of the spread-out naturist quarter knew where she was staying or

if she was still there. Oddly enough, the nudist told police, two
Indian men had been asking about the same young woman ...

— — —

Every morning Chloe and Gironde had breakfast together, croissants, big bowls of café au lait, the kind they used to serve in Paris
before they downsized to ordinary large coffee cups. They read
the newspapers quietly. It occurred to her how nice and domestic
it was, the two of them together, not talking, sharing breakfast. By
day, they were like an old content married couple, by night like
newlyweds. While he read the Marseillaise newspaper, Chloe read
La Provence, a south France newspaper in French, trying to brush
up her language skills.

That's how she read about the murder of Doo McGarrigle aka
Harry Carpenter, its connection to Diane Benham, and about the
mysterious disappearance, faked suicide of the heiress. The police
were now searching for Benham's "Canadian friend."

Oh my God, Chloe thought.

— — —

To: MichelleMaher@apu.edu
From: ChloeBower@apu.edu
Subject: Urgent from Chloe

═══

B, where are you? Have you seen the newspapers? The
police are searching for you because that guy in Monte
Carlo was murdered. I am in Arles. You can reach me
here at 06-XX-XX-XX-XX. If a Frenchman answers, don't
worry. That's Gironde. Much to tell you.
xx
C

— — —

To: Cameron@camerongetarealjob.com
From: ChloeBower@apu.edu
Subject: Urgent Cameron from Chloe

Cameron, Blackie is in serious trouble, and doesn't know it. Where is she? Where's Eddie? Call me, 06. XX.XX.XX. If a man answers don't worry. That's Gironde.

— — —

They'd gone into the nude town, Eddie and Blackie, to do e-mail, both naked. After that, they thought they'd pick up a few things at the supermarket and stop by the Sea Breeze to see Omi. They were both very quiet, and had been since Eddie told her the story about the Hersh sisters. He thought she didn't approve, that he'd creeped her out, but when he asked her, she said, "No, I'm just tired. A lot on my mind, you know."

They were just rounding the corner to the parking lot and the little strip mall with the tiny internet cafe, when Blackie saw a large man of Indian descent. He saw her too. It was not the same man who had tried to kidnap her in Arles, and at first she thought she was being paranoid. Then she saw the look and intent in his eyes, and she realized he was one of them.

"An angry Hindu," she said to Eddie.

Sanjay was about 70 or 75 meters away when Blackie and Eddie took off running. They ducked behind the strip mall, where a florist van was parked. Eddie grabbed Blackie's hand and pulled her inside. There was just enough room for them among the cellophaned bouquets and elaborate floral wreaths. Eddie hid himself between the seat and behind a large display that said, in somber white carnations on a pink carnation background, "A la Mémoire de Notre Sœur." Blackie covered herself with one in cheery yellows and purples, "Bonne Anniversaire Maman."

When the driver came out, the large fellow of Indian descent shouted something at him in English, which the driver didn't speak.

"I can't help you," he answered in French. He got in the van, auto-locked all the doors, checked his next stop—a funeral home in the coastal canal town of Sète—and drove off. He put a CD into his player and began to sing along to French pop songs.

— — —

Where was Chunky? They'd decided to split up to cover more territory. Sanjay didn't have time to look for him now. He'd just fuck everything up anyway. Sanjay ran to the rented Renault Twingo and drove out, picking up the van's trail on the road just outside the nudist quarter's gates.

— — —

Chunky was asking questions of an English-speaking waiter when the French police detectives saw him. They approached. Chunky didn't notice, and thought nothing of it until one of them tapped him on the shoulder, showed him his identification and said, in accented English, "We are police and we would like to ask you some questions."

Chunky then did a really stupid thing. His brain shut off completely and his gangster instincts took over. He ran down the wooden sidewalk, on to the nude beach. It was hard running in the sand and around the sprawled naked bodies. For some reason, he thought it would be easier if he pulled his gun out of his pocket. People screamed and, illogically, covered themselves with towels, as if a beach towel could defend them against stray bullets.

When Chunky used a Spanish grandmother's abdomen as a stepping stone, she reflexively bucked upwards, he lost his balance and came down, skidding in the sand into the breasts of a Swedish nanny.

The French police stood over him. His gun was full of sand.

— — —

The florist van stopped in Sète, just outside the side service entrance to the Cingal Frères funeral home. When the driver got out, Eddie and Blackie jumped over the front seat and crouched down to hide while the driver opened the back and took out the floral arrangement to "Notre Sœur."

The van was heavily air-conditioned to keep the flowers fresh, and they were both shivering and getting dizzy from the heavy perfume of fresh cut flowers.

"We've got to get clothes and get to a phone," Eddie said. He eased his head up to look out the driver's side window for the driver and saw the Twingo pulling up behind him in the side mirror.

"Shit. Okay. Grab that big thing, the purple-and-yellow one," Blackie said. "We're going to use it to shield us. I think we can make it into the funeral home."

"Then what?"

"We cross that bridge when we come to it," Blackie said.

Blackie maneuvered the flowers into place, and then Eddie flung open the door and they crouched behind the display, bare legs visible, as they ran into the funeral home. Once they got inside, Eddie locked the door behind them.

They were in an empty hallway. Outside, Sanjay rattled the door handle behind them. To their left, they could hear people's voices coming from an office. The low, mournful strains of funeral music could be heard coming from a curtained room in front of them.

Eddie opened a door to their right. A dead man lay on the table inside, naked under a white cloth, awaiting his final appearance. Pots of foundation, rouge, and lip gloss were lined up on a tray next to him. There was nobody else there.

"There must be clothes here. People bring something from the deceased's closet for them to wear in the casket," Blackie said.

"Over here."

Five rushed minutes later, they emerged, Eddie in the best suit of a Sète baker and heart attack victim, Blackie in the favored blue dress of a pensioner from Frontignan who choked to death on a licorice lozenge. They both looked ridiculous.

The makeup woman had returned.

"We are looking for our dead sister," Eddie said in French, then apologized for being here in error. They were directed to the funeral parlor, where one service was just ending and another, for "Notre Sœur," would begin in an hour.

Using the departing mourners from the first funeral as cover, they left through the front entrance and then jumped into the back of one of the cars in the funeral cortege. The driver looked at them, surprised.

"We were friends of the deceased. May we ride with you?" Eddie said in French.

"Ah, you knew uncle."

"Yes, he was a great man."

"Yes he was, thank you. Thank you so much," said the driver. He turned to his wife and said, "You see? He was a great man."

"How did you know him?" the woman asked Eddie. The car inched along in its sad parade.

"I knew him from his work."

"Work? He hasn't worked for years."

"I apologize. I make many mistakes in French. I meant my work."

"Well, he hardly left the house the last few years. What work do you do?" The woman asked.

Blackie understood none of the words, but she understood it was time to get out.

"I forgot something," she said.

"She forgot something," Eddie translated.

"We have to stop."

"Arrêtez, s'il vous plaît," Eddie said.

The driver braked, and Blackie and Eddie got out and looked around. There was no sign of the Indian.

"Merci," Eddie said, slamming the door behind himself.

"That bar on the corner should have a phone," Blackie said.

"Now I'm a thief. I've stolen the clothes of a dead man," Eddie said.

"He doesn't need them anymore."

Blackie had her purse with her and Eddie had his money pouch, but the rest of their things, including Ganesh, were back at the trailer. Eddie called the Sea Breeze on the pay phone by the bar while Blackie used the coin-op internet machine.

Omi said, yes, he'd go by the trailer and, if nobody was there, get their things and bring them, discreetly, to the Bar Bas in Sète.

Blackie silently read Chloe's message. She left out the part about the murdered man when she told Eddie about it.

Then she called Chloe.

— — —

"Get in," Chloe said from the passenger side of a white Twingo.

"What did you do to your hair?" Cameron asked. He had his video camera in front of his face. He was filming.

"Dyed it. Didn't want to be confused with that heiress any more. Who's the chick?" Chloe asked.

"I'm Wendy," said the girl.

"Oh. You speak English."

"Who's the guy?" Cameron asked, nodding at the driver.

"Gironde. He's French and he doesn't speak much English," Chloe said, handing the newspaper, the *Daily Splash*, over the back seat. "Page 3, right next to the topless girl."

Cameron read it. "I know, they're in Cap d'Agde. I e-mailed Jones. Eddie and Blackie are staying in a trailer owned by a guy named Omi. We're supposed to go to a bar called Naked Lunch and he'll take us there."

"No, Blackie just called," Chloe said."They *were* at the naturist quarter. Now they're in the town of Sète."

"Naturist quarter? Is that a wildlife preserve?" Wendy asked. Chloe shot Cameron a quick look.

"Yeah, something like that, Wendy. For nudists."

"Oh!"

"It's in the Bible. Like Adam and Eve," Cameron said.

At the first rest stop, Chloe took Cameron aside and said, "So what's Wendy's story?"

"She's a right-wing Christian. You ever heard of Godsmacked?"

"Yes."

"I met her in Cannes and felt it was my duty to get her away from the youth group. She's trying to convert me. I'm trying to corrupt her."

"Convert her from Christianity."

"Well, toward a less virulent strain at least."

"This is kind of Cosmic. I took a Christian pop star in Cannes for 1500 bucks."

"Peter Thorogood?"

"You've heard of him," Chloe said.

"I hadn't before Cannes. I went to a Christian rock picnic with Wendy and about a thousand Godsmacked fans. He was the star."

"Then you lured her away from the fold."

"Yeah."

"With your siren tongue and devil guitar."

"Uh huh."

"Slept with her yet?"

"No. She let me feel her breasts though, but only through her shirt. Who's the guy?"

"A bullfighter. The good kind that Eddie likes who doesn't kill the bull."

"Man. This is one crazy summer."

"What's Eddie's story?"

"Low-key but cool. No, post-cool. Real."

"Real quiet."

"Not when you're alone with him. He's just low-key, like I said before. A total noncomformist."

"Why did he leave Canada? He never wants to talk about that."

"He had a bad breakup with a girl there," Cameron said.

Wendy and Gironde returned, both speaking French. Wendy was very excited when she got in.

"Gironde fights bulls, but without hurting them," she said and then added, a little accusingly, "he believes in God."

When they picked up Eddie and Blackie, Gironde gave the keys to Chloe. There wasn't room for all of them and their stuff in the car. He was going to take the train back to Arles. He had a course with the bulls the next day.

He and Chloe kissed good-bye passionately.

"My God, who was that?" Blackie asked.

"He's Gironde, a raseteur," Chloe said. "Those clothes you're wearing . . ."

"We just came from a funeral," Eddie said.

"Does that Gironde guy have any clue what this is all about?" Blackie asked.

"No."

"What is going on?" Wendy asked. Up to this point, she'd been very quiet.

"Well, this beats almost all of Crazy Millman's adventures," Cameron said. "I mean, murder?"

"Murder?" Eddie said.

"I was going to tell you . . . I just found out myself . . . It's a case of mistaken identity," Blackie said. "Sort of . . ."

— — —

The night he was arrested, Chunky had a dream, and in it, he was feeding the Ganesh statue a spoonful of milk, trying to repeat a

nationwide miracle that had occurred with statues of the elephant-headed god in 1995. After Ganesh drank the milk, he spoke.

"Tell the truth, Chunky," the god said.

Chunky awoke with a start, surprised for a moment to see
himself in a grim hospital room. It took him a moment to come
out of his cross-consciousness stupor and remember. "Hah, I was
arrested in the nude place. I am in a prison in France."

For a moment, he was homesick for Mumbai. A memory
flashed in his mind, of dinner at the Dajgit family compound, with
all his favorite foods and the whole family, including Tara's husband, Mohan, and Doo. Chunky thought about how it would
never be the same again, the way it was before the Goonda Wars
and Doo's betrayal. Papa would talk, for a long time, about how
the golden days of the Dajgit Rowdydom were just beginning, and
how far he had come since his days as a dhobi, following his father into his life's work.

Mohan would give a funny but flattering toast to Papa and
then tell some stories from Bollywood or from his village. He was
a funny guy, and Doo was too, and Chunky missed them. Amit he
wouldn't miss much. He was kind of a snob because he was university educated and came from a higher caste. If Chunky mentioned a movie he liked, Amit would say something like, "There
hasn't been a decent movie out of Bollywood since *Pakeezah*," and
would shoot down every title Chunky might bring up to challenge
that.

Sanjay had been a favorite brother-in-law of his, but now
Chunky wasn't so sure. It was Chunky who had to do all the driving, who risked his life with bulls. Not only did Sanjay seem to
avoid danger by pushing Chunky toward it, but he had a superior
attitude toward Chunky the entire trip.

He didn't want to go back to India to prison. He'd be lucky if
he made it to prison. The police would probably shoot him, and
say they did it because he was trying to escape.

But maybe he could make a deal with the French authorities.

— — —

"You want to confess?" the French detective asked.

"Maybe, maybe not," Chunky said. "I want a deal for me and for Sanjay when you find him. We are to be tried and imprisoned here, in France, and are not to be returned to India. In India, the police will shoot us in cold blood."

"And you'd rather be in prison in France for murder than in jail or dead in India."

"Yes."

"I think that can be arranged," the French detective said.

CHAPTER 27

"You don't mind if Sam here videotapes our interview, do you?" Diane asked, nodding at Nickels.

An Asian guy pulled the camera away from his face and said, "Hi. Sam Nickels."

"Your terms," Mike said.

"Great. Would you like something to drink? A beer?"

"A beer would be nice."

Sam opened a cooler and handed Mike a beer.

"We're having lunch brought down from the fourth floor," Diane said. "So we can take our time with this."

"Ready," Nickels said.

"Go ahead, Mike."

"Well, let's start with the big question: Did you shoot Harold Carpenter in Monte Carlo?"

"I didn't kill anyone," she said. "I haven't been in Monte Carlo in two years. I have a list of the places I stayed. I'm sure the innkeepers will be able to corroborate it."

"What about your Canadian friend?"

"I don't have a Canadian friend. I had a Canadian penpal when I was a girl, but I lost touch with her years ago. There's a woman who looks a lot like me traveling around France, and she's with the Canadian."

"Why did you transfer all your money to Woy?"

"Well, it was part of a scam. I'd transfer my money to him so I couldn't be sued or lose control of my money to my father and stepmother, and so I could run away and start over again. It was his idea. We'd fake a breakup, I'd escape from rehab, and then meet up with him when he got to Paris. Afterwards, we'd go off together, hide out, and he'd write his next CD while I took care of him. When things cooled down, we'd reemerge to great fanfare. We'd be married."

"So he's got the money, the other girl, the publicity—"

"Yes. It's not fair. I will be getting that money back from him, somehow. "

"Is it true you got him into coke?"

"I take responsibility for my own stupid decisions to use. That imbecile should too."

"Are you still doing coke?"

"No. I ran out and couldn't get more. Then these fine people took me in, and I chilled and detoxed here. I smoke a little pot now and then, but mostly I've been good." She smiled at him.

While they drank mint tea (her) and beer (Mike and Nickels), she told him how she'd met Woy, how she escaped from rehab, everything she had done on her journey, and how she ended up in the Artery art squat in Paris. She talked about how novel it was to drink out of recycled jam jars and take her turns washing dishes, washing floors, working the bar at concerts and art shows, sleeping on an air mattress, learning to live with just 12 minutes of hot water every day

"At first I hated it here," Diane said. "Who were these people? Why did they share so much? Why were they being so nice? Was everyone being sarcastic or ... what's the word ... considerate? What was the scam and how could I get out of here, how could I get some money, some red meat, some cocaine?"

"Did you try to run away?"

"I thought about it, but where could I go? I had to stay. I cried in my room a lot, went through a deep blue cocaine crash and withdrawal, got in arguments. Then, and this is off the record—"

Nickels cut the camera.

"Okay," Mike said.

"Nickels here noticed my purse. It's a designer bag, and it cost 1,500 pounds. Nickels told me those bags sells for twice as much in some parts of Asia. Women go on long waiting lists there. If the bag was this season's model we could sell it to a fellow he knows in Chinatown for a 500 euro profit.

"Unfortunately, it's last season's model—I meant to buy a new one but the arrest, and rehab . . . well, anyway, we sat down and figured out a way to buy the latest designs here in Paris. You see, when the new purses come out, they are sold first here, then in New York, but in order to buy them, you have to make an appointment, be approved by the sales department, and then you can buy two handbags only. They don't sell to just anyone."

"That's to build demand," Mike said, nodding. "In New York, some women will commit everything short of murder to be the first with the new Louis Vuitton."

"And they do it to thwart scams like the one we cooked up. If just anyone could go in and buy them here then resell them to ship to Asia, it would hurt the designer's profits in places like Tokyo and Hong Kong. But Nickels knows a lot of rich American socialites who belong to Democrats Abroad. He recruited them to buy the handbags for us. We got ten and then we had to stop—"

"We ran out of socialites," Nickels said.

"They had purchased their limit. But we made 5000 euros on the deal to put toward the group's art projects and causes, and we can use the socialites again when the next new handbag design comes out."

"We debated whether we wanted to do anything to promote brand names, especially this designer's brand name," Nickels said. "His things are made in third world sweatshops without emergency exits. But in the end we decided that it was racist not to allow Asian socialites to waste their money on designer crap as freely as American socialites can, and that it was okay to deprive the designer of these profits as well."

"They think everything through here and discuss it thoroughly," Diane marveled. "To continue, I had so much fun plotting that with them, and I started to enjoy other things, the art work, even the chores. I love washing dishes! And of course, I so so like the people. They're wicked, in a brilliant way," Diane said.

She nodded at Nickels and he turned the camera back on.

"A few weeks here and you're a new woman," Mike said.

"It seems sudden, and it was in the sense that I feel like I woke up from a bad dream here. I'd been swimming with sharks, and trying to be a shark, and now I was swimming with tropical fish and dolphins and strange spiny creatures that glow in the dark. But it wasn't sudden. It had been coming for a long time, and when I had nothing else and nowhere to go, by some miracle, I landed here instead of in the hands of some drug-dealing pimp."

She stopped to take a sip of mineral water.

"Every Friday, we have shows," she continued softly. "Last Friday, we had a Russian rock band, a Puerto Rican slam poet, a French performance artist, a dessert chef, a Spanish flamenco singer—"

"A dessert chef?"

"He had to come to one of the shows and volunteered to do something for Artery. People do that here, they give just because they love the project and want to be a part of it. He made chocolate, the most delicious chocolate I've ever had. Everyone in the audience got one spoonful topped with a fresh mint leaf. I ate mine while I was listening to the flamenco singer. She was brilliant, tiny like Piaf but her voice filled the entire room. When she sang, the hair stood up on my arms and I felt the strangest, sweetest feeling in my heart. I had the taste of chocolate in my mouth, and the air was full of music . . . it was too much for me. I started crying. I thought, I must have done something right in my shite life to bring me to this place, on this perfect evening."

At that moment, Mike felt the strangest, sweetest feeling in his heart as he looked at her.

"How could I fail to appreciate it and try to understand how it works. The problem then was that I worried I wasn't a good enough person for the group, I was too damaged," she said.

Nickels spoke up. "Everyone here is broken in some way. We believe in a modified version of the Japanese way of mending broken objects. If a prized vase is broken, they mend it with gold to make the damage more noticeable because they believe mended damage makes a thing more beautiful and special."

"We mend our damage with love and art . . . and using our evil for good instead of for evil, whenever humanly possible," Diane said. "Sometimes I forget that . . . but I'm trying, and I'm good at it I think, using evil for good."

"So this is it for you, Diane? Because it isn't that nice out there. If you leave—"

"I know what it's like out there. But I will leave here eventually," Diane admitted. "I like hot water all the time, and a bathtub, not simply a shower, and I like a few little luxuries. I'll be back to visit. I'm going to be a patron. When I get my money back, I've pledged a donation of 500 pounds which gives me patron status—"

"500 pounds for saving your life?" Mike said.

"That's the maximum donation allowed. They won't let me give more than that. But when I get my money, I might start my own project, affiliated with Artery. Maybe a place like this for wayward girls and star-crossed lovers. Or small animals. I haven't decided."

"What will your family think of all this—"

"I don't know. I am sorry, but I won't talk about my family on camera."

"No?"

"I'd like to spare my father and my mother any more direct grief," she said. "But off the record? There's someone I'd like you to investigate, thoroughly. Lily Sue."

"Okay," Mike said.

"And Woy, of course."

"Woy. What kind of name is that? It sounds like Roy with a speech defect. Who were his parents? Teletubbies?" Mike said. The scandalized reporter smiled at her, and his subject, the scandalized heiress, smiled back.

"I'll help you out with some leads," she said. "You're also going to have to clear me of this faked suicide business, without implicating yourself," she said.

"How do I do that?'

"It should be relatively easy for a man of your talents. Pin it on Darius."

"Ian Darius of the *Splash*?"

"Right. That smug wanker has been trying to ruin my life for two years."

"I might be able to help with that," Sam said to Mike. "I'm a master hacker. I can hack into Darius' e-mail and—"

Sam's cellphone rang. He answered it and walked away to take the call. When he hung up, he made a call upstairs. "Incoming. Five bodies, should be here by eight."

"Incoming?" Mike said. "Five bodies?"

"Five people coming to stay at the squat," Diane explained.

"Oh."

"I have a question about the movie rights to this story," Mike said

"Our lawyers will have to work that out," she said, sweetly.

━ ━ ━

This art squat was a strange place. Wendy couldn't believe it. These people had taken a building from a bank, a long-vacant building from a bank that owned a lot of vacant buildings, sure, but still, someone else's property. In addition to falling in with atheists (or agnostics, as Cameron claimed to be), she seemed to have fallen in with communists. Man, was she going to have a few tales for her Godsmacked group when she got home, as well as a few undercover reports for XGRRRL.

She liked Cameron, that cute accent, that scruffiness, the sense of adventure that had taken him around the world twice. He taught her how to use his camera and let her shoot him sometimes, the way he was shooting her. In Cannes, she taught him how to proselytize, and, though he wasn't even a believer—yet— he was pretty good. Up to now, she'd never met a man more suited for the kind of life she wanted—as a new kind of Christian media missionary.

But, on the other hand, he was with the Devil after all, full of sophistry, a word her father liked to use. All his talk about Mithra, the ancient fire god of Persia. He believed that a lot of Christianity was "mythology," and Christian practices were superimposed onto Mithra by the Roman emperor in the third or fourth century.

But how did he know that the Mithra followers hadn't superimposed their religion over Christianity after the fourth century? Maybe it was the other way around. Did he think the universe was just an accident, because that was as mind-boggling to her as the idea to him of a father-creator who gave his only son to redeem mankind.

In the beginning, she had believed she could convert him. Now she wasn't so sure. He might be, as her father warned, one of those people who can't see the truth until they have lost everything and fallen.

But one doesn't travel the world for three years if one isn't seeking an answer. And Wendy was a girl who liked a challenge and had her eyes on the prize—bringing a hard-won specimen back to her Godsmacked group at home. Be ye a fisher of men, and she would have been so honored (pride being a sin), to drag Cameron back like a giant stunned marlin to be hung on the scales and photographed.

Within the Christian media community, Cameron could be a big star. She'd get him on to XGRRRL, just for starters, and her Dad could get some of his films on TV, if Cameron would make the right kind of films and sing the right kind of music.

They had all arrived at the squat just before dinner, which they ate in a big communal room, what had at one time been an executive office. The building was 75 years old, and had been abandoned for nine before being taken over by the squatters—and it looked it. The furniture looked like it had been dragged in from the street. None of it matched. Artwork, some very abstract and some more representational, covered the walls, except for a large map of the world over a raggedy sofa covered with a flag, and a dartboard across from the dining area.

The "dining area" consisted of two rough work tables pushed together to form an extended table about 15 feet long. Around it were padded banquettes from an old cafe, a church pew, and a variety of office, lawn, and folding chairs. All the plates matched—simple white china—but only because a sympathetic restaurant owner had made a gift of it when he upgraded to a more distinctive pattern. The flatware was mixed, and the glasses were reycled jam jars and yogurt glasses.

The people were a similarly motley collection. In a way, it reminded Wendy of MTV's *Real World* except it was, like, *really* real, and she was pretty sure *Real World* never had a 45-year-old chainsmoking divorcee in the cast. The chainsmoking divorcee was some kind of actress or comedian. Her name escaped Wendy, as did so many of their names—there were about twenty of them. There was a French-Canadian physicist-artist-solar power activist, a Russian musician also studying for his Ph.D. in economics, a tall lanky guy from Chico, California who had been raised by circus clowns, a writer from Wisconsin, a Japanese Buddhist priest, a French painter . . .

She said grace before she ate, the others abstained, and while people were passing platters of eggplant ragout and pasta, one of the young men there said, "True love waits for?" He was reading her T-shirt.

Before she could answer, the girl named Blackie said, "the condom to be in place."

"Godot," offered the 45-year-old divorcee.

"Ever," said Blackie.

Everyone laughed, even Cameron, which annoyed Wendy greatly.

"Marriage," she said.

"Seriously?"

"It's not only God's plan," she said, "It's a good common-sense way to make marriage last. If there's no premarital sex and no chance for easy divorce, people will be forced to stay together and fix their problems."

"Weren't those rules put into effect back when people, like, lived for 35 or 40 years?" a red-headed girl from Scotland asked.

"If I had married the first man I wanted to have sex with, and had to stay with him till death . . . oh my God, I would have had to hasten his death," said the chainsmoking divorcee.

"It's not like those restraints worked before, except maybe on the surface. People still cheated, abandoned each other and their children—"

"—beat each other, went off to war."

"People cheated and stayed married only because divorce laws were stricter."

"It makes sex shameful and punishes its idealists with sexual frustration and early marriage to a similarly warped individual with a stunted libido."

"Are you *all* Mithraists?" Wendy asked.

"What? No, we're, well, most of us have a core Buddhist philosophy we've built on individually."

"I'm an atheist," Ivan said.

"We're ecumenical Buddhists. Believe what you want, but remember, we're all just guessing, even atheists, so don't impose it on anyone else."

"We've been to see some Mithra sites," Cameron explained.

"I'm a Brianist," said the Scottish girl, who was some sort of guerrilla comedian. "Oh God, you know what I'd like to rent for movie night? *Life of Brian.*"

"Hey, it's a double feature. What would the second movie be?" Nickels asked.

"Do we go with a Python theme? Then *Holy Grail.*"

"Or religious irreverence—there's *Dogma.*"

Ivan looked at the new guests and said, "You guys will stick around for a while, right? Movie night is Wednesday, but we may want to show it at our Sunday night performance venue, too."

"Will Quinn be back?"

"He's at Burning Man."

"What about Jeremy?"

"He's in Marseille with Julie until October."

"Who will make popcorn Wednesday—"

The discussion went to squat and show affairs. At one point, a guy named Buster from North Carolina came in carrying big white O's.

"Someone left them on the street. They're from a neon sign. The neon element is missing, but I figured we could fill them with strings of little Christmas lights and use them during the performance venues."

"You're always finding letters," Nickels said. "What was it, a month ago you found all the letters from the Hotel Alexander sign?"

"Individual gold letters about eight inches high," Buster said, explaining to the newcomers. "You can see them in the top floor studio. We arrange them in different words and position them so the gold catches the light of the midday sun. The effect is really stunning."

"You can make a lot of words out of Hotel Alexander."

Wendy got up to help clear away dishes and take them to the washing room. A woman named Diane came in to make a plate of food to take to "our prisoner." It was some sort of joke that Wendy didn't get.

Cameron lit a joint and passed it to Blackie, with whom he'd had a lively private conversation just before dinner. Wendy wished he'd give up drugs, though, on the other hand, the bigger the sinner, the greater the redemption. There is more joy in heaven over one sinner who repenteth, and so forth.

Next to her, Chloe was using the phone, punching in numbers from a phone card. "Bonsoir, Gironde," she said, in a soft voice, and half a conversation in halting, simple French followed.

That bullfighter was pretty cute, Wendy thought. *He would have been a wild one to take home to her group.*

She poked around the office. There was a sign-up sheet for "Scavenging" for the "first Saturday of every month." An Asian-American guy told her that was when the city of Paris picked up big trash items, like old sofas, ovens, TV sets. They'd found the refrigerator on a Big Trash Saturday as well as two floor lamps and one of the TV sets they used in a video installation. They were hoping to find a microwave oven to use for popping popcorn for movie night.

Then the guy went off to sculpt.

"Hey," Eddie said from an armchair in the corner.

"Hey."

"Can I draw what you think God looks like?" he asked.

"Sure," she said. *That was very thoughtful of him,* she thought.

"You don't believe in God either, like Cameron?" she said, sitting down across from him.

"I didn't say that," Eddie replied. "I don't know, but I concede the possibility of a God, not a supernatural creature, but some natural force or consciousness or whatever. Even Einstein said that when scientists discovered the One Unifying Theory they'd find God. I like a lot about Jesus as a philosopher."

"Well, that's a start," she said. She looked at his drawing. "No, that's all wrong. I think he's clean-shaven . . ."

— — —

Diane put dinner together to take down to Mike. Passing the washing room, she saw a dark-haired woman wiping plates. When she lifted her hands, her T-shirt lifted slightly, revealing part of a tattoo.

Diane looked at her until Blackie looked back and did a double-take.

"Are you—" Diane began.

"Are you the heiress?"

"A penniless, disgraced heiress at the moment. You're my mysterious Canadian friend."

"Wow, this is eerie. Almost celestine," Blackie said, wiping her wet hands on her pants before extending one. They shook.

"Fuck me!" Blackie shouted. "Chloe! CHLOE!"

Chloe ambled out, and it took her longer than Blackie to recognize the woman, and not just because they both had different hair colors than they'd started out with. Like most people, Chloe had a warped view of what she looked like, and didn't see any immediate resemblance.

"Jesus, you're Diane Benham," she said, finally.

"We didn't kill that man in Monte Carlo," Blackie said.

"An Indian guy confessed to the killing this afternoon. I just read it on the internet," Diane said. "He says he killed the guy because he betrayed their Mumbai crime family. Wow."

"The Angry Hindu. Of course."

"I don't really see that much resemblance between us," Chloe said.

"I don't either."

"I see it," Blackie said. "You could be sisters."

"You want a beer or a glass of wine or something?" Diane asked, ushering them into her room. She went to deliver a plate of food to her "prisoner" downstairs, and then returned so they could drink wine and share the details of their strangely intertwined summers.

— — —

After several days of sleeping in his rental car, Sanjay's back and legs were killing him. Ever since Chunky had confessed, he'd had to lay real low, wearing his sunglasses and a bolero hat when he drove around, eating fast food he grabbed on the run, parking the car behind bushes or in empty lots at night. Chunky had ratted him out, but Chunky, thank the gods, had not mentioned the statue to the police. The newspaper said he simply told the cops he and his partner had killed Doo McGarrigle/Harry Carpenter because Doo had betrayed their family.

Papa had been furiously sending text messages. He wanted Sanjay to get the statue. He wanted Sanjay to break Chunky out of a maximum-security prison so he couldn't give away too much information that would be passed along to the Mumbai police. Then he wanted Sanjay to kill Chunky. He was paranoid now about Sanjay's own allegiance and sent warnings about what would happen to him once Amit arrived, then warnings that he'd better not return to Mumbai without the statue of Ganesh.

Then there were messages from Amit: He was not coming to France, so it was up to Sanjay to find that statue and bring it home. Amit's hands were full with the family business and whatever was in the statue wasn't as valuable to him as Baby Ganesh and the various family enterprises he was trying to untangle and control.

Idiots, Sanjay thought. France was a big country. How did they expect him to find this woman and the statue now? The website with the Ganesh pictures he had used as guide before, now had just a slate on it that said, "Due to extreme religious prejudice and humor-impairment, the feature *Requiem for a Nose* has been temporarily suspended. Stayed tuned for a new serial, Mithra and Me, or check our career guidance site at http://www.camerongetareal-job.com."

He was running out of money, he needed a shower, and the French cops were looking for him. Sanjay couldn't go back to

Mumbai without the statue, but how long could he stay in France? And how would he ever find that statue?

With his funds dwindling, he couldn't afford to drive around much, so he spent a lot of time at a truck stop on the N113, La Languedocienne highway, between the university city of Montepellier and the sea town of Sète, where he had lost the dark-haired girl. It was a good truck stop for hiding, and there were three different fast-food restaurants with drive-thru windows.

Here he sat, eating veggie burgers, frites, and salad out of greasy paper bags, trying to figure out what to do. Meanwhile, two more goondas were gunned down in Mumbai, one of them a Dajgit man, Dilip Kukapoor.

If he never found the statue, then what? Stay in France? Work underground, sans papiers, as so many immigrants did in Europe, selling fresh cut flowers in the warm weather and roasted chestnuts off rusty braziers made out of old shopping carts in the winter? He'd seen it on Doordarshan news, the Indians who had gone to Europe and America illegally, and the terrible hardships they endured. No, it wasn't for him. He liked eating regularly, and sleeping in a clean bed . . .

And then the gods smiled on him.

A white van with a human heart on the side pulled into the rest stop for gas. It was exactly like the van he and Chunky had followed out of Arles.

Thank you Lord Ganesh, destroyer of obstacles, thought Sanjay, turning the ignition. He put in a CD of Malkit Singh the Bhangra King, and followed Jones and five other Artery members as they pulled back on the N113 for Montpellier, and from there, to Paris.

CHAPTER 28

Wendy and Cameron, Blackie and Eddie, and some others had been sleeping in the communal rooms on a variety of sofas and air mattresses. It was kind of like a big weird slumber party. The night before, the chainsmoking divorcee had even made hot cocoa and cinnamon toast for the guests, which tasted surprisingly good and took Wendy back, deep into her past, and the chilly nights at summer Bible camp when they warmed themselves in the mess hall after evening chapel with hot cocoa, cookies, and board games like Parcheesi and Monopoly.

It was such a shame. *They were really nice people at the squat, it would have been so wonderful if they all could have been doing this for something good,* Wendy thought. They had a motto, "Using our evil for good, instead of for evil (mostly)." Evidently it was a joke because, as she pointed out at lunch that day, "You're not using your evil for good. You're using it for evil!"

"We don't think so."

"Evil, such an overused word," said another.

"So subjective," said another.

About ten other people weighed in on the subject, till Wendy's head was spinning. She hoped the dizziness was from the blizzard of conflicting ideas and not a contact high from all the cannabis she'd been around lately.

Most of the day, internet radio was piped through the Artery communal rooms via a big speaker system. Today it was some eclectic rock station out of Paradise, California. Cat Stevens was singing "Bitter Blue," and Wendy wished he hadn't become a hardcore Muslim. What a shame. When nobody was looking, she changed the station to the Christian rock network her own show appeared on, and then went out into the rest of the squat to look for a cable they needed for the movie projector that night.

About half the rooms were workspace/living areas, and the rest were exhibit or performance spaces. One of the artists-in-residence worked with lights, so there were "light installations" scattered throughout the building. Walking down a dark hallway, she was surprised and enticed by the pale blue glow spilling round the sides of one closed door. She opened it and found herself in an otherwise dark gallery full of pale blue neon cubes suspended from the ceiling, made using regular fluorescent bulbs painted with blue paint. Old white sheets bought at a charity shop were cut and tacked around the bulbs to form squares. As she walked to the end of the room, she stepped on a button, activating an old drive-in cinema speaker hung on the wall that squawked, "Enter to your left."

To her left was a door covered by a black cloth. She went into a room with more blue light cubes, this time looking as if they were suspended mid-air at different heights. When she looked closer, she saw they were held in place by thin wire frames and thin plastic wire.

It gave her such a disturbing feeling.

On the first floor, she passed a windowed exhibit room. Inside, a handcuffed man sat on a chair between two mattresses in an otherwise bare room. A cardboard sign on the wall outside said,

Hey, Let Me Out!
A Life-Action Art Installation
by
Sam Nickels

The man inside saw Wendy and shouted, "Hey, let me out! I won't file the story yet. I promise. Please? You gotta trust me by now! Hey, let me out!"

Wendy couldn't help herself. She laughed, and then moved on.

In another room, there were nothing but ladders, each covered in some different surface, one in faux leopard, another in fake dollar bills, a third in pornographic pictures of people having sex, two, three, six at a time. Even before she saw that one, she felt the place had a mildly Satanic vibe. She took out her microcassette recorder and was about to describe this when someone said, "Wendy, we found the cable. Can you help Eddie at the admission table downstairs?"

It was the Asian-American guy, Sam Nickels.

"Sure," she said, slipping the recorder discreetly into her pocket.

"Jones is on his way into Paris," someone said to Nickels as they passed on the stairwell.

The front doors, usually bolt-locked, were open. A work table had been placed in the bank foyer with two coatracks behind it, and the foyer light replaced with one that glowed a nice pink, "the pink of Edith Piaf's Paris," Wendy said, describing it into her recorder when Nickels stepped away to talk to the 45-year-old chainsmoking divorcee.

She had hardly seen Cameron the last two days. He and that girl Blackie had been busy smoothing the rough cut of his silly Mithra film. Their friend Diane had been busy on kitchen duty. The night before, Wendy herself had helped out with an assembly line making vegetarian sushi to sell at the bar during the movie.

About the only person who took any time with her was Eddie, who was working admission and the coat check with her tonight.

She sat down and waited for him. He brought her a glass of red wine and when she said, "I don't drink," he said, "It's wine. It's in the Bible. Jesus drank it by the gallon."

So she drank it too, but very slowly. At first.

"Will we check a lot of coats?" she asked "It's such a warm evening."

"I dunno," Eddie said.

People started arriving around seven, drifting in, in twos and threes. It was a word-of-mouth event, advertised nowhere but through an e-mail list. The arrivals thickened around 7:30, and by 8:00 Wendy had a pretty good idea what people check at squat parties in Paris in the summer: 82 motorcycle helmets, 16 books (including a comprehensive collection of Beckett plays), a big bag of Granny Smith apples and ripe camembert.

Eddie went to "take a leak" and left her manning the fort when the guy they called Jones, a black guy from the United States, arrived with some women.

"Who are you?" he asked.

"Wendy. Three euros admission, please."

"New?"

"Yeah."

"Jones. Welcome," he said. "We're part of Artery. We don't pay."

After him came a dark-complexioned fellow in sunglasses and a bolero hat.

"Three euros for the movie, one more if you want to check your hat."

"I'll keep the hat," he said.

"You won't be able to see the movies with those sunglasses on," she said.

"I'm blind anyway," Sanjay said. It was the first thing he thought of.

Nickels came out. "I'm locking the front doors now. You can go in to watch the movie if you want."

"I'll wait until Eddie comes back, thanks," she said.

Eddie was still on line for the john when Wendy saw the man in bolero hat and sunglasses slip out of the screening room. The way he did it, so sneakily and smoothly, made her think he probably wasn't blind.

The man turned purposefully and walked to the stairwell. Something wasn't right about the Bolero man. Wendy looked around for Eddie or Nickels, but the foyer was empty. Just as smoothly and sneakily as he, she slipped out from behind the table and went to the screening room.

It was jammed, dark and noisy in the movie room, and she couldn't find Nickels or anyone she recognized. Well, she was a reporter, she'd get to the bottom of this herself. As she went up the dark stairs, she considered possible scenarios. This man could be a thief or, worse, a saboteur for the corporation that owned the building, here to make trouble. She knew the squatters were in the wrong and that she should be upholding the principle of private property, but somehow, she couldn't listen to her conscience right now. In her gut, she didn't like this man, and she really liked the squatters a lot, in spite of all their teasing and wrongheadedness. Her first instinct was to protect them.

She heard someone shout, "Hey, let me out of here! My name is Mike Handel. I'm a reporter—"

Bolero man must be on the first floor, she thought, turning on her recorder, then hugging the wall as she crept upward. A shadow appeared on the landing above her. She froze. It was Bolero. He bounded up the stairs. Wendy followed.

—   —   —

At 8:30 P.M., Blackie had finished the last edit on the Mithra mockumentary and handed it off to Cameron to take downstairs, then she stayed behind to help Diane, Chloe, and another girl put plates of vegetarian sushi into cardboard boxes to take down to the bar.

The door to the communal kitchen flew open. A man in a bolero hat and sunglasses stood there, holding a gun.

Screams.

"Where is it, the statue," the man said, and Blackie realized it was one of the angry Hindus.

Ganesh was tucked away at the bottom of Blackie's backpack, which was under four or five others tucked behind the couch. But she never got a chance to say that. The door flew open again, knocking the Indian man forward. He stumbled into Diane, who was holding a big box of vegetarian sushi, knocking them both down and sending his gun spinning across the floor. Blackie ran to pick it up.

Wendy stood in the doorway

"I must have the statue," the man on the floor said.

"It's gone," Blackie lied. "I sold it. Chloe, this is the guy Eddie and I escaped from in Cap d'Agde."

"What's going on?" Wendy demanded. "I'm going to call the police—"

"We're rehearsing a play," Diane said, without looking up from Sanjay. "Will you take some of the sushi down to the bar, please, Wendy?"

"Okay," Wendy said, picking up a box of sushi.

After she'd left, Diane said, "I don't want the cops around here." She was thinking not only about her old rap sheet, but also that she had helped kidnap a reporter and was holding him in less than voluntary confinement as a living art exhibit.

"I don't want cops around either," Blackie said. "But what do we do with him?"

She looked down at Sanjay and pointed the gun right at his head.

"Kill him?"

"No, please, don't kill me," he said.

"We could tie him up, pin a note on him, and have the guys drop him off in the morning at the police prefecture," Chloe said.

"That's a great idea."

"Thanks. You three tie him up, and I'll take some sushi down and send up some guys to help you."

I t was autumn in Paris, two weeks after the incident with the angry Hindu in the Bolero hat. It had been a great two weeks. There'd been movie nights, an art opening, a rooftop picnic, and a steady stream of interesting visitors, but Blackie was getting itchy to move on in every way. While everyone else was at the nude figure-drawing class, Blackie took Eddie aside and broke up with him.

"The truth is, I'm kind of attracted to Cameron," she said. "That's a shitty thing to tell someone, but I'd rather tell you now than cheat behind your back with your best friend. I did that once. Don't tell Chloe. It stinks."

"I did it too once," he said.

"Really?"

"Cheated on my ex-fiancee with her sister," he admitted. "That's what made me leave, hit the road."

"Oh. Maybe that's what we saw in each other."

"It was awful, ugly, both of our families hate me. I hated me too."

"I didn't hate myself at all. But I'm mad at myself now for it. I feel remorse and don't want to do it again. So I decided just to tell you up front."

Eddie didn't seem torn up. "I'm glad to know you, and to have traveled with you, romanced you for a while."

"And I'm glad to have traveled with you too. It was a remark-able time," she said. "Sisters, Eddie. Wow. Never come between sisters, or brothers."

"Where are you going to go now?"

"Cameron is going to Arles, he wants to shoot an episode of his career guidance series at the school where those French bullfighters learn to do that raseteur thing. Chloe and Gironde are going to help him out. The students start out at, like, 13 and 14 with a bullhead mounted on a wagon. Cameron will be the tallest, oldest student in the class. I was going to invite myself along and make a mini-doc about this French bullfighting thing."

"What did your parents say?"

"They're not thrilled, but they were glad I didn't ask them for money. I told them I earned some money over here, and I'll just travel until that runs out, then I'll probably come home and go to school. Are you still planning to go to Lourdes?"

"Yeah. Wendy has invited herself along."

"No shit. The Christian? Well, that seems like a good place for her. Lucky girl."

— — —

"Gironde has invited me to come to Montpellier with him. He'll go to school and do his bull thing, and I'll study French and write. I've been writing a lot lately," Chloe said. "It's nuts, I know. We barely speak each other's language and I just met him. What is there between us but physical attraction?"

"There must be more," Blackie said.

"I'm not sure what it is. I like to think that we were attracted to each other not just by that instant physical chemistry, but the recognition of something in each other, spirit or whatever."

"Can you see yourself staying in France? Do you have a vision of yourself here?"

"I do. But I had a vision of myself with John in the future too, and before him, Will and Bobby—"

"Tell me anyway. You see yourself and Gironde surrounded by your children and grandchildren in your vine-covered French cottage—"

"It's not that specific. One day he took me around the dikes . . . the Petit Camargue near the sea is a web of dikes around the fishing villages and salt mines. We stood on one of the dikes and looked over these mountains of white salt. Fog was rising up from the salt, like ghosts, and I had a moment of déjà vu, and then I had a feeling like, I guess you'd call it sera vu, seeing myself in that same spot a year later, five years later."

"Wow. That sounds nice. If it doesn't work out, you can just blame it all on the language barrier."

"Yeah. And I figure I can always go to grad school, but when will I have a chance to live in France and be in love with a young bullfighter again?"

"Who comes to France and meets a bullfighter? This is a very rare opportunity. If you didn't do it, you would always regret it."

"I know. I think my mind was already made up before he even suggested this, when his grandmother taught me an old saying in Occitan: 'vou mai peta en societe que de craba tou sour.' 'It is better to fart with others than to die alone.' Don't laugh, but when she told me that, I wanted to have Gironde's baby just for her."

"Maybe this is it, Chloe, true love."

"Maybe. D'you ever read *The Sun Also Rises*?"

"I hate Hemingway. He was so macho and humorless."

"That's a good book though. It has the greatest last line in the world, 'Isn't it pretty to think so.' I know my track record with love, especially love at first sight, and that this is really nuts. I know so little about what he believes in. He could be a neo-Nazi for all I know."

"Have you ever seen him march with other men in drab colors?"

"No, he's probably not a Nazi, but you know what I mean. There's a lot I don't know and can't understand."

"Chloe, I'm really sorry we fought."

"Me too."

"It was fun, the crime. We were good at it."

"Yeah. Who knew? You were right though. I was kind of addicted to it, in a sin-shame-repentance cycle. I'm over it now."

"Don't give it up completely. If things don't work out with the bullfighter, we could meet next summer, roll a few pervs on a beach somewhere. Just to keep our hands in," Blackie said. "I'll probably be out of money by then."

At that point, Chloe debated about whether she should confess that she'd kept some of the Rolex money for herself.

But she didn't.

She hadn't taken credit for freeing the Filipino maid, and she wouldn't take blame for ripping off her best friend, who frankly owed her a lot of money from over the years. Somehow, it all seemed to even out.

"If you run out of money, call me. I'll wire you some," Chloe said.

— — —

Diane still had to go back to deal with court, suing her ex-boyfriend, rehab and community service. But as she said, she'd be back on the streets in no time, especially with the case her friends at Artery helped her put together. Ian Darius of the *Daily Splash* was fruitlessly claiming his innocence in the scam that faked Diane's suicide. Diane, showing her kinder, gentler self, asked people to forgive Darius and brought no charges against him.

Mike Handel was the Boy of the Hour with his exclusive Diane Benham interview, which most people thought was a very fair and sympathetic depiction of the heiress. Mike would be covering the aftermath when she returned to London and they had a joint book deal on the table, so it looked like they'd be working together for a while. He kinda liked Diane. She was turning just 18 in a couple of weeks, but she was old for her age. Maybe, he thought, she'd let him take her to dinner on her birthday . . .

— — —

Papa Dajgit spent his last afternoon in the apartment of his mistress, Bollywood actress Veena Nata. He never used to have to go to her. She always came to him. But that was before ... before he helped her break into Bollywood, before she won a Filmfare award, before the police started gunning down goondas, before his own sons-in-law betrayed him.

He would never know who betrayed him last. Only two people knew in advance he was going to visit Veena that afternoon, his mistress and his son-in-law Amit, father of his only grandson.

The minute he stepped outside to get into his car, he was shot and killed, along with his bodyguards, Fat Rishi, Ramesh, Pandit, Boomesh, and Chota. He died not knowing what became of his beloved Ganesh statue, and the rare five-carat diamond containing a single flaw at its center, a flaw that looked like a perfect lotus, and gave it its very simple name, The Lotus Diamond.

Mined in the 17th century, its first buyer was an English earl, who later sold it to an Indian maharajah when India was still a collection of states and the English were just tea traders setting up a few small posts—don't mind us, we just want to do a little business—and hadn't started taking over the subcontinent in earnest. The earl got gold then worth 3,000 pounds, a small fortune, and his pick of the young concubines in the maharajah's harem. Not long after the maharajah took possession of the gem, his first son was born and his army defeated that of a rival prince, who was captured and staked alive to the ground outside the palace before starved tigers were set upon him to the delight of all present. All in all, it had been a good year for the maharajah, and he credited the magic jewel with this.

Of course, within five years, the brother of his dead rival would have raised a new army, would defeat the maharajah. After he was dead, and his palace looted, the gem's trail vanished. Its legend grew. The last credible reports put it in India just after the end of the Raj, when Partition threw the subcontinent into chaos for a few years. It was said to be in the possession of a wealthy family known as the Gadi clan for a while, and then it vanished.

It vanished into the apron of a young bride and maid, Padmini "Mama" Dajgit, who had hidden in the Gadi house three nights in a row, watching through a closet door until she knew the combination of the safe. She had swept the safe's contents into a sack she made with a tied apron and crept out, unfurling a cloth full of glittering jewels for her young husband in their shanty in the washerman's colony. She had fulfilled her late father-in-law's lifelong plan.

Papa and Mama ran away to Mumbai, where they sold the gems one by one, using the money to buy protection, later taking over the protection business themselves. The Lotus Diamond was the only gem they kept. Papa just always felt it was good luck, a gift from the gods. He was like the lotus, he said, born in the mud, raised up to the sun.

— — —

When they came to tell Mama of Papa's death, she started crying. Not a day had gone by in the last ten years that she didn't wish him dead at least twice. But now that he was gone, she wept.

At first her daughters thought she was choking, then Tara said, "No, she's weeping. She's weeping for Papa, and Sanjay and Mohan and Chunky. . . ."

Mama Dajgit tried to blink out the name of the betrayer. "It was Amit, I heard him call the police today. Amit did it."

But all her children saw were her eyes filling with tears, and Mama trying to blink them away.

It touched them. They all hugged her. It would pass soon, but for a moment, they felt like a family, a real family.

All except for Amit, who blinked back at her.

"Shut up, old woman, or I will shut you up. This is my family now."

It took her a moment to recover from this new shock. *Amit understood her.*

She blinked: "You'll need my help. There's a lot you don't know."

"Yes," he blinked. "If you help me, I'll help you."

"Will you buy me some barfi from the old man in the dhoti on Chowpatty Beach?"

"Yes."

"I need new nurses."

"OK."

"How long have you understood?"

"Always," he blinked.

— — —

In October, a parcel addressed to Blackie's brother Kevin arrived at his dorm. In advance of its arrival, she had e-mailed Kevin to tell him to expect it.

"Take it with you next time you go home to see Mom and Dad, and put it with my stuff in Dad's basement until I get back," she wrote. "I went through hell for this little trinket, so guard it with your life."

Kevin couldn't resist opening it. It was a statue of the Indian God Ganesh.

He liked it. Blackie was on the road, she wouldn't be home for ages, and he needed another bookend for the shelf above his desk, where the books were held in place now by two bricks on one side and a book placed flat on the other. He righted the book, a book on structural engineering, and put Ganesh there. Before long, it would be garlanded with chains and its snout used as a place to put Post-It messages: *Kevin, call Sarah. She's fucking PISSED!*

After resting quietly in the ground for a million or so years, through man's evolution from simple-celled organism, through the Stone Age, the Iron Age, the Roman Empire, the birth of Jesus, the rise of the Churches and Mosques and Temples, all of Henry the Eighth's wives, the Reformation, and the discovery of the new world, then being found, cut, polished, passed between the hands of powerful men, gifted to vain queens, sought by adventurers who had been killed for it, the Lotus Diamond would now rest in a statue of Ganesh in an Indiana dorm room, through two semesters, ten dorm parties, six term papers, several tag-team love affairs, and a few drunken one-night stands.

AFTERWORD

The writing of this book was made possible in part by Mary Kaplan and the New York Foundation for the Arts with a grant facilitated by John Wells and Sara Grundman.

ACKNOWLEDGMENTS

I am most grateful to my editor, Carrie Thornton, who wrote this book as I dictated from within my full body cast at St. Vincent's Hospital; my Canadian editor, Dinah Forbes; my agents, Russell Galen, Charlie Northcote, and Danny Baror; my former editor, Jennifer Kasius; and my *USA Today* editor, Whitney Matheson.

In Paris: Varda Ducovny, the late Amram Ducovny, Daniel Crowley, Jim Haynes, Tania Capron, Fabienne Reichenbach, Bruno Blum, Brigitte Baudinet, Martin Heidler, Emilie Manorine, Ian Ayres, Professor Bernard and Marcella, Yann Panier, Nathalie Mege, and Eglantine at J'ai Lu for opening so many doors for me and being so much fun. Also, Kamel at Le Maryland on Rue du Poteau, the Hotel Pacific on Rue du Ruisseau.

Eric Périer of In Fact, visual artist and le chef of the Châteaudun art squat, who "borrowed" an unused bulding from a bank and gave it to a bunch of artists from all over the world for four years ... then lit it up in many beautiful and provocative ways. I am grateful to have been one of those lucky people who lived and worked there.

kilometerzero.org, the group I lived with there, Jeremy Mercer, who came up with the designer bag scam, Julie de Robillard, Thomas Pancake, Quinn Comendant, Ryan McGlynn, Adrian Hornsby, Tim Vincent-Smith, Musa Gurnis, Katerina Barry, Colin Askey, Maxime Petrovski, Daniel Margulies, Jim Gladstone, Claude and the inimitable Buster Berk ... I am especially grateful to Jeremy and Julie for putting me up later in Marseille while I finished this book and giving me so much support over the last year.

My other squatmates: Paolo Henriques, Irvin Salas, Roger, Immanuel, Pascale Faux, and Sudesh at Châteaudun.

Everyone at Gousset Vide.

In Arles: Audrey Natalizi, everyone at the Hôtel Gauguin, Maeva at the Hôtel Voltaire, the Narval Tabac Snack, all in Place Voltaire; the Hôtel de France and du Gare on Place Lamartine, the manadiers and raseteurs of the course camarguaise and the aficions who were so helpful.

In Amsterdam: Neville Mars of spacebrand.nl, a thousand kisses, Fonz of fonztv.nl, Jose, Gorgeous, everyone at the old Red Cross hospital anti-squat, and Tomas of Le Mot Perdu.

In the USA: New York ... Yvonne Durant, whose wise advice, witty jokes, and unflagging support kept me going during the roughest times, Bonnie and Joe at Black Orchid, Annalee Simpson, Denise DeMars, Teresa Brady, Felicia Murray, and Maggie Paley ... Austin, the Siros boys and Bouchercon organizers ... Houston, everyone at Murder by the Book and Michelle Maher of Louisiana, too ... Los Angeles, Lisa Mohan, Linda Stewart, Tim Long, Sheldon MacArthur, Mysteries to Die For, and the endlessly delicious Dark Delicacies in Burbank; Pat Tracy, Elaine, and Spike and the Wombats; and, as always, my family.

The Tuckerized Michelle Maher, Diane Benham, and Doug Mason, who donated money to good causes to buy the opportunity for me to abuse their good names in a book.

I turned to the FFCC website (http://www.ffcc.info) for background information on the course camarguaise. For Bollywood and the Goonda Wars, *FilmFare* magazine, the *Times* of India, the *Mumbai Grapevine,* and *Bollywhat?* (http://www.bollywhat.com) were indispensable.

ABOUT THE AUTHOR

Sparkle Hayter is the author of the five books in the highly acclaimed Robin Hudson mystery series. She is also the author of *Naked Brunch*. A native of Canada, Sparkle has worked as a journalist, comedian, writer, secretary, and cocktail waitress. She lived in an art squat in Paris, France for a year until it recently closed.

ALSO BY SPARKLE HAYTER

NAKED BRUNCH
1-4000-4743-9. $13.00 PAPERBACK (NCR)

A mousy secretary by day, a prowling werewolf by night, Annie
Engel is way more conflicted than your average young woman—
understandably—especially when it comes to affairs of the heart.
Get ready for a manic chase through the dank underbelly of
the big city, a place where no one seems to sleep and the scents
of fear and desire are always in the air.

"IT WILL HAVE YOU HOWLING AT THE MOON."—*NOW Magazine*

"WACKY AND IRREVERENT."—*Elle*